DEATH OF A GOOD WOMAN

Grace and Eric Cawthorne often quarrelled. One reason was that Grace had more money than Eric. Another was that she refused to live in Sheffield, where Eric was a schoolmaster, but remained in their comfortable studio flat overlooking the sea, with the result that Eric saw her only during the school holidays. Not unnaturally, Eric found consolation elsewhere. On the day this was discovered there was a long and noisy quarrel which ended with him storming out of the flat. On his return several hours later, the flat was empty, and he told a neighbour that his wife had left a note saying she had gone to stay with her sister. Next morning Grace was found dead at the foot of some cliffs near by and Eric was arrested on a charge of murder.

DEATH OF A
GOOD WOMAN

J. F. Straker

·BLACK·
·DAGGER·
·CRIME·

First published 1961
by
Harrap
This edition 1994 by Chivers Press
published by arrangement with
the author's estate

ISBN 0 7451 8635 1

British Library Cataloguing in Publication Data available

Printed and bound in Great Britain by
Redwood Books, Trowbridge, Wiltshire

FOREWORD

The name of J. F. Straker is unfamiliar today to all except the keenest students of detective fiction—even though his final novel, *A Choice Of Victims*, appeared as recently as 1984. As this re-issue of *Death Of A Good Woman* shows, Straker's work deserves to be better known, for it combines the careful delineation of character and sound plotting with the added bonus of several unexpected twists.

The good woman of the title is Grace Cawthorne, a talented artist who lives in the east wing of Mulgerry House, which occupies a lonely spot on the south coast of England. When Grace is murdered, her husband Eric is the obvious suspect and he is soon arrested. Eric is by profession a schoolteacher (as Straker was) and initially we see events from his point of view. Even in the opening chapters, however, there are several clues to the less appealing facets of his character—facets which become more apparent as the story develops. Gradually, the spotlight shifts onto Eric's lover, Sheila, who works in a private detective agency. She modestly admits to being not very good at her job, but with the assistance of Eric's solicitor, the quiet but likeable Charles Matthews, she commits herself so wholeheartedly to finding out the truth about Grace's death that until the closing pages her amateur sleuthing overshadows the professional efforts of Straker's series detective, Inspector Pitt. Suspicion shifts from one inhabitant of Mulgerry House to another and, with each succeeding revelation, the irony of the description of Grace as a 'good woman' becomes ever more apparent. Realism prevails when it is Pitt, rather than Sheila, who finally solves the mystery.

Pitt had first appeared in Straker's debut novel, *The Postman's Knock*, which was published in 1954. *The Postman's Knock* was much admired and is still widely regarded as Straker's major achievement. Solemn and cadaverous, Pitt is an unobtrusive figure, who in this book is ushered onto centre stage almost apologetically. Although he is far from being a Great Detective in the classic tradition, he is nevertheless a plausible character and Straker humanises him with many small touches. He is by no means infallible, and during his enquiries we see the consequences of his occasional misjudgements; at one point, for instance, he realises that: 'Impetuosity, so foreign to his nature, had lost him what might have been vital information'. Quiet as Pitt is, however, he is certainly a decent man. 'Even to a crook,' we are told, he 'did not enjoy having to lie.'

Yet in this book one can sense that Straker is itching to escape the procedural shackles of the conventional novel about the progress of a police investigation. He is concerned to people his story with distinctive individuals and he draws the inhabitants of Mulgerry in some depth. Nor does he achieve this at the expense of the whodunit element; the story is most skilfully structured.

Pitt appeared in only one more novel after *Death Of A Good Woman*; later, Straker wrote a number of non-series books as well as creating Johnny Inch, a policeman who eventually turned private detective. Under the name of Ian Rosse, Straker wrote one non-mystery novel and he also tried his hand at travel writing. Yet by the time *A Choice Of Victims* was published, his reputation had already been overtaken by those of younger writers. Today, most of his stories have long been out of print. That is a pity, because, as *Death Of A Good Woman* shows, Straker was a talented novelist whose work is as entertaining and enjoyable as that of many more illustrious crime writers.

MARTIN EDWARDS

Martin Edwards is the author of three novels about the Liverpool solicitor and amateur detective, Harry Devlin. *All The Lonely People* was nominated for the John Creasey

Memorial Award and has been followed by *Suspicious Minds* and *I Remember You*. Martin Edwards has also edited *Northern Blood*, an anthology of Northern crime writing.

THE BLACK DAGGER CRIME SERIES

The Black Dagger Crime series is a result of a joint effort between Chivers Press and a sub-committee of the Crime Writers' Association, consisting of Marian Babson, Peter Chambers, Peter Lovesey and Sarah J. Mason. It is designed to select outstanding examples of every type of detective story, so that enthusiasts will have the opportunity to read once more classics that have been scarce for years, while at the same time introducing them to a new generation who have not previously had the chance to enjoy them.

I

I<small>T</small> was raining heavily by the time Eric Cawthorne reached the gates and turned on to the uneven surface of the gravelled drive; he pulled up the collar of his jacket and drew it closer about his neck, bending his head to shield his face from the rain-laden gusts that blew at him fiercely across the open park from the sea beyond. The numerous pot-holes were already full of water (since all the occupants of Mulgerry House disclaimed responsibility for the upkeep of the drive, repairs were never effected), and as he splashed heavily through them he cursed again his wife's desire for rural isolation, and his own stupidity in acceding to it.

I always was a damned fool, he told himself grimly. And I'm a damned fool to be tramping around in this blasted weather. If I had any sense I wouldn't let Grace needle me the way she does. Rushing out of the house in a flaming temper won't solve anything.

Dusk had fallen, and the large bulk of the house loomed greyly against the cloud-filled sky. Mulgerry was high-ceilinged, and tall for a two-storied building; as he reached its shelter the wind lost its intensity, and he brushed the rain from his forehead and looked up. Lights shone from the large windows; dully on the ground floor, where the curtains had been closely drawn (though why "The Hump" or the Winters should imagine that anyone might be sufficiently interested to peer in at their grey, unimaginative lives only ·they and their Maker knew), brightly from the Upways' flat on the first floor, where neither Jim nor Connie had remembered (or bothered if they had remembered) that windows had curtains. But there were

no lights at all in the East Wing, and for that he was thankful. That meant Grace had gone to bed. It could not be much after seven o'clock, but Grace paid no allegiance to time. She went to bed when she was tired, got up when she felt like getting up, ate when she was hungry. And it would add to her victory over him, no doubt, to let him get his own supper.

Music blared from the Upways' open window, and despite the dampness of his whole being and the unpleasant thoughts that occupied his mind Eric smiled to himself. They were at it again. Well, maybe *The Merry Widow* was more to Lady Humpleston's taste than jazz; but for how long could she put up with the noise? For how long would their weekly rent stifle the affront to her ears?

That was what the Upways (or was it only Jim?) hoped to discover.

As he turned the corner of the East Wing the darkness enveloped him. He was not so familiar with his home that he could walk boldly forward, and he felt his way along the wall to the front door, stubbing his toe against the step as he came to it. He always did stub his toe against that step in the dark. It was so much wider and longer than he remembered it.

He let himself into the hall, switched on the light, and heaved a sigh of relief that at least there would be no resumption that evening of their quarrel; if it were to be continued it must wait until the morrow. He would put on some dry clothes, have a drink, and then see what he could find to eat. He had not thought about food while he was out, but now he was suddenly hungry.

Before going upstairs he looked in at the large living-room; it was just possible that Grace hadn't gone to bed, but had fallen asleep in her chair. She wasn't there—but for a brief moment he stood surveying the room, impressed as always by its space and dignity. Whatever Grace's faults, he had to admit she had taste. Put that room (or the whole house, for that matter) within easy reach of civilization and he would have been happy to live in it. It was its isolation that got him down, that was partly responsible for the rift that was growing so rapidly between them.

The room ran the whole width of the house—some thirty-five feet. A wide yet delicate cornice framed the high ceiling and divided it into two squares; and within each square concentric and ever deepening circles of fine moulding flowed into a wide rosette, from which was suspended a glittering crystal chandelier. Against the east wall was the fireplace, its façade an Adam chimney-piece of inlaid marble (Mulgerry dated from the late seventeenth century, the East Wing having been added later). Heavy and expensive tapestry flanked the tall windows, and there were rich Persian rugs on the polished wood-block flooring. The furniture was sparse, but in keeping with the room—Hepplewhite, Sheraton, Thomas Hope, mostly reproduction, but with some genuine pieces among them. There was no television set, but a radio was concealed in an Adam-style satinwood commode.

The pictures on the rose-tinted walls were more varied; an Amigoni panel, a portrait of George the Third by Beechey, water-colours by Blake and Paul Nash, two of Grace's seascapes, and an allegoric portrait of Grace herself painted by Jim Upway. The latter picture, nebulous and grey, with Grace's perfect oval face unnaturally lengthened and distorted, the rich corn of her hair hidden by wispy clouds, leaden eyelids drooping over dulled eyes, Eric considered to be more of a caricature than a portrait. But Grace liked it (or perhaps she was flattered at being chosen as the model), and Jim declared that it was one of the best things he had done; it so perfectly expressed her cool placidity, he said, her withdrawnness. Eric wasn't sure that that was an accurate description of his wife. Cool, yes—if by that one meant passionless. And withdrawn in the sense that she disliked crowds and crowded places. But she was placid only on the surface, as he had good cause to know.

In the past, before the house had been divided, this had been the drawing-room; they had learned that from the Hump, in one of the old lady's rare expansive moments. There had been

Humplestons at Mulgerry since the house was built, as the Hump never lost an opportunity of reminding them; implying subtly (and not so subtly if the gout happened to be troubling her) that they were twentieth-century interlopers suffered only for the rent they paid.

But it's a proper room, thought Eric, as he switched off the light. A very proper room—even if it isn't a particularly comfortable one.

He went upstairs in his stockinged feet, leaving damp imprints in the thick pile of the carpet. Outside Grace's closed door he paused. Was she asleep? Or was she lying awake in the dark, waiting for him to go in, thinking up new words and phrases with which to bedevil him?

To hell with her, he thought, she'll keep until the morning—and went along the passage to his own room.

That was another thing that rankled—their having separate rooms. It had been Grace's idea. "I have the room and the bed to myself the whole term; I get used to sleeping alone. You can't expect me to change my habits every time you come home for a few weeks' holiday. I'll put your things in the spare room."

That had been last December, at the beginning of the Christmas holidays—though she had hinted at it before. He had protested that it was unnatural, after less than two years of marriage, to keep separate rooms; but as usual Grace had had her way. And his things were still in the spare room when he had come home four days ago, at the end of the Lent term.

He took off his wet clothes and put on pyjamas and dressing-gown; but before going downstairs he looked in at the studio. It was a large room at the rear of the house, facing the sea. Two canvases stood on easels in the centre of the room; one, to Eric's unpractised eye already finished, depicted a view from the studio window, the other was the rough beginning of an interior. The latter had been in much the same state when he had left for school in January; the other was new to him, and he went over to inspect it more closely. But he was not really interested in the painting, and he did not stay long. He had only looked into the room to assure himself that Grace was not there.

He took no pains to be quiet as he searched kitchen cupboards and the refrigerator for food; the sense of grievance was still with him. Only now it was the bedroom situation, and not their latest quarrel, which was uppermost in his mind. How could a man make up a quarrel with his wife if she insisted on sleeping alone? The bedroom was the traditional locale for repairing domestic differences. If she denied him that what was he expected to do?

He cut sandwiches and made coffee and took them into the living-room, switching the radio on full blast. That was to annoy Grace; since she had a passion for classical music she could damned well listen to some now. But the cacophony of noise (Eric had no ear for music) only served to increase his irritation, and he switched the set off and sat moodily in front of the electric fire—the late March night was chilly—and ate his sandwiches and drank the coffee. Then he poured himself a large whisky, pulled his chair nearer to the fire, put his slippered feet on the Adam chimneypiece (how the Hump would have hated that!), and drifted into a sad reverie on the difficulties and intricacies of married life.

Three whiskies and forty minutes later he was still there. Only now his mood had mellowed. Sad for himself, he also began to feel sad for Grace. Sure he had grievances—her coldness towards him, her obstinacy in continuing to bury herself in that remote spot when she knew how much he loathed it; but what sort of a catch was he as a husband? Grace had a healthy income of her own, and she was beginning to do well with her painting; he didn't know just how well, but it took more than chicken-feed to furnish that room the way Grace had furnished it. Whereas he was just an assistant master in a preparatory school, entirely dependent on his salary, and with only a slim prospect of buying a partnership or a school of his own in the distant future. He was quick-tempered, thoughtless, and (according to Grace) selfish and egotistical. He wasn't even faithful to her—though Grace hadn't known that until to-day.

But money was the real root of the trouble between them. Grace had it and he hadn't. Had she been dependent on him they would have taken a small flat in Sheffield, not too far from the school, and have lived a normal married life together. But because Grace had money of her own, and because she didn't like towns, she had refused to be parted from her beloved Mulgerry. In the few months she had lived there before their marriage it had become so much a part of her life that even marriage could not wean her from it. So for eight months of the year they lived apart; hardly the basis for a successful marriage. The Upways, the Winters, the Drummonds—even the old Hump and the hermit-like Kane—saw more of Grace than he did.

We're both individualists, he thought, both strong-willed. Neither of us has more than a rough working knowledge of give and take.

When eventually he went to bed he was in a forgiving, almost a repentant, mood. Certainly Grace had not treated him fairly; to greet him so coolly, to shut him out after nearly three months' separation, wasn't playing the game. A man needed a woman; had she the right to blame him if, after such a reception, he looked elsewhere? Perhaps he should have given her more time, tried harder to melt the ice; to dash off to Sheila the very next day was neither wise nor fair. And then on his return that morning to tell her where he had been—that was the act of a lunatic! Grace had not known about Sheila until then; no wonder she had bawled him out—if such a term could be applied to Grace's scathing rebukes. And he, as usual, had lost his temper—calling her names, threatening physical violence—before finally flinging out of the house.

How much did Grace mind about Sheila? he wondered. Quite a lot, from what she had said; but was that just a pose, a marital dog-in-the-manger attitude adopted to put him in his place? She did not seem to want him for herself, so why should she object to Sheila? Or was he wrong there? Did she really love him—not passionately and expressively, but in her own peculiar and reserved way? Was it all his fault? Had he not tried hard enough to break down that reserve, been too clumsy and forthright in his attempts at love-making? Grace needed more skilful wooing than did Sheila; it would take time and patience to melt the icy barrier she seemed to have built around herself. And he was not a patient person.

Well, he would make a beginning to-morrow—if Grace would let him, if the rift hadn't already grown too wide to heal. He would start by apologizing for what he had said, what he had done; forswear Sheila (the thought of that gave him a pang, but if he had to choose between the two he must choose Grace), and devote the rest of his holiday to pleasing her, to wooing her all over again.

If Grace would let him.

He had forgotten to draw the curtains, and when he awoke the next morning the sun was streaming through the window. It seemed a propitious omen. It swept away the last remnants of bitterness, hardened his good resolution of the previous night. To hell with pride! If grovelling like a whipped cur would do the trick, then he was quite prepared to grovel.

For a few moments he pondered his course of action. Should he go in to Grace at once, overwhelm her with impetuous love, kiss away the rancour and the bitterness she must still be feeling? No, that was not the way. It was too much like his old self, his ardour might frighten and repel rather than heal. It was also too early; Grace never woke before eight o'clock, and it was not yet seven. To startle her from sleep would make a bad beginning. Better to wash and shave first (Grace always complained if he kissed her before shaving, said it made her chin sore for the day), and then take breakfast up to her. He would take his own up too, so that they could have it together. Later, perhaps—but only if the mood was right—he would take her in his arms and tell her that it was all a mistake, that Sheila meant nothing to him, that he had never made love to her, that he had only said he had because he had been hurt and angry and wanted to hurt her in return. But no love-making; he must not rush her. He must be content to wait, show her that it was her wishes, not his, that mattered to him.

It took him some time to prepare the breakfast tray; Grace did not like to see him in the kitchen, and he had difficulty in finding the things he wanted. Nor would he compromise; everything had to be just right, the way Grace liked it. There was no hurry—except in his desire for the reconciliation that would culminate his efforts.

When at last the tray was ready he stood admiring his handiwork. Gleaming china and cutlery and silver on a white cloth, wetly glistening rolls of butter, the toast a crisp, golden brown. It was a pity, he thought, that he could not add, as a finishing touch, a newspaper or the mail. But the postman never reached Mulgerry before nine-thirty, and they were lucky if the papers arrived in time for lunch.

He went up the stairs slowly, careful not to spill the milk or the coffee (he preferred tea for breakfast, but Grace liked coffee). The room was in darkness, and he put the tray down on the dressing-table and went to the windows to draw the curtains. Then, smiling nervously, he turned to the bed. Grace always woke instantly with the light.

But Grace did not wake that morning. Grace wasn't there.

For a moment Eric thought that he had missed her—that she had slipped into the bathroom or the studio while he had been downstairs preparing the breakfast. But another glance at the bed dispelled that thought; it had not been slept in, the cover was still on. His display of temper the previous evening—the banging of pans and cupboard doors, the radio turned to full volume—had achieved nothing. Grace had not heard it, had not been there to hear it. And his new mood of repentance—that too had been wasted. Although he had not known it at the time, he had come home the previous evening to an empty house.

Grace had gone.

He slumped on to the bed and ran his fingers through his

hair. He felt sick and lost and inexplicably frightened. Only yesterday afternoon Grace had threatened to leave him—and now she was gone. "I'll not stand much more of this, Eric," she had said, in that rather flat, expressionless voice of hers that even anger seemed unable to vibrate. "One of these days I shall just walk out on you." But he hadn't believed her; Grace would never walk out, for this was her home. She had chosen it, furnished it, paid for it; everything in it was hers. If one of them had to go it would be he. And in his lunatic temper he had proceeded to taunt her with Sheila, declaring that he no longer looked on his marriage vows as binding—since she, apparently, had ceased to regard him as a husband. If she wished to go there was nothing to stop her.

He had not meant it. Grace should have known he had not meant it. But whether she knew it or not, she had gone.

He got up from the bed and went over to one of the built-in wardrobes, opened it, and stared at the row of frocks and coats and costumes that hung there. A few he recognized—but only a few; they were too numerous for Grace to have worn them all in the three or four months they spent together in the year. And he realized afresh, even more strongly, how strange and unnatural a marriage was theirs; he could not even tell, by looking at her wardrobe, what clothes she had taken with her. She could have taken enough for a night, a week, a year—he wouldn't know.

He picked up the breakfast tray, put it on the bedside table, and poured himself a cup of coffee. His hand shook as he lifted the cup; he took a quick gulp, almost choking as the hot liquid scalded his throat, and hurriedly put the cup down.

Where had Grace gone? So far as he knew her sister Daffy was her only surviving relative, and he had never heard her mention any particular friends; when she had settled in Mulgerry she had apparently cut herself completely adrift from her former life and connections. There was her agent in London, of course, and that fellow . . .

Daffy!

Until that moment he had completely forgotten his meeting with Daffy. He had bumped into her at Paddington on his way home the previous morning, and she had told him she was spending the day in town, and hoped Grace would be able to meet her. Would he ask Grace to ring her at her hotel? He had promised that he would; but the quarrel had developed immediately he arrived home, and Daffy and her message had slipped his memory.

Somewhat reassured, he started to butter himself a piece of toast. Grace would be with Daffy. No doubt Daffy, impatient at not receiving the expected call, had telephoned Mulgerry (probably very soon after he had bounced out of the house), and Grace had immediately left for London. She would have had to go at once if she was to spend any time with her sister, for the latter was returning to Glasgow in the morning—that morning. And Grace in her anger had not bothered to leave a note for him to explain her absence. Probably the impecunious Daffy (it always puzzled Eric that the late Mr Lomas should have provided so amply for one daughter to the exclusion of the other) had said nothing of her meeting with him, preferring to confine a trunk call to the bare essentials—in which case Grace had no doubt experienced a triumphant delight in her sudden departure, believing that to him it would be inexplicable.

Relief made him generous, and he smiled. He did not grudge her her triumph. In any case it would be short-lived, for by now she would have learned of his meeting with Daffy, would know that he must have guessed the reason for her absence. But at least she had succeeded in giving him a few nasty moments.

He looked at his watch. Nine-fifteen. He did not know at what time Daffy's train left for Glasgow, but he thought it was around ten o'clock. That meant Grace could be home in time for lunch—unless she decided to visit her agent or to do some shopping. Well, the carefully prepared breakfast had been a fiasco. He would see what he could do with lunch; even if that too was to be wasted, the effort must be made.

He found that little preparation was needed. There was cold

chicken and salad and trifle in the refrigerator, and he uncorked a bottle of Beaujolais and placed it on the floor to breathe. Then, when he had washed up and made his bed, and done the few household chores he considered necessary, he went up to Grace's room and drew the curtains and opened the windows. Grace made a fetish of open windows. She must have closed them the previous evening because of the rain.

The windows of the two bedrooms faced east, overlooking the courtyard, on the far side of which was a stone wall; behind that a slim belt of firs screened them from the garage block and the Drummonds' flat above it. The trees gave privacy to both tenants, but they cut off the view of the park from the East Wing. The studio faced east and south; from the south windows one could look out over the lawns to the high cliffs and the sea, and it was here that Grace loved to sit. The sea fascinated her. She had no desire to be on it, to travel the oceans as he would have done had he had the money. She was content to watch it— and to paint.

It was as he opened the last window that he realized that one at least of his surmises was adrift. If Grace had closed the windows she had not done so because of the rain; it had been fine until well past six o'clock, and if she had gone to Town she must have left before that.

But if she had *not* gone to Town where was she?

After some reflection he decided that Grace had closed the windows before leaving, anticipating the rain. There had been no reason to anticipate it—the afternoon had been fine, the clouds had come up quickly and quite unexpectedly—but it was the only explanation he could think of which fitted the facts.

The facts, that is, as he wanted them to be. For if Grace were not with Daffy there could be only one explanation for her absence—that she had carried out her threat to leave him.

And that was something he did not care to contemplate.

But a moment later he was forced to contemplate it. For if he could make a reasonable guess at the closed windows, he could not account for the drawn curtains. Grace might change her clothes several times a day, but she never drew the curtains. Not even when she dressed for dinner with the lights on. There was no need to. Unless she stood close to a window she could not be seen from the courtyard.

So why had she drawn them on that particular afternoon?

2

WHEN he wandered into the garden some half an hour later the Winters were picking daffodils, a great bank of which flanked the wide terrace on the south side of the house. Mrs Winter was Lady Humpleston's sister—a big, rawboned woman nearly six feet tall, with a red face and hooked nose and a loud, crisp voice. She wore rough tweeds and stout walking shoes, and her greying hair was close-cropped. On their first meeting Eric had immediately associated her with the rangy-looking chestnut he had seen in the paddock. In that he had been wrong. Mrs Winter had never been on a horse in her life.

"Nearly over," she remarked, when Eric complimented her on the daffodils. The gardens were her responsibility; she had two men to help her, but did far more work than either of them. "Just sorting the living from the dead."

Having nothing else to do, he stood watching them. He knew better than to offer his help. The gardens were sacred; none but the Hump and the Winters was allowed to touch the flowers, let alone pick them. Mrs Winter worked briskly and efficiently, snapping the thick, juicy stems with a crisp twitch of her roughened fingers. Her daughter's efforts were less whole-hearted. She moved slowly, took longer to select the flowers she wanted, and often bungled the picking, so that the stems were broken in more than one place and drooped sadly over the hand that held them. But that was typical of Caroline, in Eric's opinion; he thought her the most ineffectual and incompetent female he had ever met. She seemed out of place as the tough-looking Mrs Winter's daughter, though she had something of her aunt's

B

contempt for the common herd. This latter was the product of environment, he suspected, rather than a natural inclination.

"It's a lovely morning," he said, wondering why he bothered with them. He didn't like them, and he suspected that they didn't like him. But to talk—even such trifling talk as this— was to shelve temporarily the uneasiness that possessed him. "So fresh after the rain."

"The garden needed rain." Mrs Winter did not cease her picking or look up. "It did a lot of good."

"Not to me it didn't," Eric said. "I got caught in it without a raincoat. Soaked me right through to the skin."

Mrs Winter stood up and arched her back. She looked at Eric, and then rather apprehensively at the windows of the ground-floor flat she and her daughter shared with her elder sister. Despite her almost masculine appearance and forthright manner, she was in some awe of her sister Alice. She was also more or less dependent on her, the late Mr Winter having failed to provide adequately for his family. And Alice did not approve of Eric Cawthorne. For one thing, he drank (or so Alice said, although Mrs Winter had never seen him the worse for it). For another, he was always quarrelling with his wife—and Grace Cawthorne was the only one of her tenants for whom Lady Humpleston had any regard. Worst of all, he was a Socialist.

Mrs Winter had no strong views on either drink or politics, and it had been her experience that all husbands quarrelled with their wives. But she had to live with her sister, and so she strove to avoid dissension. Despite Eric's belief that she disliked him, he seemed to her a personable and fairly harmless young man, and she was perfectly ready to converse with him when Alice was not around.

"It soaked Caroline too," she said. "And poor Pompey—the darling looked like a drowned rat. I hope to goodness he hasn't caught a chill. He's not strong, for all his liveliness."

Pompey was the Hump's Pomeranian; a detestable little beast, Eric thought—'vicious' was a more appropriate description of its nature than 'lively.' Mrs Winter seemed more concerned about the dog's drenching than her daughter's—which was strange when one remembered that Caroline was supposed to be something of an invalid. She certainly looked one now. She was a strange girl, Eric thought. Everything about her seemed to be exaggerated; she was tall and very thin, with a perpetual stoop that accentuated her listless appearance. She had her mother's hooked nose, a wide, generous mouth, small ears set close to her head, a slightly receding chin, and a fine, almost transparent skin. Her hair was jet black, thick and glossy, and pulled tightly back into a heavy coil at the nape of her neck. She could never have been beautiful; but with the skilful use of cosmetics and a more erect bearing she might have been strikingly arresting.

"How far did you go, Miss Winter?" Eric asked.

Usually she avoided his gaze, but now she looked at him directly and long, as though observing him for the first time. For the first time, too, he saw that her eyes were dark; he had thought they lacked sparkle, but they were brilliant enough now. Was there contempt in them? he wondered, surprised and annoyed at her steady gaze. And if so what reason had she to be contemptuous of him? The boot should be on the other foot, he thought.

Suddenly her eyes dropped, and she bent again to the daffodils. Eric was about to repeat his question when he saw the stout, dumpy figure of Lady Humpleston approaching from the far end of the terrace. He did not stay to meet her. The only good thing about the Hump, he thought, as he made his way down to the cliff-edge, is that stick of hers. You can always hear her coming; she can't creep up on you and catch you unawares. And none of the occupants of Mulgerry (with the possible exception of Grace), and least of all himself, ever wanted to be caught by the Hump.

He began once more to wonder about Grace. When he had telephoned the number Daffy had given him it was to learn that she had already left the hotel. No, Mrs Cawthorne had not spent the night there, the reception clerk had told him; all their rooms had been booked some days in advance. He rang two other hotels where Grace had sometimes stayed on her rare visits to London, but with no more success. After that he gave up.

Inevitably his thoughts led him towards Grace's favourite spot on the cliff-top. It was almost in the centre of the bay and from it one's eye could follow the coast for several miles, eastward to Gavin Head and westward to the lighthouse on Mawl Island, a rocky hump in the sea some hundred yards south of Ferring Point. It was here that Grace loved to sit, screened from the land by the bracken and bushes that grew near the cliff-edge; sometimes painting, but more often just gazing out to sea.

As Eric neared the spot a man burst out of the bushes, halting abruptly when he saw him. He was small, and swarthy of face, dressed in a rough tweed jacket and light corduroy trousers bagging at the knees. They were also dirty at the knees, as though he had been kneeling on the damp ground.

Eric halted too. For a moment the two men looked at each other. Then, with a muttered exclamation that might have been a greeting or an apology, the small man hurried off in the direction of the house, breaking into a run as he passed.

Eric turned to gaze after him. "Well, well!" he said aloud. "What has the mysterious Mr Kane been up to to put him in such a tizzy?"

None of the occupants of Mulgerry seemed to know much about Walter Kane, who had taken the basement flat at about the same time as Grace had moved into the East Wing. He appeared to have no friends and to do no work. Occasionally he would disappear for a day or two in a rather dilapidated black van he kept in the garage, but most of the time he stayed in his basement.

Connie Upway had nicknamed him "The Hermit." The alliteration of the Hermit and the Hump pleased her. "I really ought to call Mulgerry 'The Hovel,'" she said. "But it doesn't exactly fit, does it?"

Eric experienced a feeling of annoyance that Walter Kane should have invaded Grace's sanctuary, even in her absence.

Every one at Mulgerry knew of it, and by tacit agreement it was acknowledged as Grace's private property. Perhaps he didn't actually park himself here, he thought, gazing around for some evidence of the other's presence. Probably just happened to pass through it on his way back from the Head—or wherever he's been.

The tide was in, the rocks below completely submerged. He did not go too near the cliff-edge; gazing down from a height gave him a tingling sensation in the pit of his stomach. Nor did he stay long; there was nothing to stay for. Indeed, there was every incentive to get back to the house. While he had been absent Grace might have telephoned—she might even have returned. . . .

By the time he reached the terrace he was running. The Winters had disappeared, but Jim Upway was on the lawn talking to Nadia Drummond. They both called to him, but he took no notice. Grace might be home.

She wasn't home. The house was as he had left it. He looked in all the rooms, just to be certain, and then came downstairs and stood moodily in front of the open windows of the living-room, gazing unseeing at the vista of lawns and neat flower-beds and well-clipped yews.

Nadia and Jim walked across the lawn towards him and on to the terrace. As they came up to the open window Eric saw that Nadia had an electric iron in her hand.

"I just wanted to return this," she said. "I borrowed it from Grace yesterday morning. She said she would need it later in the day, but I couldn't get any reply when I brought it back. She must have gone out, eh?"

"What time was that?" asked Eric, taking the iron from her.

"Just before four. I tried again later around six-thirty, but there was still no reply. Were you *both* out?"

"I'd gone for a walk," Eric said.

His spirits rose. If Grace had left before four it seemed that his assumption could be right, that she *had* gone to see Daffy.

It didn't explain the drawn bedroom curtains, but they were unimportant in themselves. From them he had inferred that Grace had not left until after dark—in which case she could not have gone to Town. There was no bus, for one thing. And even if she had rung for a taxi . . .

A taxi! Why hadn't he thought of that before? Grace seldom went anywhere by bus; it was such a long walk to the bus-stop. He had only to telephone the car-hire firm to find out exactly when she had left. They might even know her destination.

"Wasn't Grace with you?" asked Nadia. "I'm quite sure she was out. I rang and rang and rang. Both times."

Eric smiled at her. Her news had cheered him, and it was easy to smile at Nadia. She was a pretty girl—small and very blonde, with big blue eyes which always seemed to be wide open. She wore clothes which accentuated her opulent figure, and rather too much make-up and jewellery for the country. Grace did not like her, thought her sly and empty-headed. But that didn't worry Eric. It didn't worry Jim Upway either. He was often at her side when her husband or Connie were not around.

"Grace has gone to Town to see her sister," Eric said. He said it with conviction, sure now that he was right. But in any case he wasn't going to tell them of his quarrel with Grace, or admit that he didn't know her whereabouts. He had his pride.

"Really?" Jim sounded surprised.

"Yes, really. Any reason why she shouldn't?"

"No, of course not. I just wondered . . ." Jim looked confused. But his eyes were intent on Eric's, and after a pause he said, "You're quite sure she's gone to see her sister?"

"Damn it, of course I'm sure."

"But you were out, you said."

"What's that got to do with it?" Eric was annoyed; Jim's doubts served to accentuate his own. "Her sister rang up while I was out; she had come down from Scotland, and as she was spending only the one day in Town Grace rushed up to see her. Anything unusual in that?"

"Nothing. Nothing at all." But he still looked puzzled. "Did she leave a note to say where she'd gone?"

"Of course she left a note." The lie was essential. And Grace *would* have left a note if they hadn't had that damned row, if she hadn't wanted to score off him. "Satisfied?"

"No," Jim said. But he was smiling now. "It mucks up Connie's dinner-party."

"What dinner-party?"

"Didn't Grace tell you? It's our wedding anniversary, so Connie thought we'd have a party. You and Grace, Nadia and Mike. Now we're going to be a female short."

"You could ask Caroline," Nadia said, and giggled.

"We could, couldn't we? Or the Hump. But I don't think we will. It's a wedding anniversary, not a funeral." Nadia giggled again. "What time did Grace say she'd be back?"

"She didn't. And this is the first I've heard of a party. I suppose Grace forgot to tell me. Sorry, Jim. Still, she'll probably turn up this afternoon; her sister was going back to-day. Though she *might* decide to stay another night now she's there," he added, giving himself a loophole should Grace's anger against him keep her away. He didn't want to have any further explaining to do. "If so I expect she'll ring me."

"I must flee," Nadia said. "Mike will be shouting for his lunch, and I haven't done a thing about it." Her eyes were very wide as she added innocently, looking directly at Eric, "He'll be terribly disappointed if Grace isn't at the party. He adores her, you know."

Eric gazed after her in surprise. He didn't know anything of the sort. Although the Upways were friendly with the Drummonds, he and Grace were not. Grace didn't like either of them —or so she said; and he, while attracted by Nadia's looks and provocative manner, agreed with Grace that she was difficult to talk to (when others were present, was his private reservation). As for Mike Drummond, he couldn't stand him. The man was too smooth, too conceited, and over-dressed for the country.

But—Grace and Drummond? Surely not. Nadia was just

trying to make mischief—resentful, perhaps, of Grace's aloofness. So far as he knew neither she nor her husband had ever been invited into the East Wing.

Jim too was gazing after Nadia. She had a Marilyn Monroe wiggle. He said, "If clothes were designed merely to disguise the human form they're wasted on that girl. Dressed or undressed, she's pure sex." He turned, grinning. "Perhaps 'pure' isn't the appropriate adjective." Then the grin left him. He said awkwardly, "Sorry if I sounded rather inquisitive about Grace, old man. It's just that—oh, forget it."

Eric wasn't sure that he wanted to forget it. Jim's persistence had both annoyed and intrigued him; it gave the impression that the other knew—or suspected—that Eric was not telling the truth. But why? Why should he think that? And why should it worry him if he did? It couldn't be just the dinner-party.

The dinner-party. There was something odd there too. Why had Jim immediately assumed that Grace would not be back for it? "It mucks up Connie's dinner-party," he had said—and "Now we're going to be a female short." Surely the more natural assumption would have been that Grace *would* be back in time, since she had left no word to the contrary?

But Jim had been at home all that previous afternoon—whereas he had not. Was Jim hinting that he knew more about Grace's absence than did her husband?

"What's the matter with you, Jim?" he asked. "If you've anything on your mind you'd better spill it; it'll be more comfortable for both of us. What makes you think Grace didn't go to Town yesterday?"

"I don't. Not if she left a note to the contrary." Jim paused, his darkly handsome face puckered in a frown. "Her sister's a Miss Lomas, isn't she?"

For a moment Eric wondered how Jim should know that, since he had never met Daffy. Then he remembered that Grace always signed her paintings with her maiden name, and he nodded.

"That's why I was puzzled," Jim said. "You see, yesterday afternoon I put a letter in the hall rack for the postman to collect. About five-thirty, that would be. There was no other letter there then. But later, just after dinner, I put a second letter there, and I noticed an envelope in Grace's handwriting. And it was addressed to a Miss Daphne Lomas in Glasgow."

Eric did not at first see the significance; he wondered idly why Jim should have been sufficiently interested to read the address on Grace's letter. Then he understood—and his heart sank. Some time after five-thirty Grace had posted a letter; so, despite what Nadia had told them, she certainly had not left Mulgerry before then. And since the letter had been addressed to Daffy in Glasgow it was obvious that she neither knew of her sister's visit to London nor had any intention of visiting her there.

But Jim was watching him, and he smiled. He wasn't going to show Jim he was worried. "I still don't see what all the fuss is about," he said, as cheerfully as he could. "Her sister must have telephoned after five-thirty, that's all. It seems to me you're getting steamed up over nothing, Jim. Did you think I'd murdered the poor girl?"

"Don't be an ass." But he still looked worried. "See here, Eric—I know it's none of my business, but are you sure Grace hasn't walked out on you because of the row you and she had yesterday?" He gave a rather sickly grin. "Wives do, you know. Connie played that trick on me once. Luckily she had sense enough to come back."

Eric was too startled to be offended. "Row? Did Grace tell you we'd had a row?"

"Good Lord, no! I just happened to be out here while it was on. And since it wasn't enacted in dumb show I couldn't help overhearing. The Hump heard you too." He grinned. "The old harridan simply lapped it up; I could see her ears twitching with excitement. You'd think with a bosom like hers she'd be absolutely bursting with the milk of human kindness. But not her. She thrives on other people's misfortunes."

Eric was not interested in the Hump at that moment. He was wondering whether there was now any point in maintaining the deception.

He decided that there was.

"Oh, that." He tried to sound casual. "Just a minor bust-up. It didn't last long. Still, if Grace hadn't left a note to say what she was up to I suppose I might have thought the way you did." He grinned. "But I'm sorry the Hump heard us. I hate to think I've been a source of pleasure to the old basket. What did she have to say?"

"Nothing. She hadn't time to talk, she was too busy gloating. When I realized what was afoot I cleared off and left her to it. Anyway, I'm glad I was wrong about Grace."

"So am I," Eric said. "Well, see you this evening—with or without the missus."

When Jim had gone he made for the telephone. Grace always used the same taxi-firm (the number was written prominently on the pad), and he waited impatiently for the information he wanted. But when it came it was not what he had hoped for. No taxi had been ordered for Mulgerry House the previous day.

The Upways were a constant source of wonder to their friends. In many ways they were complete opposites, yet they never seemed to quarrel. Jim was extremely handsome; tall, dark, and debonair, with wavy hair and an athlete's figure— although he disliked all forms of physical exercise. He was un-practical, optimistic, and not averse to making unkind criticisms of his friends and acquaintances if by so doing he could raise a laugh. He had a charming smile, which he employed frequently, and seemed equally at home in the company of men and women. But whereas men liked him, women adored him. Even Grace had admitted that he was attractive; and that from Grace was praise indeed. And if women had a weakness for him, he had a weakness for women; Eric knew well that he had been unfaithful to Connie on more than one occasion. Yet it was quite obvious that he loved his wife, and she him.

Connie knew nothing of his infidelities. (Once, after a heavy drinking session in The George at Tanmouth, during which Jim had confided to Eric the details of his latest infidelity, he had said anxiously, "You won't breathe a word of this to Connie, will you? It'd break her heart; she thinks I'm the cat's whiskers. If she ever found out I'd been playing away from home she'd leave me for sure. Connie's the most tolerant person I know, but she wouldn't stand for that.") She seemed as sure of her husband's love and fidelity as she was sure of her love for him. Yet she wasn't beautiful, she wasn't outwardly a romantic. She had a neat figure (and that, Eric knew, went a long way with Jim); but her face was too thin, her nose too squat for beauty. She was strong-willed and practical, a good organizer, and had a passion for sport in general and cricket in particular. Above all, she was kind.

Eric was no judge of painting, but he preferred Grace's sea-scapes to Jim Upway's abstracts and vague symbolism. Grace didn't agree. "He's a far better artist than I am," she had said, when he had first asked her about Jim. Nor had her opinion changed when, at a joint exhibition she had held with Jim at the Strange Gallery in London, her pictures had easily outsold Jim's. "It's only a question of time," she had insisted. "He'll be famous long after I'm forgotten."

Connie shared Grace's faith in her husband's talent. It was a blind faith, since she knew as little as Eric about painting. Nor was she daunted by his present lack of success. To augment his irregular and modest income she had, on coming to Mulgerry, taken a job as History mistress at the Tanmouth High School for Girls, travelling daily the twelve miles there and back on a motor-assisted cycle. Eric knew she disliked the work, disliked the journey, disliked having to spend so much of the day apart from her husband. But she never grumbled, never once suggested that Jim might go out to work himself. "It's only a temporary post," she had insisted. "I'll give it up as soon as Jim gets the recognition he deserves."

The temporary post had so far lasted for nearly three years.

Eric wondered for how much longer it must continue before she recognized it as being permanent.

The dinner-party that evening was not a success. Grace had not returned from wherever it was she had gone, and Mike Drummond was also absent. "He had to visit a most important client," Nadia told them (she always referred to her husband's customers as clients). "He's terribly disappointed he couldn't make it, but he'll try to look in later." Connie was a good cook and the food was excellent, but no one but herself seemed to have an appetite for it. Eric was too worried about Grace to enjoy his food, and both Jim and Nadia were unusually pre-occupied. Nadia always ate sparingly (she put on weight easily, and was perpetually worried about her figure), but Jim normally had a healthy appetite.

The conversation was no more spirited than the eating. Connie did her best to keep it going; but she was fighting a losing battle, and after a while she gave up trying. Even the wine did not loosen their tongues; as so often happens when the mood is not right, it had a soporific rather than an enlivening effect.

She had given them chicken Maryland, principally because it was a favourite with Jim. But as she looked at their plates and saw how little they had eaten she said dismally, "What's the matter with you all? Is my cooking really that bad?"

"It's excellent, Connie," Eric assured her. "You don't need us to tell you that. But the fact is, I'm beginning to be worried about Grace. Can't think why she isn't back by now."

"Mike's away too," Nadia said—and the sly look she gave Eric left him in no doubt as to what she inferred from that. "But that doesn't put *me* off my food. It's my weight *I'm* worried about." She ran her hands slowly over the front of her body, drawing the men's eyes to her. "You know me, Connie. Eat an ounce and put on a pound."

Connie shrugged. She had no weight problems of her own.

"And what about you, Dismal?" she said to her husband, with a tartness foreign to her. "*You* haven't anything on your mind, I hope? Because if you have I'd like to hear about it."

Yes, thought Eric, what's up with him to-night? It can't be Grace; she's my worry, not his. But something is definitely biting him. As a rule he never stops talking.

"It's Nadia," Jim said, rallying. "I ought not to have sat next to her; she does something to my baser instincts that I find it impossible to resist. The only way I can keep my hands off her is to sit on them. But it's a solution that makes eating tricky."

Nadia giggled. This was right up her street; this was the sort of badinage she understood.

"Oh, Jim!" She rolled her eyes at him, false eyelashes fluttering. "I never knew you cared. Why didn't you tell me you were having trouble with your hands? I would have held them for you."

"She would, too," Connie said, smiling. This was more like her Jim. Like most generous women, she was amused by her husband's flirtations. She even seemed to encourage them. "Well, get it over, both of you. Maybe Jim will have a better appetite for the sweet then."

Jim shook his head. "You're a lewd woman, Connie. I refuse to take sex as an appetizer for your lemon soufflé. It must stand or fall on its merits."

It was not edifying talk, but to a hostess it was infinitely preferable to silence. Connie happily collected the plates, and went off to the kitchen. But by the time she returned with the soufflé silence had blanketed them again. It was almost a relief when the door opened and Caroline Winter walked in.

"Caroline!" Connie exclaimed. "How nice to see you!"

Typical Connie, thought Eric. She can't *really* think it's nice to have Caroline suddenly thrust upon us. Caroline won't brighten up the party. But then Connie was kind to every one. She had even been known to put in a good word for the Hump.

"I'm sorry, Connie. I didn't know you had guests." Caroline's eyes slid from Jim to Eric, and again she gave him that slightly contemptuous look he had seen in the garden. Nadia she ignored completely. "I won't stay. I just brought that book I promised you."

"Of course you'll stay," Connie said, going over to her and taking her arm. "We've just finished—you can join us for coffee. Come into the other room."

Nadia and the two men followed them into the sitting room. It had a bare look. Like all the rooms in the house, it was high-ceilinged and spacious, and Connie had done her best with it; but the carpet was too small, the furniture too sparse. Instinctively Eric lowered his voice and trod softly, fearful of the echo.

"Make yourselves comfortable," Connie said. "I'll get the coffee."

They perched themselves on chairs round the room and were silent. Eric stared out of the uncurtained window at the dark night, thinking of Grace. Nadia fidgeted, Jim lolled uneasily. Caroline's eyes were fixed on the book in her hands.

"What's the book?" Jim asked suddenly. His voice sounded unnaturally loud in the wide silence, and they all started.

"Onward from Bethlehem," Caroline said. Her soft, clear voice had a childlike quality that would have been irritating if one heard it too often. But Caroline was not a great talker.

"H'm! Sounds religious. Is it?"

"Not exactly."

"It's the story of a man born in Bethlehem on the same day as Our Lord," Connie said, coming into the room with the coffee tray. "That's about all the religion there is to it. Didn't you read the reviews?"

"I never read reviews—you know that. They make me buy books I can't afford and probably won't enjoy anyway. I think I must have rather peculiar tastes in literature."

Connie laughed. "You can say that again, darling."

As she poured the coffee and handed round the cups Eric saw that Caroline's eyes never left her. Even when Connie sat down and began to drink her coffee the girl continued to watch her. Her lips were slightly parted, and there was more animation in her face than Eric had seen there before. It did not take a psychologist to appreciate that Connie was important to her.

But her interest was her undoing. Her eyes still on her hostess, she replaced her cup insecurely on its saucer. It teetered perilously, and then toppled over into her lap.

"Oh, dear!" Connie exclaimed, hastening to her aid. "It's all over your dress."

Caroline's embarrassment was painful to watch. Knowing how she felt, that her one desire was to be out of range of their inquisitive and censorious eyes, Connie did not attempt to deal with the damage on the spot. "You'd better go and change, dear," she said, taking the cup from her. "I'll come down with you. Don't worry about the frock. We'll soon get the stain out."

When they had gone Eric said, "I can't make that girl out. Sometimes she's all Humpleston, or Winter, or whatever family it is she gets her damned arrogance from. But at others—well, look at her just now. As clumsy and awkward as a ruddy kitchen maid."

"She's not a girl, she's a woman," Nadia said. "She won't see thirty again." Nadia was twenty-eight. "Got a crush on Connie, hasn't she, Jim? Never took her eyes off her." She shrugged, and her dress slipped a little further off one shoulder. She put up a bejewelled hand to adjust it, hesitated, and then decided to leave it as it was. "Well, I hope it's healthy."

"Of course it's healthy. It's your mind that isn't." Jim was annoyed. "And why shouldn't she be fond of Connie? Connie's the only person here who accepts her as an adult human being. Her mother treats her like a child, the Hump bullies her, and the rest of us avoid her like the plague and sneer at her behind her back."

Eric nodded. "That's true. Though I fancy she does a bit of sneering herself at times."

"Does she? I hadn't noticed. But you can't wonder at it with the Hump as her mentor. 'There have been Humplestons at Mulgerry for nearly three hundred years,'" Jim mimicked the old woman. "Pure feudalism; they're all tainted with it. Did you notice how she walked in on us without bothering to knock? She's always doing it. Can't seem to appreciate that she no longer has the right to wander about the whole damned house at will." He stretched lazily. "That's one of the reasons why I want to get out of here."

"What cheek!" Nadia had recovered from the shock of Jim's unexpected rebuke. "Doesn't Connie object? I would."

"She objects all right; but she's too kind-hearted to tick the girl off. And as Caroline always comes laden with gifts it's rather tricky. Quite expensive gifts too, some of them. God knows where she finds the money to buy them. I doubt if the Hump is over-generous with pocket-money."

"What sort of gifts?" Nadia asked.

"Every sort. Books, jewellery, things to wear—even the odd chicken. Regular fairy godmother, she is. Connie tried refusing them at first. But Caroline was so upset that it seemed kinder to accept." He turned to Eric. "I suppose you know she once walked in on Grace?"

"Did she?" Eric was startled out of his reverie. "No, I didn't know."

"Grace found her upstairs. She'd brought a message from the Hump." He laughed. "Grace was livid. I don't think she's tried it since."

After that the conversation languished again. Jim switched on the radio; from force of habit he had the volume full on. Nadia stuffed her fingers into her ears. "Heavens, what a row!" she squealed. "I can't hear myself think."

"Don't worry," Jim said, grinning. "You'll not be missing much."

But he turned the volume down slightly. Nadia leaned over the arm of her chair, heedless that in so doing her short skirt rode far above her silken knees, picked up a cushion she had discarded, and threw it at him.

Eric said, "The noise campaign is still on, I gather. I could hear that thing going full blast yesterday evening."

Jim laughed ruefully. "It's still on, but it doesn't seem to be taking effect. The old girl rants and raves, but she won't break the tenancy. And honestly, Eric, we just can't afford to live here. It's crippling me."

Crippling Connie, you mean, Eric thought. "Can't you sub-let?" he asked.

"No. It's in the agreement."

The door opened slowly and Connie came in. She looked white and strained. Her husband stared at her.

"What's up, darling? Seen a ghost?"

"I'm all right," Connie said unsteadily. "At least——" She switched off the radio and turned to Nadia. "Do you mind if I take Jim downstairs for a few minutes? There's—there's some one he has to see."

She did not look at Eric.

No, said Nadia, she didn't mind. But when they had gone she said, "Some one he has to see? Who could that be? One of Jim's girl friends making trouble, do you think? He's got plenty."

"Has he?" Eric wasn't going to discuss his friend's misdeeds with Nadia. "I wouldn't know."

"Then you're about the only one who doesn't. You and Connie. It beats me how she can be so blind."

He ignored that. "It's more likely to be trouble with the Hump. It's been brewing for some time."

Jim was as pale as Connie when they returned. Before either of their guests could question them Connie said, "I'm terribly sorry, Nadia, but would you think me dreadfully rude if I asked you to go now? Something important has cropped up that we have to discuss with Eric. Something private."

Nadia did mind. Other people's private affairs were always of interest to her. But she had no option. She said, "Shall I wait in the other room?"

Connie shook her head. "We may be some time. It would be best if you went home."

Nadia shrugged and stood up. "It's the first time I've been thrown out of a party," she said. "And I haven't even mis-behaved." She looked at Jim. "Or have I?"

c

He shook his head without answering.

Connie saw her to the door, and then came and stood beside her husband. Eric saw that she was crying.

"It's Grace, isn't it?" he said, his voice hoarse. It had to be Grace; they wouldn't look at him like that otherwise. "What's happened? Where is she?"

Jim stepped forward and gripped his arm.

"She's downstairs, Eric. No, wait a minute! She—there's been an accident."

Connie was weeping copiously now, and a cold shaft of dread pierced Eric's heart. An accident! That was the way people always broke it when . . .

"You mean—she's dead?"

Jim nodded. "I'm afraid so. The police have just found her. She was lying on the rocks at the foot of the cliff."

3

ERIC was never to forget that last look at his wife. She lay on a stretcher in the big hall, where the police had brought her to await the ambulance. The Upways and the doctor had stopped him when he had bent impulsively to lift the blanket that covered her; and at first he had been glad of their restraint. "No need for that now, sir," the police inspector had said solicitously. "Leave it until to-morrow. Your friend here has identified her for us." And he had stood back, with Connie's hand grasping his tightly, and had stared unseeing at the men grouped round the stretcher.

It was when the ambulance men bent to lift her that he knew they had been wrong. He had to see her; not to-morrow, but now. He was no longer afraid to look. That vague form under the grey blanket was Grace; he could not let her go without a final farewell.

This time they made no attempt to stop him.

It was Grace—and yet it was not Grace. Not after what the rocks and the sea had done to her. But even in that battered and broken body he could still see her. Her head was set at an odd, unnatural angle, giving her a grotesque, questioning look (later he was to learn that her neck was broken). It was a relief that her eyes were closed; he had feared that even in death they might accuse him. Her face was swollen, there were ugly red blotches on her cheeks, her hair was matted and discoloured. But it was still Grace. Cold and withdrawn and passionless as ever. No longer sleek and beautiful—but still Grace.

They took her away after that; when she had gone he felt very much alone, even a little frightened. He was aware of

vague, shadowy forms—some close beside him, some lurking in the vastness of the hall—but they had nothing to do with him. Grace was not among them, would never be among them again. Grace had left him for good.

The finality of that thought appalled him. He buried his face in his hands. "Why did she have to do it?" he sobbed. "Why? Why? *Why?*"

Connie was beside him, her arm around him. Now that she was needed she had forgotten her own tears. "Don't, Eric," she pleaded. "You mustn't blame yourself."

There were still two policemen left. One of them, the tall, uniformed inspector, said kindly, "We won't worry him now, Mrs Upway. It'll keep until the morning. Maybe the doctor here can fix him up with a sedative. A good night's sleep'll do him a power of good."

Eric took his hands from his face and looked at the man.

"I don't need a sedative," he said—and was surprised at his own calmness. "I'm not ill. My wife is dead, but there's nothing wrong with *me*."

The inspector looked shocked. Eric did not care what he or the others thought about him; he wanted to be rid of them. Only a few moments back he had been scared of being alone. Now that was all he wanted.

Without a word he turned toward the massive oak doors that led to the drive and the East Wing. But Jim stopped him. "You're not going home to-night, old man," he said firmly. "You're staying with us."

Eric did not protest. He could be alone anywhere now; one place was as good—or as bad—as another. With Jim's hand on his arm he turned and walked steadily up the broad staircase to the Upways' flat.

He sat on the worn settee and listened to the murmur of their voices as they whispered together. He knew what they were saying. But he did not want their sympathy. He didn't want it, and he didn't deserve it.

"I don't want sympathy," he said. "I don't want sympathy

and I don't want cosseting. It's kind of you to let me stay here, but if you don't mind I think I'll go to bed."

Connie came and sat beside him. "Not just yet, Eric," she said, a hand on his knee. "It will make the night so long. You —you wouldn't like to talk about it, would you? It might be better than bottling it up inside you."

"There's nothing to talk about." His voice was detached, impersonal, dead. And that was the way he felt; as though there were no blood in his veins. "Grace killed herself, and it's my fault. What else is there to say?"

"A lot." Connie's fingers bit into his flesh. She did not wear her nails long, as did Grace and Nadia, but he could feel their pressure. "In the first place, there's no reason to suppose that Grace *did* kill herself. Obviously the police don't think so. They think it was an accident."

He looked up quickly. An accident? It would not bring Grace back if that were so, but it would put him on better terms with himself, help him to lose the dread feeling of guilt.

Eagerly he clutched at the straw. "What happened?" he asked. "Tell me."

"Some one walking along the cliff-top this evening saw her lying on the rocks, and phoned the police," Jim said. He had poured out a stiff whisky, and he thrust it into Eric's hand. Mechanically Eric sipped it, surprised that he could enjoy the taste and stimulus of it. "Just below where she always sat. You know."

Eric nodded. "Was—was she drowned?"

"No. She broke her neck when she fell—or so the doctor said." He saw the other wince, and added, "I'm sorry. But it's better for you to hear the details from us rather than from others."

"And it *must* have been an accident," Connie said. "Grace would never have committed suicide; you know that as well as I do. Why should she, anyway?"

"Because we had a row," Eric wanted to say. But he didn't say it. For one thing, it sounded almost conceited—that Grace might kill herself simply because he had quarrelled with her. And for another—well, Connie was right. Grace wasn't the suicidal type. She was so calm, so controlled.

"We had a row," he said, omitting the 'because.' "But there was nothing new in that. Perhaps it was just coincidence that made me think——" He finished the whisky at a gulp, and held the empty glass out to Jim. "I could do with another of those. May I?"

"Sure thing," Jim said.

"Of course it was a coincidence," Connie assured him. "I expect she got too near the edge and slipped."

"I was there only this morning," Eric said. "Standing just where she must have stood. But the tide was in and the rocks were covered. If I'd only known!"

"How could you have known?" Jim handed him the whisky. "And what could you have done if you had known?"

"But why wasn't she washed away by the tide?"

"She fell between two boulders. They held her." Jim decided that this was an aspect of the tragedy best ignored. "Anyway, you have nothing to reproach yourself with, old man. You're completely blameless."

But I'm not, thought Eric. Maybe I wasn't responsible for her death, but I was a rotten husband. I didn't make her happy, I could never see her point of view. I thought she was selfish and cold and unbending. I even told her so, only a few hours before . . .

"Why did you go there this morning?" Connie asked gently. "Did you think she might be there?"

"No. Instinct, perhaps—or because I was worried about her." He stared at the whisky in his glass, watching the bubbles rise, his mind back at the cliff. Suddenly he looked up. "Kane!" he exclaimed. "*He* was there!"

"Kane?" Connie and Jim echoed the name simultaneously.

"He was there this morning. I saw him. He came out of the bushes just as I got there. But why? What was he up to? Nobody ever went there but Grace."

"Did you speak to him?" asked Jim.

"He didn't give me the chance; bolted back to the house as soon as he saw me. But he was up to no good—I'll swear to that. The look on his face——" Eric stood up. The hand holding his glass shook in his agitation. "By God, if he had anything to do with it I'll—I'll——"

"Steady, old man." Jim put a hand on his shoulder, and pushed him gently back into the chair. "Don't go jumping to conclusions. Grace was killed last night, not this morning."

"How do you know that?"

"Well, I don't *know* it, of course." Jim looked embarrassed. "But it seems a reasonable assumption. If not, why didn't she come home?"

Yes, that was true. At some time after half-past five Grace had posted her letter, and then gone for a walk. And only about an hour later he had come home. Even as he was searching the house for her she must have been dead. Why hadn't he known? Why had not some instinct, some form of second-sight, warned him that she was dead? Yet the possibility had never occurred to him. He had thought she was in London with Daffy.

"I'd still like to know what Kane was doing there," he said.

"Well, you could ask him. But I don't think it's important." Jim hesitated. "Eric—you know you told me Grace had left a note for you. That wasn't true, was it?" And, when Eric shook his head, "I hope that won't give the police wrong ideas."

"The police? How does it concern them?"

"It doesn't, of course. But they might think it does. They might think it odd that you should have invented it."

Eric shrugged. "I don't see that it matters. In any case, I'm not likely to mention it to them."

"No. But I did." Eric looked at him in astonishment, and he went on quickly before the other could interrupt, "I'm sorry, old man—but it was your own fault. You shouldn't have been so damned positive. They asked me why no one had reported her as missing, and naturally I told them what you had told me—that she'd left a note saying she had gone to London to see her sister."

"I thought she had," Eric said. "And I knew she would have left a note if she hadn't been mad at me. So I just invented it; it was a sort of sop to my pride. Silly of me, I suppose—but I didn't mean any harm by it. Surely they'll understand that?"

"Of course they will," Connie said soothingly. She frowned at her husband. "I don't know why Jim is making such a fuss over nothing. Now—how about some sleep? Do you feel ready for it yet? I know I do. This has been a terrible shock for all of us, but for you——" A lump came into her throat. "Oh, Eric dear, I'm so dreadfully sad for you."

He squeezed her hand. "I know. And I'm grateful, even if I don't seem to be. But don't worry about me, Connie; I'll get over it. Other men lose their wives and survive, and I suppose I'm no different from them." He sighed. "In a way, perhaps, I'm luckier than they are. You see, I don't believe I really loved Grace. I was fond of her—very. I admired her, too. But Grace wasn't easy to love, she was too—too self-sufficient. She didn't *need* me. Or perhaps it was my fault. Maybe I'm not capable of loving—not fully, not in the way you and Jim feel about each other. Some people aren't." He laughed harshly. Even to his own ears it was an odd noise, and very out of place. "I'm being brutally frank, aren't I? I'd better go to bed."

There was an embarrassed and rather shocked silence.

"I'll mix the sedative," Connie said.

He did not drink the sedative. It was there by his bedside, but he was not ready for it yet. There were things he had to sort out in his mind, both of the future and the past, before he went to sleep. Grace had been his wife. However strained their marriage had become, he could not erase her as suddenly and completely from his mind as she herself had gone out of his life.

Marriage to Grace had been fun at first. Not only fun, but exciting. She was beautiful, she was charming, she was clever, she was rich. And they had thought (or he had thought) that they were in love, that it would continue like that for ever.

It was hard to say when he had realized that it would not, that 'for ever' was too long. Even the first sharp difference— when Grace had refused to leave Mulgerry, so that he was forced to spend most of the year away from her—had not disillusioned him. There will be the holidays to look forward to, Grace had said, when they had come to their first good-bye; just like a second honeymoon. And that's how it will continue, holiday after holiday. We shall never get bored with each other, never reach the stage where we have nothing to say, when going to bed will merely mean going to sleep and have nothing to do with love.

It sounded fine, but it didn't work out like that. They had so little in common. He disliked life in the country; he wanted to go out of an evening, meet people, do things. But Grace was happy only at Mulgerry, she never wanted to leave it; the house and her painting filled her life. She was fond of buying new clothes (clothes and antiques and picture-galleries were the lures that occasionally took her to London), but there appeared to be no purpose behind their purchase. They were not bought for some special function, but because she saw them and desired them. She adorned herself solely for her own satisfaction.

They had had their happy times together, of course, particularly during the first months of marriage; they could cope with their differences then. But gradually the differences developed into quarrels, and the quarrels became fiercer, more bitter; things were said which were harder to forgive and forget. Grace had never given him as much of herself as he had wanted— there was a virginal shyness about her; now she gave even less. Gradually they drifted further and further apart, with Grace making no effort to stop the drift, and he himself becoming more and more indifferent. There was so little response to his attempts at mending the marriage that it seemed useless to try.

After the first two terms Grace no longer came to spend an occasional week-end in Sheffield; later, because of Sheila, he did not press her. Sheila became an outlet for the ardour that Grace disdained to accept. She was younger than Grace; warm, friendly, and sympathetic. She never sneered at him for his lack of culture; she wasn't interested in the arts, she was interested in people. Perhaps it was that interest which had led her to join a firm of private detectives, although it seemed an odd profession for a girl as young and as pretty as Sheila. But she said she liked it. What was more, she seemed able to make a success of it.

He was not in love with Sheila, he thought. He had been in love with Grace—and then, gradually, out of love. Yet Sheila never completely took Grace's place—or the place Grace *should* have had. She gave him all her affection; but always at the back of his mind was the thought that they came from the wrong woman, that from Grace they would have been even more desirable. He was fond of Sheila, grateful to her for filling the gap in his life. But he wasn't in love.

He sat up and pulled the curtains aside. The moon reflected a pathway of light on the sea; he could hear the waves breaking gently against the cliff, a soft murmur that grew and faded in turn. A vision of Grace came to him—not the Grace he had married, but the Grace who had died; Grace as he had seen her last, with her neck broken, and her face distorted and disfigured.

Violently he slammed the window shut and drew the curtains, blotting out the sight and sound of the sea. With a gulp he swallowed the sedative Connie had left for him. He no longer wanted to think. He wanted to sleep, to forget.

The police came the next morning after breakfast, when he was back in the East Wing; the tall, uniformed Inspector Halton, whom he had seen the previous evening, and two men in lounge suits whom Halton introduced as Detective-Inspector Pitt and Detective-Sergeant Rivers, both of the Criminal Investigation Department.

"C.I.D.?" Eric said, surprised. "Why?"

"It wasn't a natural death, sir," Pitt said. He was a solemn, cadaverous-looking man with iron-grey hair, whose clothes hung limply and awkwardly on his long, thin body. "There will have to be an inquest."

"We won't trouble you more than is absolutely necessary," Halton said. "A tragic business, sir. But you'll have got over the first shock, I hope."

"I'm all right." He spoke brusquely because he *was* all right. He was a great deal better than he had any right to be, and the knowledge of this made him angrily guilty. He was aware that the sun was shining, that most of his holiday still lay ahead to do with exactly as he pleased. Last night seemed æons ago. "How can I help? Oh, sorry—sit down, won't you?"

They sat down, looking very out of place on Grace's chairs. (Only they weren't Grace's chairs now. Whose were they? His?) There was a short silence, and he became uncomfortably aware that they were all looking at him.

Pitt said quietly, "When did you last see your wife, Mr Cawthorne?"

"At half-past three the day before yesterday. I went for a walk then, but she stayed at home. At least—well, she was here when I left."

"And you expected her to be here when you returned, eh? What time was that?"

"Just after seven."

"But in fact she wasn't here. Instead, there was a note saying she had gone to London to see her sister. Right?"

"No, wrong." This was going to be tricky, but there was no point in beating about the bush. "She wasn't here, but I invented the note for the benefit of my neighbours."

"Just as you invented her visit to London?"

"Yes. Except that I honestly thought that was where she had gone." He told of his meeting with Daffy, and her message to Grace. "And if she'd gone to London she ought to have left a note. But she didn't, so I invented one. People talk, you see, particularly in a small community like this. I didn't want them to get wrong ideas."

Pitt's face was expressionless as he said, "Why should they? Because you and your wife had quarrelled?"

Eric flushed. "It doesn't take a Sherlock Holmes to deduce that, does it?" he said rudely. "Yes, we'd had a row. What of it? Husbands and wives often do." He frowned. "I suppose you heard all about it from the—from Lady Humpleston. I understand she was eavesdropping as usual."

Pitt ignored that. "Apart from the fact that you and your wife had quarrelled, do you know of any reason why she should decide to take her life?"

"No. And not because of the quarrel, either. It wasn't all that important to her, you see." He paused. This was difficult ground. If he wasn't careful he could become involved in a complicated explanation of how it had been between him and Grace. "I mean, it was only a trifling domestic dispute, whatever anyone may have told you to the contrary. My wife was a most calm and collected person; she seldom did anything on the spur of the moment. So you can rule out suicide, Inspector. It must have been an accident. I suppose she got too near the edge and slipped."

"You didn't seem to think it was an accident last night, sir," Halton said quietly.

Eric flushed. "I wasn't myself last night, Inspector. I hadn't had time to think."

"I appreciate that, sir. That is why I was surprised that you should immediately assume that your wife had committed suicide. Unless there were good reasons to the contrary, would not accident have been the more normal assumption? And you say there were no reasons."

"None at all."

Halton did not pursue the argument, but Eric was worried. They had a good point there. Somehow he must convince them they were wrong. A charge of suicide, even if it should prove to be unfounded, would publicize the unhappier intimacies of his life with Grace. And that was something he was most anxious to avoid.

He was even more worried when Pitt said, "There's one small point that suggests your wife had no intention of returning."

"Eh?" Eric was startled. "What's that?"

"There was no latch-key in her handbag. We found the bag, unopened, wedged between the rocks, but the key was missing. And there were no pockets in her dress where she could have put it. How do you account for that?"

"I don't. She certainly locked the door when she went out; I had to use my key to get in. Perhaps she forgot to take it with her—although it was unlike her to be forgetful. Or perhaps she expected me to be home by the time she returned."

"Perhaps," Pitt said, and stood up. Halton and the sergeant stood up also. The sergeant, a much younger man than the other two, said, "This is a charming room, sir. Your wife had considerable taste."

"And money, too," Pitt added. "She seems to have been quite a connoisseur of period furniture."

Eric wondered why they should assume that it was Grace's taste and money, and not his. Had some one at Mulgerry supplied that information? The Hump, perhaps.

Halton said, "I understand Mrs Cawthorne had quite a reputation as an artist. But Inspector Pitt here would know more about that. He's something of an artist himself."

There was the ghost of a smile on the detective-inspector's face as Eric looked his surprise—disbelief, almost.

"Even policemen have interests outside their work, Mr Cawthorne—though they don't have much time to indulge them. Mine happens to be painting. Mind you, I'm only an untalented amateur; not in your wife's class, I'm afraid. I went to her last exhibition at Strange's, by the way. Some of her seascapes were delightful."

Eric felt flattered by this reflected glory. He said, becoming more expansive, "There's more of her work upstairs in the studio. Would you care to see it?"

Pitt was gazing at the Paul Nash. When he turned his

smile had more body to it, softening the gauntness of his face.

"Thank you, sir. I'd like that very much."

Eric led the way upstairs, the two inspectors following; the sergeant stayed below. "One of the reasons my wife took this place was because of the studio," he said, opening the door. "It's big, and there's plenty of light."

While Pitt looked at the canvases stacked against the walls Halton admired the view from the south window. He was not interested in paintings. Eric stood idly with his hands in his pockets. This was Grace's studio. Of all the rooms in the house, this was the one in which he should have felt her death most keenly. But he did not. He felt only a desire to be rid of the two policemen, and was already regretting the whim that had led him to invite them upstairs.

It was then that he noticed the empty easel. "Good Lord!" he exclaimed: "It's gone!"

"What has gone, sir?" asked Halton, turning.

"One of my wife's paintings. It was standing on that easel only yesterday morning. I saw it." He went over to the canvases by the wall, and searched quickly through them while the two men watched him. "No, it's not here. What the devil can have happened to it?"

"Perhaps you've got the day wrong," Halton suggested. "If it was the morning before yesterday that you saw it your wife could have moved it later in the day."

"No, it was yesterday. I'm quite sure of that."

"Was the picture finished?" asked Pitt.

"I don't know. It looked finished to me, but I'm no judge. It was a view from that window, I remember."

Pitt walked over to the south window and looked out over the sea. He stood there for some time, as though impressing the view on his memory. Halton said, "Has any one—other than yourself, of course—been in the house since yesterday morning?"

"No one. Oh, yes—Mrs Upway was here this morning. She

very kindly came in to do some housework. But she wouldn't have moved it. And where could she have moved it to?"

"It might be a good idea to ask her," Pitt suggested.

Eric nodded. It was not the loss of the picture that worried him, but the inexplicable manner of its disappearance. It increased his rapidly growing irritation, and he said sourly, "Is there anything else I can do for you gentlemen? Or shall we call it a day?"

They were prepared, said Pitt, to call it a day.

During that day and the next Eric hung around Mulgerry, waiting for the inquest to free him; the house had already become something of a prison. It was a depressing time; he had nothing to do, and no one to do it with. Jim Upway, whom he turned to automatically for companionship, was no great help; he too seemed moody and depressed, and strangely monosyllabic. The evenings he spent in the Upways' flat, listening to the radio or talking to Connie. He would have preferred to spend them in a pub, either with Jim or alone, but he did not wish to offend Connie. It was obvious that she had appointed herself his friend and consoler, and he was not so rich in friends that he could afford to upset her.

The Upways were, in fact, his only friends at Mulgerry. Mike Drummond came over the first day to utter conventional regrets, a mouthful of clichés on love and death and marriage; after that he kept away. Eric preferred his absence to his clichés; he had no liking for the fellow. Nadia flashed him a mechanical smile when they met in the grounds, but she was always in too great a hurry to stop and talk; she avoided sorrow as she would have avoided the plague, it could interfere with her pleasure and her comfort. And pleasure and comfort were the be-all and end-all of Nadia Drummond's life.

Lady Humpleston sought him out once.

"A terrible tragedy, Mr Cawthorne. But it is your wife I am sorry for, not you. She was a good woman. And she had a proper sense of values—which you, I fear, have not." She gazed at him fixedly with her bright, beady eyes, one hand gripping the handle of her stick, the other clenched beneath her enormous bosom. "You would not otherwise have driven her to do this dreadful thing."

"Just what do you mean by that?" he demanded angrily.

"You know quite well what I mean, young man. I heard you shouting at her that afternoon, threatening her. So did your friend Mr Upway. And I don't mind telling you that I repeated what I had heard to the police."

"I'm sure you did," Eric said. "And plenty more beside, I've no doubt. You wouldn't let the truth ruin a juicy piece of scandal, would you?"

It was the first time he had allowed himself to answer her back. The effect was soothing to his frayed temper. In the past she had been Grace's landlord—to offend her might have had unhappy repercussions for Grace. Now there was no longer need for restraint.

Lady Humpleston drew herself up to her full five feet one inch.

"There is no need to be rude. I told them only what I had heard, what I knew to be the truth; that was unpleasant enough without any embellishment." She leaned precariously forward, her chin aggressive, her eyes accusing. "You killed your wife, Mr Cawthorne, just as surely as if you had actually pushed her over the cliff. And if you are able to be honest with yourself you will admit it."

She stumped off before he could think of a suitable retort, so flabbergasted was he by her accusation. After that they did not speak again. If they met by accident she looked through him as though he were not there. Once he permitted himself the childish gesture of making a rude face at her; but as usual she ignored him, and he felt that she had got the better of the exchange.

Mrs Winter ignored him also—probably under instruction from her fiery sister. Caroline did not speak to him; but on the few occasions they met her eyes watched him closely. To the contempt he had thought to see in them before was added a new expression, one he could not fathom. It was too hard for compassion, but there might have been something of sympathy in it. He did not know.

She's an incomprehensible creature, he thought. But it doesn't matter; there is no need for me to understand her. In a few days I shall be away from here. After that I never want to see Mulgerry or its inhabitants again.

The inquest proved less of an ordeal than he had anticipated. There were few witnesses (the man who had found the body, the doctor, the police, and himself), and no awkward questions. Yet on reflection he was not greatly surprised. Grace's death had been an accident; at the worst it was suicide. No one else had been involved; there was no blame to affix. It was a matter of routine, and routine did not call for fireworks.

It came as a shock, therefore, when the coroner's jury returned an open verdict; there was insufficient evidence, the foreman said, to determine how the deceased came by her death.

"Does that mean the case isn't closed?" he asked Jim, as they left the court together. "Have I got to go through all that again?"

"I wouldn't know. But I doubt it. At least the police are unlikely to bother us further. They'll have got all they want from Mulgerry by now."

"If they haven't they'll get no more from me," Eric said. "I'm clearing out, Jim—for a while, at any rate. It's only the inquest that's kept me here this long. Mulgerry holds nothing for me now."

He did not add—it did not even occur to him that it was true —that Mulgerry had held little for him for some time past.

"Good idea," Jim said heartily. "Where will you go?"

Eric shrugged. "Somewhere on the Continent. It doesn't matter where; the important thing is to get away." A movement behind him caused him to turn sharply. Sergeant Rivers stood there, a thoughtful frown on his face. "Well, Sergeant? Did the verdict surprise you?"

D

Rivers shook his head. Eric guessed that his harassed expression was due to the fact that the burden of detection had now fallen squarely on his shoulders. Inspector Pitt, he had heard Rivers inform the coroner, was too ill to attend the court.

"Not particularly, sir," Rivers said. "Did I hear you tell Mr Upway you were going abroad?"

"I don't know what you heard, Sergeant, but I certainly said it." Eric's tone was curt. He objected to the other's eavesdropping on a private conversation. "Any objections?"

"Not officially, sir." Rivers hesitated. "But it might be more convenient for us if you didn't. There are still a few loose ends to tidy up."

"Then tidy them quickly," Eric told him. "I'm sorry, Sergeant, but I'm not putting your convenience before my own. I'm off just as soon as I can get a passage."

The funeral was the next day, with Eric and the Upways the only mourners. Eric felt guilty about that. Daffy should have been there—would have been there, presumably, had he thought to write to her. He had belatedly given the police her address; but either they had made no effort to contact her, or Daffy had gone off on one of her business trips. Whatever the reason, he had not heard from her.

Jim had been wrong in his assumption that Mulgerry had seen the last of the police. Rivers was there when they returned from the cemetery. He did not bother Eric, but he spent some time talking to the other occupants, the Upways included.

"He's got ants in his pants, that sergeant," Jim said, when Eric asked him later about the interview. "Can't seem to leave well alone."

"What did he want this time?"

"Damned if I know. Same old stuff all over again."

Rivers was back the next day also, but this time he came direct to the East Wing. Eric was packing when the bell rang, and made no attempt to hide his annoyance as he opened the front door.

"Haven't you chaps finished yet?" he demanded.

"Not quite sir," Rivers's voice was unusually solemn. "I have——"

"Now look here, Sergeant," Eric said, his tone less truculent. The man was only doing his job—and with no great liking for it either, from the look on his face. "I don't wish to be awkward, but I'm going abroad to-morrow and there's much to be done. Come in if you must. But for the Lord's sake make it snappy, there's a good chap."

Sergeant Rivers shook his head.

"I'm afraid you don't understand, sir. I am taking you into custody. I have a warrant for your arrest on the charge of murdering your wife on March the twenty-ninth last."

4

THIS was his second visit to a magistrate's court. On the previous occasion he had been a mere spectator, and the proceedings had struck him as dull and sordid; drunkenness, motoring offences, and petty thefts were not crimes over which he could work up much enthusiasm. He had left long before the court rose. But he could not leave now. This time he was in the dock; not a spectator, but the star performer.

He still could not believe that it was actually happening to *him*. In a daze he had gone with Rivers to the police-station, vehemently protesting his innocence; but Rivers had advised him to say nothing at that juncture, and he had taken the advice. In the charge room he had listened incredulously to a summary of the reasons for the arrest; increasing friction between himself and Grace, culminating in threats against her life uttered a few hours before she died. (That would be the Hump, damn her interfering old eyes! But it wasn't true; not in intent, anyway. What exactly had he said? Something about being rid of her. But surely only a half-wit would interpret that as implying murder?); that he had accounted for her absence (and thus obviated any suggestion of a search) by declaring that she had gone to London and had left a note to that effect. (That damned note! If only he could have foreseen what a repercussion its invention would have!); that he was known to be having an affair with another woman in Sheffield (how on earth had they managed to ferret that out?); and, since Grace had apparently left no will, he would inherit her money. (It was true about the will, but he had never given a thought to Grace's money. Even now he had no idea of the state of her bank-balance; although if the police were making it a motive for murder it must be reasonably substantial.) There was also the fact that he had been out of the house at the time Grace had died, and could not support his statement that he had merely gone for a walk. He had listened to the station sergeant's scratchy pen as he made out the charge sheet, had listened to the charge being read to him, and the subsequent caution. But he had refused to make a statement, apart from again protesting his innocence, and had demanded bail. "You can't be bailed here," the sergeant had said. "You can apply for bail when you come up before the magistrate to-morrow."

And to-morrow was to-day.

The magistrate was speaking. He had to speak again, sharply, before Eric realized he was addressing him.

"Do you propose to employ a solicitor yourself or do you apply for legal aid?"

"I hadn't thought about it," Eric said. Just what would his defence cost? He had less than a hundred pounds in the bank; and whatever the state of Grace's balance, it certainly would not be available to him now. The police had made a stupid blunder; why should he pay for their mistake? "I'd like legal aid if I can get it."

The magistrate called Inspector Pitt into the witness-box. The inspector's gaunt face looked even more drawn than usual, and he had a frequent cough that obviously hurt. But when the magistrate invited him to be seated he refused.

Eric did not listen closely to the discussion that followed; it concerned his financial standing, and he was well acquainted with that. He was searching the court for familiar faces; Jim or Connie come to sympathize, perhaps, or the Hump to gloat. But he saw no one he knew. Mulgerry, it seemed, was not interested in his fate.

"Very well," the magistrate said. "I shall grant you legal aid."

Eric thanked him, and listened while Sergeant Rivers, who had taken the inspector's place in the box, gave evidence of arrest, heard the clerk read his deposition aloud, watched him sign it and step down.

"You will be remanded in custody for a week," the magistrate told him.

"In custody? Can't I be granted bail?"

"You can not." The magistrate's tone was decisive.

He had spent the previous night at the police-station. But he did not go back there now; he went to Tanmouth Prison. He had passed it many times; it stood on the crest of a hill, an old, gaunt building of grey stone, high-walled, just out of the town on the Tanbury Road. He had even permitted himself to wonder about its interior, about the lives its inmates led. But now, as Sergeant Rivers took him through the big gates and he heard them clang dismally and (it seemed to him) finally, he no longer had need to wonder. He was about to find out.

They went into a small reception room, and he was handed over by Rivers to a prison officer. All his possessions were taken from him and checked, and after he had certified the list as correct he was given a bath and weighed and measured. It reminded him of his preparatory school—the compulsory bath, the weighing and measuring that had taken place at the beginning and end of every term, the handing over of his pocket-money, the general air of order and discipline. But there the resemblance ended. He was given the choice of wearing prison clothes or his own, and elected for his own; it made his new circumstances seem less degrading. Then, after being kitted out with the few items he needed, he was taken across the courtyard to the hospital block (Why hospital? he wondered. I'm not ill. Later he was to learn that all prisoners remanded on a capital charge were housed in the hospital block so that they might be kept under mental observation) and ushered into a cell.

If the long stone corridors momentarily revived the memory of schooldays the cell did not. It was small, with barred windows. The furniture consisted of an iron bed with a dubious-looking mattress, an unvarnished, triangular-shaped table-cum-

washstand with a shelf beneath, and a clothes cupboard. The
walls were whitewashed, the floor of stone.

"Best room in the place," said the prison officer, a round man
with a cheerful face. "Lovely view."

Eric did not share his opinion of the view. There were flowers
growing in the beds among the flagged paths, but the high stone
wall that bounded the prison area was the dominant feature.

"What happens next?" he asked.

"The Governor'll see you soon." The officer pointed to a push
button in the wall. "Anything you want, just ring. We pride
ourselves on our service."

Eric was in no frame of mind to appreciate humour, but as
the door closed and he heard the key turn in the lock he would
have welcomed the man's return. It was the loneliest moment in
his life.

The Governor was a big man, heavily built, with a red face
and one of the squarest jaws Eric had seen. Looks the sergeant-
major type, he thought—and prepared to be shouted at. But the
Governor's voice belied his looks; it was soft and cultured, with
the faintest trace of a Scots accent.

Eric listened, not very attentively, while the more important
rules and regulations that would govern his stay in the prison
were explained to him. "I see you are wearing your own
clothes," the Governor said. "You may also choose whether to
work or spend the time in your cell. In the latter event you will
be allowed the normal half-hour of exercise every morning and
afternoon."

"What work?" Eric asked.

"Sewing mail-bags."

He shuddered. "I don't think that's my line of country," he
said. "I'll stick to my cell, much as I dislike it. I suppose I
couldn't have an armchair? It's a bit grim without one."

"If you're prepared to pay for it, yes," the Governor said.
"You may have food sent in if you prefer it to prison food, and
you can purchase cigarettes, sweets, and the like from the
canteen."

Eric relaxed slightly. At least the Governor seemed a decent fellow. "How about a drink occasionally?" he asked, expecting a blunt refusal. But the other nodded. "Beer or wine with your meals," he said. "But *only* with your meals." And added, with a faint smile, "You'll have to pay for it, of course. It's not on the house."

Eric elected for an armchair, and went back to his cell to lie on the bed and brood. He had plenty to brood over. Although the reasons for his arrest, as detailed by the sergeant, had sounded formidable, it was preposterous that anyone could seriously believe he had murdered Grace. *Would* anyone believe it—apart from the police? The Upways, for instance? No doubt the Hump had welcomed his arrest—she had in fact done her best to bring it about—but then she was a sadistic old woman from whose generous bosom hate had long since ousted the kindlier passions. And what about the staff at school? How would they react when they read their morning papers on the morrow?

That afternoon Charles Matthews, the solicitor who had undertaken his defence, arrived with his clerk. He was a man of about Eric's age, rather like Jim Upway in his good looks, brisk and friendly in an impersonal way. Eric did not immediately warm to him as a person, but was heartened by his obvious efficiency.

"I've read the charge," Matthews said, almost without preamble. "Let's have your version."

His version? He hadn't got a version. Everything the police had said was true—except that he had not murdered Grace. And suddenly he was aware of the formidable task that confronted them. There could be no disputing the facts. All that was left, then, was to argue their implications, their alleged culmination. And what sort of a defence was that?

"I haven't got a version," he said dully, looking round the bare visitors' room in which they sat—two chairs, and a table between them. "I've no idea what happened."

"I don't suppose you have," Matthews said drily. "What I

want is your account of the events preceding your wife's death
in so far as you were involved. And please be frank, Mr Cawthorne. Don't gloss over something merely because it may show
you up in a bad light. The more frank you are with me, the
better equipped I am to help you."

Eric told him. Prompted by intelligent questions from the
other, he was both frank and detailed, sparing neither Grace nor
himself in laying bare their life together. Nor did he spare the
other occupants of Mulgerry.

The solicitor made no immediate comment when he had
finished. He sat thoughtfully studying the notes his clerk had
handed to him and energetically tapping a pencil between his
teeth. They were very white teeth, Eric noticed. Even, and
rather pointed.

Eventually Matthews said, "In the main you agree with the
police, then—except, of course, as to the manner of your wife's
death. How *did* she die, do you think? Any ideas?"

"I imagine she got too close to the edge and overbalanced.
What else could have happened? Suicide's out; she wasn't the
suicidal type. Exactly the opposite, I should say. As for murder
—why? She had no enemies that I know of." Eric paused.
"Does that make it more difficult for you? If the police arrest the
wrong man—as they have done—I imagine the defence could
try to counter by exposing the right one. But what if it was an
accident, if there is no murderer to expose? What then?"

"It's not the job of the defence to discover who murdered
your wife, Mr Cawthorne—if indeed she was murdered. What
we have to do is to prove that you did *not*, or to discredit the
police evidence sufficiently to make it impossible for a jury to
convict you on it." He looked directly at Eric. "This walk you
took. Were you anywhere near where your wife lost her
life?"

"On the way out, yes. Not coming back."

"And you were away for three and a half hours altogether.
How far did you go?"

"Not far. I was in no hurry. I went out along the cliffs and back by the road, and for part of the time I was sitting on the grass. I only hurried when it started to rain."

"And you met no one?"

Eric flushed. He detected doubt in the other's tone.

"Not along the cliffs. There were people and cars on the road, of course, but they were all strangers to me. You see, apart from the Mulgerry lot and odd tradesman, I don't know any one in this part of the world."

After the solicitor had gone he was taken back to his cell, and once more lay down on his bed. But he was not left undisturbed for long. At five o'clock the door was unlocked, and he was ushered out into the corridor to join the other men in the block and be marched off to get his supper. It was the first time he had had any contact with the other prisoners; they were all men on remand, either from magistrates' courts or Quarter Sessions or Tanbury Assizes. Only a few, he noticed, had elected like himself to wear their own clothes.

The meal was much as he had expected; bread, margarine, and tea, with a sausage-meat rissole. He took it back to his cell to eat; he had no appetite, but this was the last meal of the day, and he did not want to add hunger to the other miseries he feared would help to keep him awake. He decided to lay in a store of chocolate. Five o'clock was an indecently early hour for an evening meal.

Despite his fears, he slept long and well. Neither his thoughts nor hunger nor the springless bed disturbed him; and if he had any bad dreams he had forgotten them by the morning. At seven-thirty he had breakfast; it was much the same as the evening meal, with the addition of porridge. Since he had chosen not to work there was nothing to occupy his time, and after several hours of sitting in his newly installed armchair, or lying on his bed, mailbags became an almost inviting prospect. It was a relief when he was called out for the morning exercise.

The exercise yard was the one he could see from his cell window; small, and laid out rather like an ornamental garden, with a paved path going round and through it in a figure of eight. Some of the men closed into groups and talked as they walked, but Eric walked alone. One lean, ascetic-looking individual in prison clothes bade him good-morning, and seemed anxious to add to his greeting. But Eric did not respond. He might be forced to mix with criminals, but he could not be forced to talk to them—forgetting, in his snobbish sensitivity, that they might be as innocent as himself of the crimes of which they were accused.

As he came off exercise a prison officer stopped him.

"A visitor for you, Cawthorne," he said. "A lady."

That will be Connie, Eric decided; she's the only one who would bother. But it wasn't Connie. As he entered the visitors' room a blonde, petite girl with a ridiculously tip-tilted nose and a warm, eager smile rose to greet him.

"Sheila!" he exclaimed. "What on earth are you doing here?"

"I read the papers," she said. "I just *had* to come, darling, I was so dreadfully unhappy for you. I cried nearly all the way down in the train. I don't think I've really stopped crying yet."

Her eyes were bright and eloquent enough for him to believe that. He wanted to take her in his arms, but the prison officer was still with them, standing just behind him.

"I don't know what to say—except that I'm glad to see you." He smiled at her nervously. "I don't have to tell you, do I, that this is all a ghastly mistake? I'm as innocent as you are."

"I know that, Eric. I wouldn't be here otherwise, however much I——" She stopped, and gave the officer a brilliant smile. "Can't we be alone for a little while, please? I'm sure you're very sympathetic, but it's so difficult to talk freely with a third person present."

The officer shook his head. "I'm sorry, miss. It's against regulations. And you only have fifteen minutes."

"Is that all?" She gave him another smile for good measure, and turned to Eric. "We must make the most of it, then. You had better start by telling me everything. I can't help you until I know the facts. And that's why I'm here—to help you, I mean."

He did not take her offer of help seriously, but it was good to have her sympathy. He told her briefly. When he had finished she said softly, "Poor Eric." There were still traces of tears in her eyes.

"It doesn't look hopeful, does it? But at least they seem to have picked a competent solicitor to defend me."

"That isn't enough." She was suddenly brisk and purposeful. "Eric—your house is empty, isn't it? Good. Then may I stay there while—while you're here? If I were to get to know these people I might be able to ferret something out. After all, that's my job."

He had forgotten her job, and said so. But this was a very different matter from the kind of investigation she was used to. "And there's nothing to find out, Sheila. It was just an accident."

"Was it? Obviously the police don't think so. They must have positive evidence of murder to arrest you. If it could equally well have been accident or suicide they wouldn't have arrested *any*one."

He saw the sense of her argument, but it did not cheer him. Rather it depressed him. If murder could be proved would it not merely increase his own danger?

Recalling that he had put the opposite argument to the solicitor, he shook his head.

"I'm not thinking straight," he said sadly. "Perhaps being in a mess like this turns one into a pessimist, so that all roads look wrong. But thanks for wanting to help me—I certainly need help. Is this the sort of murder they hang one for? I can't remember."

"No." She spoke sharply, afraid that any sign of weakness or despair would shake what little confidence he might have in her. "And stop being a pessimist. It's not like you."

The officer said, "Your time's up, miss, I'm afraid."

Although she had been vaguely aware of him standing silent and still at Eric's back, she had not given him a thought or looked at him again after that first plea for privacy.

"Couldn't you stretch it a little longer, please?" she begged. "It's so terribly important. You know that."

He did know it. He knew too that a prisoner must be given every reasonable facility for preparing his defence, although in his experience this had been confined to visits from solicitors.

He nodded. "A few minutes, then."

Sheila smiled her thanks, but did not waste time in words.

"About the house, Eric. It's all right for me to stay there, isn't it?"

"Of course. But don't count too much on it, my dear. I shan't. None of those people would have killed Grace. If it *was* murder, then it must have been an outsider who was responsible."

"We'll see. May I have the key?"

His hand stopped half-way to his pocket. "I haven't got it," he said. "They took it from me when I came in here. But the police have one; I dare say they'll give it to you if they don't need it themselves. No—better still, go and see the Upways. Connie has a key—I gave it to her after Grace died so that she might pop in now and again to keep the house tidy. She'll help you if anyone will. But you'd better check with the police first. They may object to your moving in."

She smiled and stood up. "I'll do that."

"And see the solicitor too, Sheila. He ought to be kept informed. I don't know his address, but his name is Charles Matthews."

"I'll find him. And don't worry too much, darling. We'll work something out between us—you, and I, and Mr Matthews."

She gave the officer a grateful smile, and was gone.

5

SHEILA LOVEDAY had been an orphan since she was fifteen, and this had made her more self-reliant than most girls of her age. At twenty she had joined a London private detective agency, with branches in Birmingham and Sheffield; and it was at Sheffield, when she had been working there for nearly two years, that she met Eric Cawthorne and fell in love. Eric was glad of her companionship, but did not at first want her love. He did his best to play fair with her, pointing out that he was married and that he had every intention of staying that way. But Sheila was a determined and attractive young woman, and Eric no misogynist. That last term he had seldom mentioned his marriage, and to the girl it had seemed that his obvious affection for her was blossoming into something stronger, something more akin to her feelings for him.

And now, Sheila thought sadly as the taxi bumped up the long drive to Mulgerry, it could be over almost before it had begun. Prison walls made a most efficient barrier to love. To Eric she had optimistically blown her own trumpet as a detective, but to herself she had to admit she was not a very talented performer. Yet this was her big chance. If she could win freedom for Eric she would win Eric for herself; there was no longer his wife to keep them apart.

How much had he loved Grace? she wondered. Surely not completely, or he could not have found room for *her*. With no competition, why should she not have all his love? She had never wished Grace harm, never tried to persuade Eric to leave her. Now that Grace was dead, was she not entitled to some reward for her honesty?

It was Jim who opened the door of the Upways' flat to her. His eyes brightened as they invariably did at the sight of a pretty girl, and he welcomed her effusively without asking either her name or her business.

"I'm Sheila Loveday," she told him. "I've just been to see Eric Cawthorne. I'm—I'm a friend of his."

His face clouded, but only for a moment. Sheila guessed that the cloud was because of the element of tragedy that the mention of Eric's name must inevitably bring with it. She was used to sizing people up quickly. Jim Upway, she decided, was ill at ease with tragedy.

"Poor old Eric," he said. "How is he? Bearing up?"

Before she could reply Connie came running up the stairs and into the flat. "Caught you at last, have I?" she said cheerfully. She gave her husband a kiss and nodded to Sheila. "Glad to meet you, rival."

Jim introduced them. Connie too looked grave at the mention of Eric's name—but with sadness, not annoyance. "If there's anything we can do we'll do it gladly," she said. "Eric's arrest was an awful shock to us. How could the police be so stupid? But then they don't know Eric, of course."

Sheila warmed to her; she was obviously sincere, both in her desire to help and in her belief in Eric's innocence. Jim she found pleasant and attractive, but he did not inspire in her the same confidence. He's probably rather shallow, she thought— and selfish. I doubt whether he'd put himself to any great inconvenience for a friend.

But he listened as carefully and as sympathetically as his wife to her account of her visit to the prison. "Eric thinks my coming here is a waste of time, that there's nothing to find out," Sheila concluded. "He's certain his wife's death was an accident. But the police think it was murder, and that's good enough for me."

"Let's get this straight," Jim said. "If Grace was murdered then Eric was the only one with the least suspicion of a motive for doing it. No, wait a minute," as both girls started to protest.

"If we agree that it *wasn't* Eric, doesn't that make murder most unlikely? The rest of us here would be very bad starters indeed. Right down the course."

"Why 'us'?" Connie asked. "You're not including me, I hope."

"As an unlikely suspect, yes," he said firmly. "Who more unlikely than you? Though now I come to think of it you have no alibi. You were late that evening."

Connie nodded. "So I was. I had trouble with the bike. And you haven't an alibi either. You were here on your own."

"Agreed. And that probably goes for the others too—with the possible exception of the cackle of hens down below." He stopped, frowning. "Now I've forgotten where I was going."

"I think you were trying to prove that it wasn't murder," Sheila said. "So far you seem to be heading the other way."

He laughed. "I do, don't I? All right, I give you opportunity. But not motive. You try to find motive, Miss Loveday."

"The name is Sheila," she told him. "And what do you know about other people's motives? They certainly wouldn't broadcast them."

Jim shook his head in mock despair. "You know all the answers, don't you? But I still don't believe Grace was murdered."

They went on arguing, and Connie listened. But it was clear that neither would convince the other, and presently she said quietly, "Aren't you getting away from the point? If you're right, Jim, there's nothing we can do. But if Sheila's right—if it *was* murder—there is. So let's do it. We may not succeed, but at least we can try."

"Bless you!" Sheila said.

Connie took her over to the East Wing and showed her the house; but she sensed that Sheila wanted to be alone, and did not linger. "We'll be around when you want us," she said. "Just let us know when you need our help."

"I will," Sheila said gratefully. "And Connie—you won't tell the others why I'm here, will you? I don't want them to be on their guard against me; we'll only get results if they talk freely. As far as every one but yourselves is concerned I'm just a friend of the family."

At the front door Connie said, "I didn't say this in front of Jim because I didn't want to cramp your style. But do you honestly think you're more likely to get at the truth than the police?"

"I don't," Sheila admitted. "I feel hopelessly inadequate. You see, I'm not even a very good detective in my own sphere. But I've got to try. The police seem to think they're sitting pretty, that it's roses all the way. If I can only rake up just one little thorn to prick them with I'll have achieved something."

When she was alone she went into the big sitting-room, and sat down in one of Grace's armchairs and gazed up at Jim's portrait of the dead woman. It was after seven and growing dark, but she did not switch on the light. She could think better in the dark.

She was not impressed by Grace's room and Grace's furniture. No doubt it was beautiful, but it did not seem a happy room. There was nothing cosy or inviting about it; it was cold and distant, like the face of the woman in the picture. If Grace had really been like that, she thought, then Eric had never experienced love. A frigid affection, perhaps, an intellectual communion of the mind; but no warmth, no body, no passion. No love as she understood it.

Poor Eric. And poor Eric indeed, to be dependent on her for his liberty. (At this moment she had forgotten the solicitor.) Waiting and watching and shadowing—all that she could do. But would it be enough? How did one set about investigating a murder?

A noise in the hall startled her. For a moment she held her breath, listening; but the loud beating of her heart was all she could hear. Forcing herself to be brave, she got up quietly and went out into the hall.

The front door was open. Silhouetted against the dusk, one foot on the step, stood a young woman. Relieved that the intru-

E

der was not a man, Sheila stepped forward and switched on the light.

"Good evening," she said.

The newcomer was obviously as surprised to see Sheila as Sheila had been to see her. Her mouth was open, her eyes wide.

"I—I'm Nadia Drummond," she stammered. And, as an afterthought, "Good evening."

Sheila had heard about Mrs Drummond, both from Eric and from Connie. She was prepared to dislike her, but she would not show her dislike. "Won't you come in?" she said politely.

The other hesitated. Then, with a muttered word of thanks, she stepped into the hall and closed the door behind her. "I'm afraid I was trespassing," she said, holding out the key. "Er—I found this in the yard."

Sheila did not inquire into the reason for the trespass. It could have been plain curiosity or it could have been something more; but that must wait. There had been the unhappy thought at the back of her mind that after Grace's death Eric had turned to Nadia Drummond for consolation; hence the key. But she quickly put the thought from her. It was unworthy, both of herself and of Eric.

"How odd!" she said, leading the way into the sitting-room. "I wonder how it got there."

"Some one dropped it, I suppose." Nadia was gazing about her, goggle-eyed. "My, what a grand room! Just like a saloon."

It was Sheila's turn to look surprised. "Saloon?" she said. She had seen nothing like Grace's room in any inn she had visited. Then light dawned, and she said hurriedly, "It is, isn't it? Haven't you been in here before?"

"No, never. Grace wasn't—well, she wasn't very friendly, was she? Quite civil, of course," she added, anxious not to offend unwittingly. "But she never got real matey. Not like Connie Upway, I mean."

"That's true. Grace was rather aloof with every one, I think. A lonely person—though the loneliness was largely her own fault. She just didn't know how to make friends."

How near to the truth was that description? she wondered. Eric had seldom discussed his wife with her, but it tallied with Jim Upway's portrait. Not that the truth mattered. What was important was to gain Nadia Drummond's confidence, to make her talk. If Grace Cawthorne had been murdered some one at Mulgerry must know something about it.

It could be Nadia Drummond.

She smiled. "I'd better introduce myself. I'm Sheila Loveday —a friend of the family. Now, how about a drink?"

"I'd love one." She watched Sheila pour out a large whisky, making no protest at the quantity. "This is a dreadful business, isn't it? Do you think—I mean, is it possible he really did kill her?"

"No." Involuntarily Sheila bristled at the suggestion. But she would not achieve her object that way. "At least, I don't think so. But then I like Eric, so perhaps I'm prejudiced."

"Oh, so do I. He's a real sweetie. But he did have a quick temper, didn't he? I mean—well, they were always quarrelling. It could have been her fault, of course. He was always very nice to *me*."

I bet he was, thought Sheila, eyeing her opulent curves and silk-clad legs so generously displayed. I bet most men are. Or is that being catty? Only I do wish she wouldn't refer to Eric in the past tense, as though he were already finished and put away.

"It's a ghastly mess, whatever happened," she said. "You're right about the quarrels, of course. But then nearly all married couples bicker at times, don't they? The police must have had more cause than that to arrest Eric. The question is—what?" She hesitated. "Don't you think it strange, Nadia (you don't mind me calling you Nadia, do you?) that no one seems to have seen either of them that afternoon?"

It was a shot in the dark, but it worked.

"I saw *her*," Nadia said. Volubly she told her story of the borrowed iron, and her unsuccessful attempts to return it. "And I thought that was odd, you know, because she'd been so insistent about wanting to use it that evening. But of course I never dreamt anything like *that* could have happened. It never does, does it? I mean, not to people one knows."

She sounded almost regretful.

It's very odd indeed, Sheila thought; Eric had forgotten to mention the iron. In the first place, why did you choose to borrow from the unfriendly Grace, who never invited you into the house, when you could have as easily borrowed from the friendly Upways? And secondly, where was Grace between three-thirty, when Eric left the house, and some time after five-thirty, when she posted the letter? Did she go out twice that afternoon—both before and after five-thirty?

The letter. Maybe they could get a line from that, if Eric's solicitor could manage to lay his hands on it. It had been written to Grace's sister—but where was it now? In the hands of the police, probably, if it contained anything of interest.

Sheila suddenly felt cold. Was that it? Was it something Grace had put in the letter that had prompted the police to arrest Eric? Unable to sit still with that disconcerting thought in her mind, she got up and started to walk slowly up and down the long room.

"I really ought to be going," Nadia said.

"Going? Oh, no!" Sheila searched desperately in her mind for a plea with which to detain her visitor. "Stay a little longer. Sitting alone in this enormous room gives me the willies. Let me get you another drink."

Nadia did not protest. "My, but that's strong," she said, as she slipped the whisky. "One more like that and I'll be tiddly." She giggled. "Lucky Mike's out to supper to-night. I can't see myself doing any cooking after this."

Sheila tried to visualize the absent Mike. Flashy, she thought. That type always went for provocative, sexy women.

She said, "In that case why not stay and have something to eat with me? I don't know about you, but I'm starving. I've hardly eaten all day."

Nadia accepted with alacrity; not because she was hungry— whisky took away her appetite—but because she wanted to stay.

Mike didn't approve of her drinking, he said it loosened her tongue so that it flapped wildly. But she liked talking, and she liked whisky, and she was beginning to look on Sheila as a friend. She had never found women easy to get on with, but Sheila was different. Not stuck-up, like Grace Cawthorne and the Humpleston crowd.

They scrambled eggs and made coffee, and Sheila laced the coffee with brandy. Afterwards they stuck to brandy. Sheila felt rather guilty at her freedom with some one else's drinks, but she thought Eric would approve; it was all part of the softening-up process. And when Nadia was on her third brandy she decided it was time to be more direct in her quest for information.

"How did you know the key belonged to the East Wing?" she asked pleasantly, trying to sound casual.

"The key?" Nadia, an elbow resting precariously on the arm of her chair, tried to focus her mind on the question. "Oh, that. Well, I didn't exactly know, of course. But Mike——" Her elbow slipped from its support, jerking her sideways. Brandy splashed over the rug, and she looked down at it glassily. "Damn! I—I'm terribly sorry, Sheila!"

"Don't worry," Sheila said hastily, cursing the interruption. "It won't hurt the rug. What were you saying about your husband?"

"Mike?" Nadia drained the remaining brandy, and eyed the empty glass thoughtfully. "What about him?"

"I don't know. It was something to do with the key you found."

"Was it?" She put the glass down slowly and carefully on the table at her side, as though scared that her aim might be inaccurate. "Oh, yes. Well, I was right, you see. It was hers."

Sheila said, "And if it hadn't been? What would you have done? Tried all the other doors until you found one it *did* fit?"

"Oh, no. If it wasn't hers I didn't mind." She sighed gustily. "Anyway, I only wanted to be sure. It doesn't matter now, does it?"

"Because Grace is dead, you mean?" Sheila ventured. The picture was becoming clearer.

"Yes."

Where do we go from here? Sheila wondered. Do I ask the sixty-four thousand dollar question and risk being told to mind my own business, or do I scout round it a little longer? To delay her decision she went over to the liquor cabinet and poured a little brandy into her glass. She had deliberately not kept pace with Nadia, but now a drink seemed almost a necessity.

When she returned to her chair she saw with surprise that Nadia was crying. Great tears welled out of her eyes and rolled down her cheeks unheeded.

"What is it?" Sheila asked. She knelt beside the other and took one of her hands in her own. "What's wrong, Nadia?"

Nadia brushed a hand across her eyes and swallowed hard. "She—she did it to spite me," she spluttered. "She didn't love him—I know she didn't."

Sheila sighed. But it was a sigh of relief, not of despair. She said quietly, still holding the plump, bejewelled hand, "They were lovers, weren't they? Grace and your husband?"

"I—I think so."

"Had it been going on for long?"

"Ever since we came here." She started to fumble for her bag. It had slipped to the floor; Sheila gave it to her, and she opened it and dabbed at her eyes with a handkerchief. "He—he was always running over here to see her. Except when Eric was at home. He kept away from her then." She started to cry again at the thought of her husband's deceit. "We'd only been married a year," she sobbed. "I—I thought he loved me."

"Did you ever see them together?" Sheila was too impatient to waste much sympathy on her. It seemed incredible that the cool, haughty Grace whom Eric had depicted, and who stared down at them so aloofly from the wall, could have been engaged in a hole-and-corner liaison. Certainly Mike Drummond could be no flash boy; he must be quite something to have ousted

Eric. And presumably that explained Grace's coolness towards her husband.

Nadia shook her head.

"She was too clever for that." She picked up the glass from the table and stared at its emptiness. Sheila took it from her, filled it generously with brandy, and put it back into her receptive hand.

"Sorry," Nadia said. "Silly of me to cry." She put the glass to her lips and sipped slowly but steadily, as though the brandy were water. Sheila watched her uneasily. I hope I haven't overdone it, she thought. I don't want her passing out on me.

But Nadia did not pass out. When the glass was again empty she waved it vaguely in the direction of the table. "Thass better," she said, slurring the words.

Sheila took the glass from her. "Why didn't you put your foot down, Nadia, when you discovered what was going on?"

"Oh, I did. He said I'd got it wrong. He said it wasn't Grace he was interested in, but her paintings." She sniffed derisively. "Paintings! You don't find him visiting Jim Upway, and he's a much better artist than Grace. Every one says so. He——" A hiccough startled her into silence. " 'Scuse *me*!"

Sheila said, "You didn't find that key in the yard, did you, Nadia? Where was it?"

"In his pocket. I was going to——" She paused, suddenly alarmed at her own frankness. "You won't tell Mike, will you? He'd be furious."

"I won't tell him anything," Sheila promised.

A ring at the front door startled them both. "It's probably Connie," Sheila said. "Hang on a minute while I get rid of her. You won't want to see her now, eh?"

"I don't want to see *any*body," Nadia said ponderously.

It wasn't Connie. A fat, dumpy little man stood there. He stared at Sheila in surprise when she opened the door.

"Yes?" she said.

"I'm sorry if I've disturbed you," the man said. He had recovered his poise, and smiled, showing blackened teeth spaced with gold. "I didn't know anyone had moved in. But I saw the light, and I thought perhaps my wife—well, she was always very friendly with the Cawthornes, and it would be just like Nadia to pop across and make sure everything was ship-shape now that they——" He paused, finding the sentence difficult to complete. "The name's Drummond, by the way. Mike Drummond. We live just across the way, above the garage."

Sheila wanted to laugh. This fat, smarmy little man the great lover, who had conquered the unconquerable Grace? It was altogether too absurd.

"Yes, your wife is here," she said, restraining her laughter. "Come in, won't you?"

He hesitated. Sheila stared at him, fascinated. He wore a well-cut, well-pressed suit of loud check, with a check tie. His reddish hair was very thin on top, and he had no chin; from lip to throat was a straight line.

"It's a bit late, isn't it? Perhaps I'd better—— Ah, there's Nadia. Must have heard the old master's voice, eh?" He gave a jaunty salute. "Hyah, girlie! Coming home?"

Nadia had come into the hall and stood eyeing him uneasily, one hand against the wall for support. They continued to stare at each other. Then Nadia said slowly, "I suppose so," and began to sidle along the wall toward him. Suddenly she hic-coughed loudly. The sound startled her as much as it did her audience, and she looked from one to the other in astonish-ment—only to hiccough again. " 'Scuse me," she said, and began to giggle.

Her husband frowned. Then the frown vanished, and he said cheerfully, "Tiddly, eh? And all for free." He turned to Sheila. "She can't take it, you know, Miss—I'm afraid I don't know your name."

Sheila told him. "She hasn't really had much to drink, have you, Nadia?" Nadia took no notice, but continued to giggle. "We've had a nice long chat. I've enjoyed it immensely."

"Glad to hear it," Drummond said. But he did not sound glad. Moving easily for such a dumpy creature, he took his wife by the wrist. "Come along, girlie. Time I took you home, I can see that. And maybe you and *me* can find something to talk about too."

6

CHARLES MATTHEWS's offices lay in a quiet cul-de-sac leading off the High Street. The Georgian front had a charm and dignity of which Sheila approved; and although the outer office smelled and looked like the outer offices of so many other solicitors' offices into which her work had taken her, the room in which Matthews received her was modern and light, with a pleasant view of the sea from the casement windows.

Sheila's approval extended to Matthews himself. She approved of his good looks, and she approved of his dignified manner. He was also a good listener, interrupting her only when, in her eager haste, her meaning became uncertain.

"Of course, it was a stroke of luck that I happened to be in the house when she tried the key," she concluded. "I don't suppose she'd have talked so freely if we'd met under other circumstances."

"Or without the brandy," he added.

Sheila nodded. "I felt rather mean about that. But it worked, and now we've got to make the most of it."

"And how would you suggest we do that?" he asked cautiously.

She stared at him, surprised by the question. "Don't you *know*?"

"To be honest, Miss Loveday, I don't." He smiled. "Maybe I'm not at my best this morning; I'm not used to beautiful lady detectives invading my office so early in the day. They usually call in the afternoons—Saturdays and Bank Holidays excepted, of course."

"To-day is Wednesday," Sheila said, returning the smile.

"Ah! That explains it. But seriously, how can the fact that his wife was having an affair with another man improve Mr Cawthorne's case? I should say it tends to complicate it."

"But I don't believe she was. That's the whole point. She *couldn't* have fallen for a dreadful creature like that. No woman could."

"Mrs Drummond did, apparently."

"She's different." The solicitor smiled, but did not argue the point. "No. Drummond had that key for quite another reason. I'm sure of that."

Matthews shrugged. "Well, we can ask our client. Maybe he can explain it. And now, Miss Loveday——"

"And there's another thing," Sheila interrupted him. "This morning I had a look at the spot where Grace Cawthorne died, and it's quite obvious to me why the police think she was murdered. It *couldn't* have been an accident. The ground slopes sharply *up* to the cliff-edge, not *down*; you almost have to clamber up it. And it hasn't broken away, or anything like that. She *must* have been murdered, Mr Matthews."

"So many italics," the solicitor murmured. "But it's a good point—although it doesn't rule out suicide, of course. In fact, suicide would be our best line of defence were it not that every one, our client included, vetoes it." The swivel chair swung round, and he stood up. "I was just about to leave for the prison when you called. Would you care to come with me?"

"Yes, I would. But aren't you going to get in touch with Miss Lomas first? That letter may be important."

"Very important, I imagine." He smiled. "I haven't been entirely idle, Miss Loveday. I contacted Miss Lomas last night."

"And the letter?"

"She's bringing it down from London this morning; she travelled from Glasgow overnight. But I'm not waiting for her. I'll leave word with my clerk to send her along to the prison as soon as she arrives. Our client may as well hear at first hand what she has to say."

As they drove out to the prison Sheila thought, He's nice, and quite unlike most of the solicitors I've met. But I hope he's not too young and inexperienced; he can't be much more than twenty-five or six. And I do wish he wouldn't keep referring to Eric as 'our client.' Eric may be his client, but he isn't mine. He's my lover.

Lover! It was an odd word when you thought about it. She remembered the first four lines of a rhyme she had learned in the kindergarten at school—'A farmer farms, a dyer dyes, a builder builds, a flyer flies.' But—lover! As though loving were a profession.

But then most words sounded odd if you thought about them long enough.

"We've an awful lot to discuss in fifteen minutes," she said. "We'll have to talk fast."

"We'll have all the time we want," he assured her. "This is an official visit to prepare our client's defence, and the regulations ensure that we must be granted every facility."

"They only gave me fifteen minutes yesterday," she protested. "And I was helping in his defence too."

"Yes. But not officially."

They were not shown into the same room as on her previous visit. Nor did the prison officer remain in the room. He waited in the passage outside, looking at them through a small window. "In sight but out of hearing," Matthews explained. "That's the official jargon."

Sheila was relieved to see that Eric looked less depressed, although he could not be described as cheerful. "Is it very bad, darling?" she asked, heedless of the solicitor's presence.

"It could be worse, I suppose." He had smiled on seeing her, but the smile did not last for long. "The Governor's decent enough, and the officers are as humane as the system permits. It's the boredom that gets one down. That and the noises. Keys rattling, locks turning, boots stamping—they never let up. If I ever get out of this place I'll have a house with thick carpets everywhere, and no locks."

"You'll get out," she assured him. "Mr Matthews and I will see to that."

"You have a first-rate team," the solicitor said. Eric was surprised at the change in the man; he was almost jovial. Was that Sheila's effect on him? "Miss Loveday is an excellent detective. Let her tell you what she's discovered."

Eric merely nodded when she told him about the cliff; he knew the terrain better than she, but because he had wanted to believe that Grace's death was accidental he had subconsciously ignored anything that indicated the contrary. Nadia's confidences, however, he greeted with astonishment and disbelief. "Grace and that awful bounder?" he exclaimed. "Rubbish! Absolute rubbish! The woman must be off her rocker."

"She's not, Eric. It may not be true, but *she* believes it. Having seen her husband, I agree with you. But how did he come by that key?"

"Pinched it, perhaps. I wouldn't put it past him."

"But why? What would he want it for?"

"I don't know." He sounded irritable. "But I do know that Grace wouldn't have given it to him. And I certainly didn't."

"How many front-door keys were there?" Matthews asked.

"Well, there was mine. They took that off me when I came in here. The police have the one that was normally kept in the lock, and I gave the spare to Connie. Grace had one, of course; she kept it in her bag. That makes four in all."

"Your wife could have had another cut, of course," Matthews said. "But there was no key in her bag when the police found it."

"You see, Eric? It *must* have been Grace's." Sheila was all excitement. "What do we do now, Mr Matthews? Tell the police?"

"Tell them what?"

"Why, that Drummond killed Mrs Cawthorne." Without waiting for a reply, she turned to Eric. "Isn't it obvious? Nadia was right in one respect—her husband *was* infatuated with Grace. Where she went wrong was in thinking that Grace felt the same about him. She didn't. She would have nothing to do with him—and that's why he killed her."

"I doubt it," Matthews said. "From what Mrs Drummond told you the infatuation began a long while ago—as soon as they moved in. Why should Drummond wait until now to murder her? Why not when she first refused him?"

"I don't know. Perhaps he hoped she'd change her mind. Does it matter?"

"It could. And, if you're right, how did Drummond come by the key?" He looked from one to the other. "I suppose you haven't considered the possibility that it was his wife who killed Mrs Cawthorne? She seems the more likely candidate of the two. The jealous wife eliminating her rival."

"Supposed rival," Eric corrected him. "Yes, it's possible. But it still doesn't account for the key. Grace would never have given it to *her*. And if, as she says, she found it in her husband's pocket—well, we're back where we started."

"Yes." Matthews shook his head. "We keep on coming back to that, don't we? Of course, if we assume that your wife did not repulse his advances—not at first, anyway—we can make it fit into place. Then she *might* have given him the key. Later, perhaps, she regretted it. That very evening she could have told him the affair was over, asked him to return the key. You have then a reasonable set-up for a murder."

"No," Eric said firmly. "In the first place, Grace couldn't stand the fellow; she was civil enough to him when they met, but that was as far as it went. And secondly, whatever Nadia may say I don't believe Drummond was keen on Grace. I don't like the man, but to give him his due I should say he is far too fond of his wife to run after other women. I'm not saying he didn't kill her, mind you; I wouldn't know about that. But if he did it wasn't because of any infatuation."

Sheila sighed. She had worked herself into a feverish pitch of excitement, and so much cold water shocked her into depression. She rubbed her eyes hard to stop the tears from coming.

"No need to despair, Miss Loveday," Matthews said, his voice sympathetic. "Because we can't explain that key it doesn't mean it's not important."

"Of course it's important," Eric said. "You both talk as though Drummond had had it for years. But not if it's Grace's he hadn't. Unless she committed suicide—and I'll not believe that for one moment—Grace had that key in her bag when she went out that evening. The question is, what happened to it after that? Did she lose it and Drummond find it? Or did he take it from her by force? And if so, why?"

The officer came in before they could reply. "There's a Miss Lomas here, sir," he said to Matthews. "She hasn't got a permit, but she says you're expecting her. Shall I ask her to wait?"

"No. Show her in here, please, will you?"

Daphne Lomas had her sister's clear-cut features without her good looks. She was tall and stout and untidy, with tree-trunk legs and a weatherbeaten face. Grace had been her half-sister, and the younger by twelve years; but despite the difference in years and looks and build there remained a family resemblance.

She nodded casually to Eric, looked with interest at Sheila, and addressed herself to the solicitor.

"Mr Matthews? Well, here I am—although I've an idea the police wouldn't approve if they knew. They've called at my place several times, but I was away. Up in the Highlands. I was away when your telegram came, too; but I happened to ring up my landlady, and she read it to me over the telephone. Thank you." This was for the chair the solicitor proffered. "Am I right in thinking that a witness for the prosecution shouldn't be 'got at' by the defence?"

"Quite right, Miss Lomas."

"Well, you've got at me." She sounded pleased.

"You are not yet a police witness," Matthews pointed out. "I hope you never will be. But that depends on the letter. Have you brought it with you?"

"Wait a minute," Eric said. His voice was harsh. "Daffy—you know it isn't true, don't you? I didn't kill Grace."

"I don't know anything of the sort," she retorted briskly. "What I *do* know is that you hadn't even the common decency to let me know Grace was dead. You left it to your solicitor to tell me—a week later."

"I'm sorry. I'm afraid I forgot; too wrapped up in my own worries, I suppose. But I did give the police your address. And don't you ever read the newspapers?"

"Sometimes. But not that kind of news. And neither police nor newspapers excuse your own silence."

"I know that," he said impatiently. "But you haven't answered my question. Do you believe I killed Grace?"

"I'm keeping an open mind on that. But I've no doubt she gave you plenty of provocation. Grace was a difficult person to live with. I know—I tried it for six months, and that was just six months too long." She caught Sheila watching her. Sheila was wondering how the woman could be so briskly cheerful and impersonal about her sister's murder. "Who is this young woman?" Miss Lomas demanded.

The 'young woman' bristled with indignation. It was not so much the words as the tone and the look that annoyed her. But before she could burst into an angry retort Matthews said smoothly, "This is Miss Loveday, a private detective. She is trying to help us get to the bottom of this unhappy business."

"Oh, is she?" It was clear that Sheila was not Miss Lomas's idea of what a private detective should look like. "What's wrong with the police? Isn't that what we pay them for?"

Eric said, trying hard to keep his temper, "The police happen to be on the other side, Daffy."

"That's not quite true, Mr Cawthorne," Matthews said. "Strictly speaking, they're not on any side except that of law and order. In this case——"

"In this case they're certainly not helping *me*." He was fond of Daffy, but somehow she always managed to irritate people, himself included. "What about this letter, Daffy?"

"Yes." She fumbled in her bag and produced a piece of paper. But she did not give it to him. She said, "It's not exactly complimentary to you, Eric. Quite the opposite, in fact. Are you sure you want to read it?"

"We all want to read it," Matthews said. He leant forward and took the letter from her. "Excuse me."

Eric read it after him. It was short and, as Daffy had said, uncomplimentary to himself. "He actually threatened me physically," Grace had written, describing their quarrel; "I was really frightened." But it was the final passage that mystified him.

> It's now nearly five-thirty, and Eric hasn't returned. However, at the moment I'm not concerned with Eric. Something happened this afternoon; something so unexpected and devastating that it complicates everything. Or perhaps it isn't a complication; it could be a solution if only it goes the way I hope it will. And until it does I'm telling no one. Not even Eric.

"What on earth was she referring to?" Eric asked, handing the letter to Sheila. "Do *you* know, Daffy?"

"Of course I don't know. How could I?"

"Whatever it was it's important," Matthews said. " 'Unexpected and devastating,' according to Mrs Cawthorne. Miss Loveday, this looks like a job for you."

The girl nodded. She was rereading that final passage. She said slowly, "Either she went out and met some one—or some one came to the house—or some one telephoned. It must be one of those, mustn't it? But which? And how do I find out? Surely anyone who saw Grace or a visitor that afternoon would have said so by now? They must know how important it could be."

Matthews shrugged. He did not answer the questions, but turned to Eric.

"That letter cuts both ways, Mr Cawthorne. The final passage is in your favour, in so far that it poses a question that will have to be answered. But if it comes into the hands of the police— and it is a criminal offence to suppress material evidence—the rest of the letter strengthens the case against you. I suppose you realize that?"

F

"Of course." Eric's face was white and strained. "But I didn't threaten her. Or if I did I didn't mean it. I lost my temper and shouted at her, but I would never have struck her."

"I'm sure you wouldn't," Miss Lomas agreed. "You haven't the guts. If you'd slapped Grace a few times right from the start of your marriage you wouldn't be in this mess now. That was what she needed."

He did not take offence at the remark. He said, "And yet you are quite prepared to believe that I killed her?"

"That's different. It wouldn't take guts to sneak up behind her and push her over the edge. Not that I'm saying you did, mind you. But you could have done it."

"Spoken like a true friend," Sheila said softly.

Miss Lomas's eyes suddenly blazed.

"It's my sister who was murdered," she snapped. "And I'm not his friend, I'm his sister-in-law. That doesn't give him the right to demand my implicit belief in his innocence. He won't get it, either; not until I know all the answers. As for you, young woman—I'd advise you to stop insulting your elders and stick to your detecting. If you *are* a detective," she added truculently, but with less wrath.

It was Sheila's turn to be angry, but once more the solicitor headed her off. "When did you last see your sister, Miss Lomas?" he asked.

"Oh, months ago. We kept up a desultory correspondence, but we seldom met. We liked each other better at a distance."

"Have you ever visited her at Mulgerry?"

"No. I was never invited. When we met it was usually in Town."

"You were in Town last Monday week, I believe—the day she died. Did you speak to her on the telephone?"

"No. I had run into Mr Cawthorne at Paddington that morning, and sent her a message by him asking her to ring me. But she didn't, and that was that."

"I forgot to give her the message," Eric said.

Miss Lomas nodded. "And that's another piece of forgetfulness that rebounded with force," she said grimly. "If Grace had come up to Town she would probably still be alive to-day."

Sheila had been watching her closely, a new suspicion forming in her mind. She said, her voice throbbing with suppressed excitement, "When your sister failed to telephone you, Miss Lomas, you didn't by any chance come down to Mulgerry to see her?"

Miss Lomas's weatherbeaten face positively glowed with anger. "That, young woman, is an extremely insulting suggestion," she barked.

Sheila was not intimidated. "It wasn't meant to be insulting. And it wasn't a suggestion, but a question. Would you mind answering it?"

The older woman snorted. "I have already told you once that I've never been to Mulgerry. And I mean *never*. I suggest you mind your own business for a change, and leave it to Mr Matthews to——"

"This *is* my business," Sheila said quietly. She was no longer excited; her calmness surprised her. "Your sister was a rich woman, wasn't she? Far richer than you."

"I haven't the faintest idea," snapped the other.

The solicitor said evenly, "It's rather important, Miss Lomas. The police attribute several motives to Mr Cawthorne for the murder of his wife, and one of them is her money. Unfortunately, although he knows she was rich, he doesn't know *how* rich. If you can help us——"

"But I can't." Miss Lomas clicked her tongue impatiently. "If her own husband doesn't know what her paintings fetched how do you expect me to?"

"We're not talking about her paintings, Daffy. We're talking about her inheritance."

"Inheritance?" She stared at him in obvious bewilderment. "What inheritance?"

"The money that was left her by her father, of course," Eric said impatiently. "And that's something that has always puzzled me. Why did he leave it all to her, instead of sharing it with you?"

"He didn't. Not that I would have minded if he had. Did Grace tell you how much he left?"

"No. What was it?"

"One hundred and fifty pounds. Seventy-five pounds each. *That* was Grace's wonderful inheritance that you all seem so interested in."

They took Miss Lomas back to her hotel. Her bombshell had left them stunned; although Eric, when he had recovered from his surprise, had at first been jubilant. "That's one nail they can't drive home into my coffin," he had said, with the first flash of humour he had exhibited that afternoon. But the solicitor had quickly destroyed his optimism. "There is plenty of evidence that you *thought* she had inherited money," he had pointed out. "That is all the police need. And isn't there material evidence of wealth? If she didn't inherit it there must have been some other source."

As Miss Lomas prepared to leave the car Matthews said, "Do you happen to know if Mrs Cawthorne made a will?"

"She made one, but she tore it up. That's something I *do* know. She mentioned it the last time we met."

"What made her destroy it?"

"Your client, Mr Matthews," she told him, with a sideways glance at Sheila. "She had discovered that he wasn't the ideal husband she had originally thought him. The rot had set in—and I can't imagine anything has happened since to make her change her mind."

Matthews was on the pavement, holding the car door open for her. He said, "She was defeating her own object, then. Provided we can clear Mr Cawthorne of the charge against him"—he too gave Sheila a quick glance—"as I'm sure we can, he will automatically inherit as next of kin."

One foot on the step, Miss Lomas halted in her descent.

"Will he, Mr Matthews?" She smiled faintly and shook her head. "You know, I wouldn't count on that if I were Eric."

7

As he got back into the car Matthews said, "Mind if I drive you home? I'd like to take a look at Mulgerry."

"Mind? I'd love it. Queueing for buses is the end when you're tired." Sheila sighed. "And I *am* tired. Up to now I've enjoyed my profession; it's rather fun, really. But it's different when you're working for some one you love. It isn't fun any more."

Charles Matthews was no more impressionable than the average young man; but Sheila Loveday was a very pretty girl, and her sadness depressed him. To cheer her he said, "Don't let it get you down. You're not doing too badly, you know. Two suspects in one morning is well above average. I doubt if the police could do better."

"Two?"

"Drummond and Miss Lomas. Didn't you practically accuse the good lady of having come down to Mulgerry in secret to murder her sister?"

Sheila blushed. It made her look even prettier, Matthews decided.

"Well, she could have done," she said. "No one saw her; but then nobody saw anyone that afternoon, it seems. She might have killed her for her money; or because she had always been jealous of her, her father having provided for Grace and not her (that was what I *thought*—I didn't know then that he hadn't provided for either of them); or because she just didn't like her. And she didn't, did she? She made that quite plain."

"You didn't like her either, did you?" the solicitor said, smiling. "Miss Lomas, I mean. You made *that* plain."

"I suppose I was rather rude. But she was rude too—both to me and to Eric. Mr Matthews—where do you suppose Mrs Cawthorne got her money from if it wasn't from her father? She must have had money. She couldn't have lived in that style without it."

He shook his head. "I don't know. It's one of the many problems facing us. Another is Miss Lomas's cryptic remark as she left us. Why shouldn't Mr Cawthorne inherit? What can stop him?"

"Perhaps she hasn't the same faith in his innocence that you and I have," she suggested.

"I don't think it was that." He did not quibble over her assumption that his faith in her lover was equal to her own. "It was something more subtle."

He completely approved of the East Wing at Mulgerry, although his chief comment on the luxurious sitting-room was that it had taken more than peanuts to furnish it. "I like the dignity and spaciousness," he said. "And I was always a sucker for a house by the sea. That's why I chose my present offices. They were as near to the sea as I could get."

As they came down the stairs from the first floor he noticed a door next to the kitchen. "What's this?" he asked, trying the handle. "A cupboard?"

"No. According to Mrs Upway, it leads down to the basement. That's where the servants' quarters used to be."

"And now?"

"Now the basement is a flat. It's occupied by a Mr Kane. He's the man Eric saw out on the cliffs the morning after Grace was killed. I haven't met him yet."

Matthews tried the handle again. "It's locked, of course. But who has the key?"

"I don't suppose there is one. Not now. Or perhaps Lady Humpleston keeps it. Mrs Upway said that the old lady made as few alterations as possible when she divided the house into flats. She still hopes that one day she may be able to afford to have it to herself again."

The solicitor frowned. "It ought to be nailed up," he said. "Even to an amateur an ordinary house lock isn't hard to open. Kane could get in here any time he chose."

"Well, he didn't come that way to murder Grace," Sheila said. "She was killed out on the cliff."

"I know. But what about the picture that disappeared so mysteriously the following day? He could have stolen that."

"So could Drummond," she pointed out. "*He* had a key. Perhaps he wanted that picture in memory of Mrs Cawthorne." She could never make up her mind how to refer to the dead woman. "He could hardly ask Eric, could he?"

"Drummond's a problem," Matthews said. "Do we ask him about the key, or don't we?"

"I promised his wife I wouldn't."

"H'm!" The solicitor smiled. "It isn't ethics that deters me, I'm afraid, but the problem of how to proceed if he denies ever having had it. As he undoubtedly will if he has anything to hide. I think we'll let the police handle that one."

It was on their way back from the cliff-top that they met Lady Humpleston. Dressed in her habitual black, with her beady eyes and prominent nose, she looked like an overgrown crow barring their progress.

"You're Miss Loveday, I suppose," she said, ignoring the solicitor and addressing herself to the girl. The two women were of about the same height; Sheila saw that there were bristles on her chin and at the corners of her tight little mouth. "I'm told you have moved into the East Wing. But maybe you are not aware that there is a clause in the tenancy forbidding sub-letting." She clicked her tongue sharply. "I cannot have any Tom, Dick, or Harry moving into Mulgerry without even bothering to consult me."

Matthews was furious. He put a hand on Sheila's arm. "Miss Loveday is neither Tom nor Dick nor Harry," he said sternly. "She is a friend of Mr Cawthorne, and is staying here at his wish. There is no question of sub-letting."

Lady Humpleston turned on him, lifting her stick and banging it down angrily. "And who are you, young man?" she demanded.

"The name is Matthews. I am Mr Cawthorne's solicitor."

"Oh, are you! Well, I wish you joy of your client. But he doesn't happen to be my tenant, Mr Matthews. I let this house to his wife, and he has no right whatever to instal his——" She darted a quick glance at Sheila. "His *friend* here."

The girl flushed. She said quietly. "You are very free with your insults, Lady Humpleston. Why?"

The old woman stared at her, momentarily nonplussed. It was a difficult question to answer. Before she could do so Matthews said, "It is a question of Mrs Cawthorne's rights under the tenancy. Who are your solicitors, Lady Humpleston? I will go into the matter with them."

Lady Humpleston hesitated. Then she shook her head.

"No. Now that Miss Loveday is here she may as well stay," she said ungraciously. "I imagine it won't be for long; once that dreadful man's trial is over he won't be needing the East Wing. The Government will house him." As she turned away she added "To my mind it's a disgrace that they don't hang *all* murderers."

Sheila stared after her wide-eyed, too astonished to be angry. "What a beast!" she exclaimed. "What a perfectly horrible old beast!"

Matthews laughed. "She is, isn't she? If some one at Mulgerry had to be murdered I'm surprised it wasn't her. But I wonder why she didn't want me to see her solicitor."

"Probably afraid she'd have to hand back any rent Grace may have paid in advance. Mrs Upway says she's hardup."

"Could be. But more likely a fiddle over income tax."

After the solicitor had gone Sheila went upstairs and began to search methodically through the dead woman's room; it was just possible that somewhere in the house there was a clue to the 'complication' Grace had mentioned in her letter to her sister, and the bedroom seemed the likeliest place in which to find it. The extensive wardrobe made her envious; suits and frocks, furs and coats and jackets and hats, lingerie and stockings in profusion. What will Eric do with them all? she wondered. Give them to Connie and Miss Lomas? No, Miss Lomas was too big. And I'm too small, she decided, holding up a magnificent evening gown against herself and wistfully eyeing the effect in the long mirror. But in any case I couldn't wear them. Not with Eric. They would always remind him of Grace.

There was surprisingly little jewellery, but what there was was good. The box was not locked, and she examined each piece with interest, unaware of its market value but delighting in the jewels and their exquisite settings.

It was in the glove box that she found the key. It was large and heavy, and very much out of place among the nylon and suede and soft skins. And because of that she knew at once that it had been hidden there. The whole room was eloquent of Grace's care for her clothes. She would not have secreted this enormous key among her gloves unless she had had a very good reason.

But—hidden from whom? Eric, presumably.

For a moment she stood in thought. Then she remembered the door next to the kitchen that had aroused the solicitor's interest, and she hurried downstairs. To her surprise the key turned easily and noiselessly in the lock. Gently she turned the handle and opened the door.

Since it led to the basement she had known there must be stairs. What surprised her was that they were carpeted. Nor was the carpet a threadbare relic of the past. It was of a modern design, and almost new. The light from the hall did not penetrate far down the stairway, but she could see that it curved to the right. There was probably a second door at the bottom.

She closed the door, noting the brass bolt on the reverse side, locked it, and went into the sitting-room to ponder on the significance of her discovery. The door's well-oiled locks and hinges indicated that the stairway was in current use; indicated too (as did the carpet) that its use was meant to be silent and secret. Yet there had to be collusion before the door could be opened. Grace had had the key, the unknown Kane a bolt.

Grace and Walter Kane!

Sheila sat down suddenly on a Sheraton armchair; it creaked alarmingly in protest at such cavalier treatment, but she did not heed it. She was appalled at this revelation of the woman Grace Cawthorne must have been. Eric had described her as cold, implying an antipathy to sex; he had dismissed as absurd the suggestion that she had been indulging in an affair with Mike Drummond. Having seen Drummond, Sheila had been inclined to agree with him. But it seemed now that they had both been wrong; Grace had had not one lover, but two. And there might have been others. With Eric away from home so much it would not have been difficult.

Here was a motive for murder the police had not considered. Jealousy. But Eric was not the only one, apparently, who had had cause for jealousy. Had Kane or Drummond killed Grace because of her liaison with the other?

Drummond she had met. But what sort of a man was Kane?

Acting on impulse, she ran out of the house and into the yard. On the far side of the archway were the stone steps that led down to the area in front of the basement; they were smooth from long use and steep, with no railings to hold on to, and she descended them carefully. Without stopping to consider what she was doing she lifted the heavy iron knocker and let it fall; and only then did she pause to wonder what she should say when the door opened.

But the door did not open. She banged the knocker again, more firmly this time, her courage increasing with the knowledge that her knock was unlikely to be answered. Relief struggled with disappointment as she waited. But there was no sound from within, and she turned away and went slowly back up the steps.

As she crossed the yard her pace quickened. She had been curious to meet the man whom both Jim Upway and Eric had described as rough and uncouth, and who had yet had sufficient appeal to attract a cultured woman such as Grace. But if the man was out his flat was empty, and she had her own means of entrance. It was possible that the flat would tell her more than the man.

Heart thumping loudly, she unlocked the door and started down the carpeted stairway. As she rounded the bend the gloom deepened; but she could see the door at the bottom, and her groping fingers found the latch and held it. Then she paused. Suppose the flat were not empty? What if Kane had merely been asleep when she knocked, or had heard her and refused to answer? How would he react to this intrusion?

She depressed the latch and leant gently against the door. It opened smoothly and quietly; holding it slightly ajar, she squinted through the narrow opening at whitewashed walls, a stone floor covered with rush matting, and another door set in the far wall. For a few seconds she held her breath, listening. There was no sound from the basement. Reassured, she opened the door wide and stepped into the room.

It was obviously the old kitchen. An enormous range, rusted and dirty, stood against the end wall, with a modern electric cooker in one corner. The big windows that overlooked the area were shuttered and barred, so that the only light came from small fanlights above; but there was modern strip lighting on the ceiling which would, Sheila imagined, more than compensate for the lack of daylight.

The room was sparsely furnished; two wooden chairs, a big chest and a cupboard, and a massive oak table that stood, its top smooth and polished, beneath the shuttered windows. There were numerous strips of wood on the floor, a roll of white paper, and a collection of bottles, jars, and tins which looked as though they contained paint or varnish. Against the near wall was a carpenter's bench, with an assortment of tools hanging from hooks above it. And near the bench, on a small trestle table, was an old-fashioned smoothing iron.

Sheila went over to it, fascinated, and picked it up. It was extremely heavy. She remembered having once seen a tailor in a

London shop-window using an iron such as this. But what was it doing here, in what was obviously a workshop?

She tiptoed quietly round the room, searching for some further indication of its use. The chest and the cupboard were locked. On the floor around the workbench were wood-shavings and some scraps of material, mostly muslin. The muslin puzzled her almost as much as the iron had done; she picked a piece up and fingered it, noting its fineness. Even the pumice-stone at one end of the bench seemed more at home than did the muslin and the iron.

She was still fingering it when she heard a noise outside; some one was coming down the area steps. The muslin still in her hand, she hurried to the stairway, closing the door behind her. Then she hesitated. Safety was only a few feet away; there was no need to panic. Kane might come into his workshop, but he would not use the stairs; Grace was dead. Why not stay by the door and listen? Even if she could not see the man she might learn something from his movements.

She heard the front door slam, and the murmur of voices in the hall. So Kane was not alone. There came the sharp sound of iron-tipped boots on stone, suddenly muffled. A man spoke. His voice came to her clearly, and she knew they were now in the room she had just left.

"Okay. So he says he'll do it." The voice was harsh and uncultured. "But I still don't like it. How much does he know?"

"No more than he has to." Sheila caught her breath. That was Mike Drummond's voice; there was no mistaking the rich, plummy tone. "And that's nothing to what we have on him. You scare too easy."

"I don't trust him. And I don't like murder."

"Who does? But if it falls into your lap you've got to use it."

The voices were silent, but she could hear the men moving about. There was the sound of a key turning in a lock (that will be the chest or the cupboard, Sheila decided), and the first speaker said, "That okay?"

"It looks okay to me," Drummond said. And then, "No, not now. Later."

They did not speak again after that, and presently she heard them leave the room. Opening the door slightly, she saw that the men had not closed the door leading to the hall. It would not be safe, then, to venture again into the room, to see if they had left or taken anything. She must content herself with what she had got.

And that was plenty, she decided, when she was once more back in the sitting-room. When they spoke of murder, had they been referring to Grace? Or was there another murder yet to come? "He says he'll do it," Kane (she supposed it was Kane) had said. Did not that in itself point to a further victim? But whatever the correct interpretation of that brief conversation, to keep such information to herself was out of the question. It was far too dangerous. Matthews must be told, and at once. He would know what to do.

When she telephoned the solicitor's office it was to learn that he was out.

"Please ask Mr Matthews to ring me immediately he returns," she told the clerk. "It's terribly important."

Was there enough evidence now, she wondered, as she stood staring out at the wide, deserted lawn, to clear Eric? What she had overheard was not sufficient in itself, of course; but at least it would give the police a lead away from Eric that they could hardly ignore. If only she had heard a little more, if only the meaning had been less ambiguous! And if only they had mentioned just one name to work on!

She had supposed that one of them had killed Grace out of jealousy of the other (she had not decided, not even considered, why the victim should have been Grace and not the rival). But was that theory still tenable? They were not rivals now—they were conspirators.

The lawn was no longer deserted; a tall, drooping figure walked slowly across it towards the cliff, a Pomeranian trotting obediently at her heels. That would be the Winter girl, Sheila thought. What should she do now? Go out and talk to her, and probably get herself snubbed? Or stay where she was, and wait for Matthews to ring her?

She went out. The clerk had not expected Matthews back within the hour. And although Caroline Winter was an unlikely source of information, she—well, one never knew.

Caroline did not snub her. Neither did she welcome her. "I heard about you from my aunt," she said, not looking at her.

Sheila laughed. "You didn't hear anything good, then. Somehow I don't think she liked me."

"She didn't."

"Oh!" Was this the expected snub? "Well, I hope you don't use second-hand opinions. I'm not that bad."

"She dislikes most people outside her own circle," Caroline said. "Strangers in particular."

She's certainly frank, Sheila thought. Or was that intended to put me in my place—under instruction, perhaps, from the aunt? But the conversation was going the way she wanted it, and she persevered.

"By her own circle, do you mean the people here at Mulgerry?"

"No. She dislikes them too."

"But why? What's wrong with them? The Upways, for instance—how could anyone possibly dislike Connie?"

Caroline's rather dragging step faltered for a moment, and then went on. But the soft voice was no longer lifeless as she said, almost eagerly, "You like her too?"

"Of course. As I said—who wouldn't?"

"She's so kind," Caroline said. "So—so *good*. I wish——" She paused, and looked at Sheila. The dark eyes were shining. "Connie is the only person here I care about, Miss Loveday. She's my only real friend."

She's not entirely a drip, then, thought Sheila; Connie at least can rouse her. "And Jim Upway?" she asked, watching her companion closely.

"My aunt objects to his radio." If Handsome Jim arouses any

emotion in her breast, thought Sheila, she's a good dissembler. Her manner was once more one of cool but well-bred indifference. "She says it makes Mulgerry sound like a slum tenement."

Sheila laughed. "I'm told that that's intentional. They find it too expensive here, and Jim hopes to provoke her into terminating the lease." Remembering that this was Lady Humpleston's niece she was talking to, she added apologetically, "I'm sorry. Perhaps I shouldn't have passed that on. Please treat it as confidential. It probably isn't true anyway."

She half expected Caroline to be annoyed. She was not prepared for the girl's evident distress.

"They want to leave Mulgerry? Oh, but they mustn't!" More quietly she added, "I was very lonely here before Connie came, and now—well, I'd be lost without her."

"You have your mother and your aunt."

"Yes, I have them."

She did not sound enthusiastic. To distract her mind Sheila asked her about Kane and the Drummonds; after what had happened earlier that afternoon, these were the people in whom she was chiefly interested. The Upways were a pleasant couple, but they were unimportant at the moment.

But Caroline, it seemed, knew nothing of Kane or the Drummonds. She spoke of them as though they were people from another and inferior race, and it was obvious that she shared her aunt's contempt for them.

"I'm surprised Lady Humpleston let them come here if she dislikes them so much," was Sheila's comment.

"We're very isolated," Caroline said. "It doesn't suit most people. Aunt Alice had to let to whom she could. But I think she would have disliked them no matter who or what they were—simply because they were here. Perhaps you can't understand that—but I can. She is devoted to Mulgerry, and she cannot reconcile herself to the knowledge that it's no longer entirely her own. Even Mummy and I sometimes feel like interlopers." She added bitterly, "We're the poor relations, you see."

They were passing the spot where Grace had died. Left to herself Sheila would have avoided it, but Caroline did not deviate. There was no indication that it possessed any special significance for her.

"From the short conversation I had with your aunt it was plain she disliked Mr Cawthorne also," Sheila said. "That surprised me. His father is a peer."

The sarcasm was wasted on Caroline. "A life peer," she said shortly. "And a Socialist."

It was an explanation which obviously satisfied her.

What an odd creature she is, thought Sheila. Hard—and yet strangely soft where Connie Upway is concerned. She resents her aunt's treatment of her, but she can sympathize with the motive that inspires it. Perhaps that is because she has so much of the old lady in her; the same indifference, amounting at times to contempt, for those outside her own social sphere, the same habit of speaking her mind. But whereas the old lady is downright rude, I fancy Caroline's outspokenness is more the frankness of youth.

Except, of course, that she isn't so young. Why do I keep thinking she is? She must be quite a few years older than I am.

"Mrs Cawthorne's death must have been a great shock to you all," she said. "Was she popular?"

"With some people she was," Caroline said, after a slight pause.

Her tone indicated that they were the wrong people—the Drummonds and Kane, was Sheila's immediate thought. But when she mentioned their names Caroline shook her head.

"I was thinking of Aunt Alice," she said.

"Oh! Why did she single *her* out?"

"According to my aunt she had all the virtues. Breeding, taste, poise." Caroline's tone was brusque. "What it really amounted to was that Mrs Cawthorne was never short of praise for Mulgerry. She won Aunt Alice over completely."

Deceived her is what you really mean, Sheila thought. But had Grace in fact deceived the old lady? Or was Caroline's opinion distorted by her obvious dislike of the dead woman?

The truth, perhaps, lay somewhere between the two.

"You didn't like her, eh?" she said.

"No. I'm sorry if that offends you."

"Why should it? Oh, I see; you think she was a friend of mine. But she wasn't. I never even met her."

"Then why are you here?" Caroline asked, astonished.

Sheila tried to explain. It wasn't easy. She wanted to enlist the other's sympathy, but she suspected that Caroline would be shocked to learn that she and Eric were in love. She had to tone that down. Having already denied Grace's friendship, she had to admit to Eric's.

If Caroline thought the explanation unsatisfactory she did not say so. She did not say anything until they had turned, and were on their way back to the house. Then she asked, rather haltingly, "Mr Cawthorne—he isn't in any real danger of being convicted, is he?"

"He is unless we can find some way of clearing him," Sheila said. She was puzzled by the question; it implied a belief in Eric's innocence. And why should Caroline believe that unless she had cause? "Miss Winter—forgive my asking, but can *you* think of anything that would help?"

Caroline did not answer at once. She was calling the dog, which had discovered something of interest in a distant clump of bushes. But she was plainly embarrassed by the question when Sheila repeated it.

"I don't know," she said. "I'm not sure if it will help—but I did see Mr Cawthorne that afternoon."

"Where?" In her excitement Sheila clutched at her companion's arm. "Where, Miss Winter?"

"Near Gavin Head." Caroline turned and pointed east. "That's it—where the cliff juts out at the end of the bay. It's about three miles from Mulgerry."

"What time was this?"

"About a quarter to six. I did not actually look at my watch, but I've thought about it since and I'm sure that's right. I took

G

Pompey out after tea, and it's just over an hour's walk to the Head."

Sheila's excitement faded. She let go of Caroline's arm, and began to walk slowly on. There was no alibi for Eric here. No one knew exactly when Grace had died, except that it could not have been before five-thirty. At that time Eric, according to Caroline, had been nearly three miles away. But the police would say he had killed Grace on the way back. And there would have been time. By his own admission he had not returned home until after seven.

"In what direction was he going?" she asked.

"Towards Bineford. It's a small village on the Tanmouth road."

That helped a little. It bore out Eric's statement that he had returned by the road. But it wasn't enough.

Caroline said, "I expect you are wondering why I did not mention this to the police, Miss Loveday."

"I am, rather."

"It was wrong of me not to, I suppose. But at first I wasn't sure; Mr Cawthorne was some distance away. It was not until a few days later, when I saw him in the garden and recognized the jacket he was wearing, that I knew I had been right."

"And you still said nothing? Why?"

Caroline took her time in replying. Eventually she said, her voice low, "I—I was advised not to—that it was immaterial."

And I know damned well who advised you, Sheila thought. That grisly old aunt of yours has made up her mind that Eric is guilty, and she doesn't want any member of her precious family involved in the trial. She knows damned well you could be a key witness.

But another thought had come to her. She said, "After you saw Mr Cawthorne, what did you do yourself?"

"I went on out to the Head, and then came home."

"This way? Along the cliff?"

"Yes."

"But you didn't see Eric—Mr Cawthorne—again?"

"No."

Sheila looked around her. The bracken and gorse along the cliff-top were liberally dotted with clumps of bushes and stunted trees, but there were large areas of open ground.

"If Mr Cawthorne had changed his mind and had come back this way, either ahead of you or behind you, do you think you would have seen him?"

Caroline too looked around her, considering her answer.

"It depends, doesn't it?" she said. "If he was walking straight home, and if he wasn't too far ahead, I *must* have seen him. But if he had wanted to keep out of sight—or if he were some distance behind . . ."

She shrugged her thin shoulders, and left the sentence unfinished.

That was a double-edged sword to use in Eric's defence. "What time did you get home yourself?" Sheila asked.

"At ten to seven. I remember the time exactly. I was very wet, and wondered how much time I had in which to change for dinner. Aunt Alice is very insistent on punctuality."

"And you didn't see Mrs Cawthorne at all?"

"No," Caroline said shortly. It was plain that the question offended her.

"I'm sorry," Sheila said. "Maybe I should not have asked that. But it wasn't meant as an accusation, I assure you."

Caroline was not a talkative person by nature, and when Sheila lapsed into silence she was silent too. They were back in the grounds of Mulgerry when Sheila put her final query.

"Just why did you dislike Mrs Cawthorne?" she asked.

The other flushed. "I'd rather not discuss it," she said.

"Perhaps not. But you can't dismiss it as easily as that, Miss Winter. You may not realize it, but by withholding from the police what could be vital evidence you have done Mr Cawthorne considerable harm. (You may also have done yourself harm, but I'm not concerned with that.) If you want to make amends—and I'm sure you do—you might at least be frank with me."

"I have been frank. The fact that I disliked his wife cannot affect Mr Cawthorne one way or the other."

"Are you sure? If it throws fresh light on her character or activities it might be all-important."

"Very well." A stern, almost savage expression took control of Caroline's thin face. "If you must know she—she was an adulteress."

It was not the accusation but the word that startled Sheila; Caroline gave it a Biblical sound, dwelling on the sibilants. She said, "I'd already guessed that, Miss Winter. But I take it you're not guessing. You know."

"I saw them together." She shuddered at the recollection. "It —it was horrible."

"And the man? Who was he?"

"I don't know," Caroline said bleakly. "I'd never seen him before."

8

Nothing showed above the high wall but the heavens; no building, no tree, nothing. By now he was becoming fanciful about it, believing that there *was* nothing on the other side. Certainly there was nothing for him. The wall contained his world; people could come into it, but he could never leave it. And if by some chance he were to climb the wall he would drop into a bottomless abyss, so that for the rest of time he would be falling—falling—everlastingly falling.

He lay on his bed and looked at the wall now, divided into neat little sections by the bars of his cell window. The dusk lent fancy to his imagination, and he longed for the night to blot out the wall and free him from his confinement within it. The day was always so long. The night could be long too, but at least it was split by snatches of sleep. In the day he could not sleep. Perhaps the Governor had been right; work would have helped to pass the time. But how could mail-bags occupy his mind?

At exercise that afternoon he had determined not to repel, as he had done before, any sign of friendliness extended to him by a fellow-prisoner. He had to talk to some one. But no one had bothered him; perhaps the word had got round that he was not a 'mixer.'

When he had passed the man he had snubbed that first morning he had apologized for his rudeness.

"That's all right," the man said pleasantly. "We're all a bit touchy when we're new."

Eric was grateful for the cultured voice; it made easier what might be an awkward conversation. "Aren't we all new?" he asked. "I thought every one in the hospital block was on remand."

The other shook his head. "Not all. Some are sick men from the other blocks. But all of us out here are on remand. They don't mix us with the convicted men."

"And how long have you been here?"

"Nearly two months."

"Two months!" Eric was aghast. "I thought the longest period of remand was eight days."

"So it is. But sometimes they keep on remanding you. They did that with me. Now I'm waiting for the Assizes. They're on next week."

"You must almost be looking forward to the trial," Eric said. "Two months! I bet you'll be glad to see the last of this place." The other did not answer, and Eric realized that he had made a possible gaffe. The trial might not mean the end of prison for his companion; it might be only the beginning. To cover his mistake he went on quickly, "Time seems endless here—as I suppose it is. Did you elect to work?" And, when the other nodded, "What hours do you do?"

"Nine till twelve and one till four. Six hours a day—for which I am credited with the princely sum of three shillings a week. But it's worth it. It makes time pass just that little bit quicker."

To pass the time! What a goal to work for!

It was darker now; the wall had almost vanished. He tried to visualize Mulgerry, and Sheila moving about the East Wing. But he found he could not picture her for long; after a little while she began to merge into Grace. And Grace stayed with him. He did not resent that; it was fitting that Grace should be with him now. Some one had killed her, and he was being accused of the crime. They were together in adversity.

Which is more than we were before, he reflected unhappily.

Sheila had dinner with the Upways that evening. It was a good dinner, for Connie was a good cook. Sheila, who had eaten little all day, was hungry, but her appetite gave her a guilty feeling. How could she enjoy food when Eric was shut up in prison, existing on prison fare, his mind full of the injustice that had been done to him? Yet she did enjoy it. When she apologized to the Upways for her appetite Connie said, "And a good thing too. Starving yourself won't help Eric; you'll do better on a full stomach. How did things go to-day? Any luck?"

"A little, I think." She was not sure how much she should confide in them. They were Eric's friends, they would not wilfully do or say anything to harm him. But Jim, she felt, was unreliable; he might talk out of turn. "I've been trying to get hold of Mr Matthews—he's Eric's solicitor—but he hasn't been back to his office. I'll have to see him in the morning. It could be important."

"I saw you talking to Caroline on the lawn this afternoon," Jim said. "You won't get much out of her. She's dumbness personified."

"She's not," Connie said indignantly. "She's just shy, that's all. Get her alone and she's quite a different person."

"I'll take your word for it. Getting Caroline alone isn't my idea of bliss. I'll settle for Sheila."

The two girls laughed. But several times during the meal Sheila saw Connie watching her husband with a puzzled look. She thought she knew why. Jim had the reputation of being a gay and witty person, but that evening both wit and gaiety were spasmodic, and rather artificial. And though he had rubbed his hands with glee when Connie had called them to the table, Sheila noticed that he ate little. Once she had chanced to glance at him while she and Connie were talking together; he was staring vaguely ahead, a frown on his handsome face, the soup cooling unheeded in front of him.

Connie excepted, it seemed that every one at Mulgerry had something on his or her conscience.

"I agree with Connie," she said. "Caroline isn't dumb. I should say she's pretty shrewd, really—though rather warped in her values."

"Why do you say that?" Connie asked, surprised. "It's perfectly true. But how did you discover it so quickly?"

"Because she considers adultery the ultimate sin," Sheila wanted to say. "She'd sooner condone murder, I think." But she did not say it, because she would then have had to say more. And I may be a little prejudiced where adultery is concerned, she thought wryly. I may not have committed it, but there were occasions with Eric when it was perilously near.

She shrugged. "I just gathered it from her general conversation."

"Anyone who lived with the Hump would be warped," Jim said. "It's inevitable. What did you talk about?"

"Don't pry, Jim." Connie gave her guest an apologetic look. "Sheila will tell us anything that it's proper for us to know. But you mustn't press her."

"There's nothing secret about it," Sheila said. She told them how Caroline had seen Eric on the night Grace died. "But I can't see that it's of much value. Perhaps Mr Matthews can make something of it."

"It's more *for* Eric than against him," Jim said. "That's certain. But I agree it isn't particularly strong. I remember seeing Caroline going off with that blasted dog when I posted my letter. She takes it out every evening; it belongs to the Hump, but no one but Caroline will bother with it. And I don't blame them. It's like its mistress—it howls whenever I turn on the radio."

Shelia was reminded that she had betrayed their confidence in that, and apologized. But Jim only laughed. "It doesn't matter a hoot," he said. "If she repeats it to the Hump it will show the old devil we mean business." He looked quickly at his wife. "Or rather, that we *did* mean business. I'm not so sure now."

Visions of her daily ride to Tanmouth, continuing indefinitely year after year, floated before his wife's eyes. It was almost unbearable in the winter. "You mean you want to stay here?" she asked sadly.

"I might. It's pleasant enough. I only wanted to leave because I couldn't afford the rent." Sheila had a shrewd suspicion that Connie paid the rent, and that this was just another example of Jim's egotism. "But things are looking up. I've been commissioned to do a couple of pictures, and there may be more to follow. And I've an idea the price will be more than right."

"How much is that?" demanded the practical Connie. But she did not conceal her pleasure at this recognition of his talent.

Jim blew her a kiss. "That, my love, is my business." He turned to Sheila. "I'm a strong believer in a husband's right to keep his earnings secret from his wife. It avoids bickering."

"If you'd told me this before I'd have spread myself on the feast in celebration," Connie said.

"You've spread yourself nicely as it is. And I didn't tell you before because I didn't know. I only heard this morning."

"Who are the pictures for?"

"Some boardroom or other, according to my agent."

"Congratulations," Sheila said. "Caroline for one will be delighted. She was most upset when I told her you were thinking of leaving. You have a friend for life there, Connie. She said Mulgerry would be unbearable without you."

"I can't think why." But it was plain that Connie was pleased at the compliment. "She does far more for me than I do for her."

"You talk to her, that's why," Jim said. "No one else does. And you always look pleased to see her. I bet those two old witches downstairs—yes, I said witches—treat her like dirt. They only speak to her when they want something done."

He's certainly devoted to his wife, Sheila thought; praise for Connie is as welcome to him as praise for himself. Or is that only another example of his egotism? The great Lord "I" taking credit for the achievements of his minion? If so it's partly Connie's fault in always putting his interests and desires before her own. She's as much a mother to him as a wife.

She tried to find out more about Kane (he and Mrs Winter were the only occupants of Mulgerry she had not yet met), but they could tell her little she did not already know. "He looks like a scarecrow," Connie said. "He doesn't seem to have any decent clothes, and those he has don't fit him."

"Perhaps he's a miser as well as a hermit," Sheila suggested.

"Perhaps. But I can't help feeling sorry for him. I'm sure he doesn't get enough to eat; a man living on his own never does. If he weren't so shy I'd invite him up for a meal occasionally, just to put a little meat on his bones."

"Put a little more on Sheila's," Jim said. "Her plate's empty."

Lady Humpleston dined punctually at seven-fifteen. She enjoyed her food. So did her sister, but to a lesser degree; the burden of having to prepare and cook it took some of her appetite away. Caroline's part in the domestic ritual was to lay the table, to fetch and carry during the meal, and later to clear away and wash and wipe up; she had little interest in the food itself. This seemed to Lady Humpleston a fair division of labour, since she had to bear the largest share of the cost herself.

That evening Caroline ate even less than usual. Her aunt made no adverse comment on this (it was not to her advantage to urge her relatives to healthier appetites), but she had other criticisms to make.

"I saw you talking to that Miss Loveday this afternoon," she accused her. "I'm surprised at you, Caroline. You know very well I don't want her here, that I'm doing my best to get rid of her."

To argue was to invite additional recrimination. Caroline contented herself with an apology.

Lady Humpleston grunted. "What did she want?"

"She asked me about the people living here."

"And that included me, I suppose?"

"Only incidentally, Aunt Alice. She was more interested in the others."

"I'm sure she was." Lady Humpleston turned to her sister. "There was a solicitor with her this morning. I think they are trying to rake up evidence to prove that Eric Cawthorne didn't kill his wife. Most annoying. If they succeed it will mean more visits from the police, more poking and prying." She sighed, and reached for the sauce-boat, helping herself liberally. "Happily that is an unlikely contingency. This sauce isn't piquant enough, Ellen. You're too mean with the capers."

"Perhaps he *didn't* kill her," Mrs Winter said briskly. Briskness was her stock-in-trade; it gave her confidence. She had developed it during her married life to deal with her husband's creditors, and she used it now as a shield against Alice's bullying. "We don't know, do we?"

"The police know, and that's good enough for me. He killed her for her money, of course. That—and this Loveday girl."

"He didn't," Caroline said. Frightened by her temerity, she added weakly, "Miss Loveday told me they were just old friends."

"Of course she did." Lady Humpleston, delighted at this opportunity to be sarcastic, overlooked the abrupt contradiction. "And you believed her? How naïve!"

Caroline flushed. Her mother said nothing, but went quietly on with her dinner. She had long since ceased trying to fight Caroline's battles for her. It took all her strength and determination to fight her own.

"The man is not only wicked, he's a fool," Lady Humpleston continued. "The girl's young, and pretty in an obvious way, of course; I've no doubt she's also shallow and cheap. Just something he picked up, I suppose." She made Sheila sound like a germ. "How could he be so stupid as to prefer her to his wife? Mrs Cawthorne had background; I believe her father was in the diplomatic service—or was it the Church? You only had to look at her to know that. She had dignity and poise, and a proper appreciation of the things that matter in life—matter to intelligent people, anyway." Lady Humpleston believed in extremes. She had not been quite so vocal in praise of Grace during the latter's lifetime, but she piled on the virtues now to stress her point. "Yes, she was a fine woman—a *good* woman, one might almost say. But she was certainly at fault in her choice of a husband—like others we know of, eh, Ellen?" Her sister ignored the dig. "He was a real trial to her, poor thing; one cannot but admire the way she put up with him. Many young women in her position would have turned to another man for consolation. But not Grace Cawthorne. She had too true a sense of duty."

Throughout this peroration Caroline had grown increasingly restive. Now she could stand it no longer.

"Stop it! Stop it!" She jumped to her feet and banged on the table with her fists, her dark eyes blazing. Mother and aunt stared at her in shocked astonishment, which in the aunt gradually turned to wrathful indignation. But Caroline did not wait for the wrath to explode into words. She almost hurled her chair from her and ran to the door.

There she turned. "Good woman indeed!" she shouted. "She wasn't anything of the sort. If you want to know what your precious Grace Cawthorne was I'll tell you. She—she was a *whore*!"

The Drummonds had finished dinner. Nadia's culinary repertoire was not so varied as Connie's or Ellen Winter's, nor was her cooking so good, and they lived mainly on joints and steaks, and cooked meats bought by Mike at the delicatessen in Tanmouth. Mike did most of the shopping. Nadia hated the bus journey.

Normally they watched television after dinner. Mike disliked it, but he suffered it to please her. This evening he did not.

"I want to talk to you," he said curtly. "You can watch that thing later."

Nadia did not protest; she had known this was coming. He had left the flat before she awoke that morning, leaving a note to say he would be back to dinner. The thought of the impending row had been with her all day; it would be a relief to get it over, even though she did not feel well. Sheila's 'softening-up' process had left her with an aching head and a queasy stomach.

"A nice fool you made of yourself last night!" he said. "Letting that damned girl get you stinko. You must have known what her game was. She wouldn't waste good liquor on a stranger for nothing."

"There wasn't any game. She was just being friendly."

They did not quarrel often; Mike was too indulgent and she too lazy. And on the few occasions when he found it necessary to reprimand her she would use her bodily attractions to distract and, inevitably, inveigle him from his purpose. But that evening she felt too ill for such wiles. She slouched untidily in her chair, careless of her appearance.

"Like hell she was! Not if she's a friend of Cawthorne. What she wanted from you was any little bit of gossip or scandal that might help him to get off."

"So what? It doesn't affect you, does it? Or did *you* murder Grace? No, of course you didn't. You were much too fond of her for that."

He scowled. "For God's sake shut up about my being fond of her. I've told you before, I couldn't stand the woman. She was a damned sight too stuck-up for me."

Nadia shrugged. "All right. You couldn't stand her and you didn't kill her. So what's giving you the jitters?"

"I just don't like people nosing around. And I don't like my wife getting drunk, and trading domestic secrets for brandy. It's —it's degrading."

"Ah!" She pushed herself up in her chair to stare at him angrily. "So I'm degrading now, am I? But it isn't degrading, I suppose, to carry another woman's key in your pocket so that you can visit her secretly whenever her husband happens to be away? You call that being friendly, eh?"

"So that's where you found the damned thing." He was too worried to deny the accusation. "And I suppose you blabbed it out to the girl?"

"What if I did? It was the truth, wasn't it? When she caught me opening the front door I had to tell her *something*."

He waved a fat hand. "Okay. But why tell her the truth? Anything but that." A new thought occurred to him, and he eyed her suspiciously. "What were you up to, Nadia? What was the idea, busting into the East Wing like that?"

"Nothing. I just wanted to make sure it was Grace's key. *I* don't go sneaking into another woman's house at night. I leave that to you."

Again he ignored the accusation. He heaved himself off his chair and went to stand by the mantelshelf, thoughtfully stroking the thinning red hair at the back of his head. He said, "You want to watch your step, girlie. Telling that girl—well, it could cause trouble. Real trouble."   —

"Not to me it couldn't." She knew from his tone, from the use of the diminutive, that his anger was cooling. As so often in the past, from being the accused she became the accuser. "Hadn't you better watch *your* step, Mike?"

"I know what I'm doing," he muttered.

"Maybe you do. But I don't—and I think it's time I did. Just what were you up to with that key? Did *she* give it to you?"

"No." He considered her for a moment, weighing in his mind domestic happiness against the probable indiscretion of her tongue. "I—I took it."

"Took it? You mean she didn't know you had it?"

"She couldn't. She was dead." He saw the horror dawning in her eyes. "Hey, don't get me wrong! I didn't kill her, girlie—I swear I didn't! But I had to have that key, and there it was in her bag, and so—well, I took it. It wasn't any use to her."

So far she had managed to keep apart from Grace's death, and the suffering and suspicion that went with it. But now it had been brought to her doorstep, right into her house. Mike was mixed up in it. She could not even be sure that he had not killed the woman. He had lied to her before. He might be lying now.

"When did this happen?" she asked. "I don't understand."

"I told you, didn't I? I took it from her bag after she was dead. I had to have it before the police came."

"But—if you didn't kill her, how did you know that she was dead? How did you know where to find her?"

"I didn't." He shook his head in perplexity; he should never have started this. He dared not tell her the truth. Yet without it how could he hope to make her understand? "I—well, I just found her, that's all. I can't tell you any more than that, girlie, I'm afraid."

"You can't, eh?" she said scornfully. "What do you think I am? A fool? You just happened to be walking along the foot of the cliffs, all among the rocks, and you came across this body in the dark—and you simply took the key out of her bag and walked away and never said a word to a soul! Is that it?" She almost screamed the last sentence at him, and paused to recover her breath. "I don't believe a word of it. You're lying."

"I'm not," he said desperately. "And of course it didn't happen like that. I was on the cliff-top, not down below. I saw her body lying on the rocks—I had a torch with me—but luckily the bag hadn't fallen with her. So I took the key out and threw the bag away, expecting it to be washed out to sea with the tide. Apparently it wasn't. Somehow it got jammed among the blasted rocks."

Nadia pictured Grace Cawthorne's body, mangled and broken and tugged at by the sea, and she shuddered. Grace might still have been alive when Mike saw her; yet he had done nothing to save her, had told no one. But it was not the callousness of his behaviour that horrified her so much as the knowledge that it was her own husband who had done this. And by involving himself in the tragedy he had inevitably involved her.

"And why were you out on the cliffs at night if it wasn't to meet Grace?" she demanded. "You knew she'd be there, didn't you?"

"Yes. That is, I knew——" He stopped, and held out both arms in supplication. "Please don't ask me any more, girlie. You'll just have to trust me."

"Trust you? I'll never trust you again as long as I live. No, don't touch me, you—you ghoul!" She was not sure that 'ghoul' was the word she wanted, but her recollection was that it had an unpleasant association with cemeteries and the dead.

"What did you want that key for? To rob a dead woman's house?"

"Of course not. It's not stealing to take what belongs to one, is it? And Grace had something of mine, something I didn't want the police to find. If she'd been alive she'd have given it to me without question."

"So that's why you couldn't come to the Upways that evening, is it? An important client, you said—who turns out to be a corpse. What was this thing of yours that you were so anxious the police shouldn't find?"

He shook his head. "I can't tell you, girlie. I just *can't*. Later, perhaps—but not now."

Ungracefully she scrambled out of her chair and faced him, hands on hips, unmindful of her appearance. She was near to tears, but she fought them back.

"There's a damned sight too much you can't tell me," she said furiously. "Well, I'll tell *you* something. If you want to keep this to yourself you can. And you can keep yourself to yourself also. Until I know exactly what's been going on I don't want you anywhere near me. And I probably won't want you then. Good night!"

The wiggle was still there as she walked from the room, but it no longer carried the same message. He heard the bedroom door slam and the key turn in the lock.

He shuddered and sat down. His knees felt weak and his mouth was dry. There was fear in him; fear that he had lost his wife, fear that through her he might lose his liberty.

"You bloody fool!" he told himself. "You miserable bloody fool!"

9

I DON'T get it," Eric said. "I'm sorry, but I just don't get it." He looked round the walls of the room, on which only a list of prison regulations for visitors relieved the bareness. The ashes of a fire long since dead littered the grate, there were the familiar bars on the high windows. "If it were not for all this I'd think I was dreaming." He gave Sheila a rather sickly smile. "Come to that, I'd think *you'd* been dreaming too."

"I'm sorry," she said. "But I'm afraid it's true."

"You're not the first man to have trusted his wife, Mr Cawthorne, and to find his trust misplaced," Matthews said. "It happens every day."

"I know. It's just that I could have sworn Grace wasn't like that. A *grande passion*—yes, that could have happened to her; although if it had I don't think she would have continued to live with me. She would have considered that degrading. No, it's this—this galaxy of lovers I boggle at. And look at the men involved. Kane and Drummond!" He turned to Sheila. "Can you see yourself falling for either of that pair?"

"No," Sheila said.

"Neither would Grace. As for this third man, the one Caroline saw——" He shrugged. "I wouldn't know about him. Did Caroline describe him to you?"

"No. After she'd told me the bare facts I couldn't get another word out of her."

"It doesn't matter. I don't suppose I'd recognize him, anyway; if he was a stranger to Caroline he was probably a stranger to me also. I didn't know any of Grace's friends apart from

H

her agent, and he's over sixty and a cripple. I didn't even know she *had* any friends."

"I'm afraid this is very upsetting for you," Matthews said. "I'm sorry."

"Strangely enough, it isn't. Perhaps I'm even slightly relieved; it lessens the guilt of my own behaviour." He gave Sheila a look which made her blush. Matthews saw it, and frowned. "Even her death doesn't seem quite so tragic—although I don't know why it doesn't."

Sheila had thought that his pride, if not his heart, would be bruised by their news of Grace's infidelity. Men were so insistent on their wives being virtuous—even when they had ceased to love them and had strayed themselves. It was a relief that he should take it so calmly.

"When did Kane and the Drummonds come to Mulgerry?" the solicitor asked. "I've been wondering whether there was any previous association with your wife."

"Not that I know of. But Kane moved in about the same time as Grace, and the Drummonds a few months later. They had to wait until the garage flat was ready." He turned to Sheila. "I think I know now why Caroline looked at me so oddly the morning after Grace was killed. It was because she'd seen her with this man."

"What sort of look?" Matthews asked.

"Pity—contempt—a little of both, perhaps. I was the deceived husband—rather a comical figure in fiction, I believe."

"Caroline doesn't take adultery quite so lightly," Sheila said.

Matthews said thoughtfully, "Are you inferring, then, that this—this act of adultery Miss Winter says she witnessed occurred very recently? On the day Mrs Cawthorne died, perhaps?"

"Not necessarily. It was the first time I'd seen Caroline since the Christmas holidays, so it could have happened during the term. But I see what you're getting at. You think this is the 'complication' Grace mentioned in her letter, eh?"

Matthews nodded. "And it's strengthened by your belief that

your wife would not have continued to live with you if she had fallen in love with another man. Doesn't that also point the same way?"

Eric flushed. "I'm afraid not. Although we shared the same house, we didn't occupy the same bedroom. I thought I'd explained that to you."

"I'm sorry," Matthews said. "I had forgotten."

"But it makes sense!" Sheila was always ready for a fresh line of pursuit. "Perhaps this man called at the house after you'd gone, Eric—or perhaps he telephoned—and Grace arranged to meet him out on the cliff because she didn't want you to find them together when you returned. Yes—and that was where Caroline saw them," she said excitedly. "It must have been. And afterwards they quarrelled, and he killed her. Perhaps he didn't mean to—but it happened. Isn't that what you were thinking, Mr Matthews?"

"Something like that," he agreed cautiously. "But it's all rather hypothetical, I'm afraid. And if a stranger was involved it's a job for the police."

"If they'll tackle it," Eric said. "Right now they seem too taken up with me to go job-hunting."

"Maybe. But there's one lead they can't ignore, and that's Kane and Drummond. If Miss Loveday heard aright they were either planning a murder or had recently taken part in one. We can't tackle that, but the police can and must. And the sooner they know about it the better." The solicitor thumbed the pages of his notes. "About this communicating door, Mr Cawthorne. Ever seen it open?"

"No. I asked my wife about it, and she told me it was locked and that there was no key. I never gave it another thought."

"Ever been in Kane's flat?" Eric shook his head. "So you've no idea what all this paraphernalia means, eh?"

"None at all. Sounds like a load of junk to me."

Matthews smiled. "I'm with you there. Flat-irons and muslin don't go with a carpenter's bench, somehow. So let's leave that problem to the police too, shall we? I doubt if it has any real bearing on your wife's death. The man may have an unusual hobby, but that doesn't make him a murderer."

"Aren't we leaving rather a lot to the police?" Sheila said. "How about doing something ourselves?"

The solicitor was unperturbed.

"Certainly. But remember, our task is not to discover who killed Mrs Cawthorne, but to show that Mr Cawthorne did not. And I fancy Miss Winter's statement will help considerably in that."

"You do?" Sheila looked her relief. "Well, that's a blessing. I was afraid it was too inconclusive."

Eric said nothing. He was staring out of the window, a thoughtful frown on his face.

"Let's examine it more closely, shall we?" Matthews continued. "Mr Cawthorne left the house at around three-thirty—Mr Upway saw him go, so there is no disputing that. At some time after five-thirty Mrs Cawthorne went out; if we put it at five-forty that would give her time to seal the letter to her sister, address the envelope, and put it in the hall rack. She would reach the cliff-top by five-fifty at the earliest, then."

He took an Ordnance Survey map from his brief-case and spread it on the table.

"At five forty-five Miss Winter saw Mr Cawthorne near Gavin Head; about three miles from Mulgerry, not more than an hour's steady walking. But you, Mr Cawthorne, took two and a quarter hours—which bears out your point that you were strolling rather than walking, and that you took an occasional breather. On the return journey via the road you took an hour and a quarter—if, as you say, you were back by seven o'clock. Now, look at the map. Here's Gavin Head, and here's Bineford. It's nearly four miles that way, yet you did that journey in nearly half the time."

"I got a move on when it started to rain," Eric said.

"Exactly. That's what I'm getting at. It's a perfectly reasonable explanation of your movements that afternoon."

"But how can I prove I was back by seven? No one saw me, did they?"

"If they did they haven't said so. And that's a pity. It's not a vital time, luckily, but it makes your case stronger if the police can check and find it correct. You didn't see or hear anything on your return that would make that possible, I suppose?"

Eric closed his eyes. It was easy to look back. In his cell it was easier to look back than to look forward, for there he could see no future beyond the wall. Now that was changing; they were giving him hope. But the immediate past was too close to the present—would probably always be too close—for him to forget it.

He walked up the long drive again, stumbling through the puddles with the rain beating on his face. He could see the house, tall and grey against the overcast sky. There were lights shining from the windows—though none in the East Wing. (Eric shuddered. That no longer meant that Grace had gone to bed. It meant she was dead.) Music flowed noisily from an upstairs window, and . . .

"*The Merry Widow*!" he exclaimed. And, as Matthews and Sheila looked at him in astonishment, "The Upways had their radio on. Full blast, as usual—I heard it as I came up the drive. They were playing the waltz from *The Merry Widow*."

Matthews slapped his hand delightedly on the table.

"Fine. We can check that with the B.B.C. They'll be able to tell us at what time it was broadcast."

"The police might say I looked it up in the *Radio Times*," Eric objected.

"Not light music," Sheila said. "They don't usually publish the items. Only the name of the orchestra."

"That's true." The solicitor paused, and then said impressively, "Mr Cawthorne—do you remember at what time it started to rain that evening?"

"You're a one for times, aren't you? Somewhere around six-thirty, I should say. Might be a little before."

"At six-fourteen exactly," Matthews said. There was such

triumph in his voice that they looked at him in surprise. He's like a little boy when he's pleased with himself, Sheila thought. "I've the experts' word for that. And it rained heavily, didn't it?"

"It certainly did. I was soaked."

"And unexpectedly?"

"Very. It caught *me* on the hop, anyway."

"It must have caught Mrs Cawthorne too. She wasn't prepared for it—she took no coat with her when she went out." He paused again, his eyes dancing with suppressed excitement. "What do you suppose she would do, Mr Cawthorne, if she were out on the cliff-top and it suddenly started to rain?"

"Hurry home, of course," Eric said. "Grace was fond of the rural life, but she was also fussy about her appearance. She didn't like getting her hair wet, and there is no shelter there. Not unless she crawled under the bushes. And that would do more damage than the rain."

"Exactly. But she didn't hurry home, did she? Which brings us to the inevitable conclusion that by the time the rain started she was dead. You see? At a quarter-past six she was dead."

"Of course!" Sheila exclaimed delightedly. "And——"

But the solicitor was not to be robbed of his final triumph. He said firmly, interrupting her, "And half an hour previous to that Mr Cawthorne was seen at Gavin Head, about two and a half miles from where his wife was killed."

"I could have made it if I'd run," Eric objected.

"Perhaps. But why should you? And how could you know that your wife was there? Even supposing you were filled with an overwhelming and sudden urge to murder her, is that where you would have gone? Wouldn't you have made for the house? That was where you'd left her—and that was where you'd expect to find her."

He looked from one to the other expectantly, inviting their approval. Sheila gave hers whole-heartedly, her waning faith in his ability completely restored. But Eric said nothing. Perplexed by his lack of enthusiasm, and worried lest the solicitor should be hurt by it, Sheila said hastily, "That's terrific. Why didn't I think it out for myself?"

"You provide the information, I interpret it," Matthews said lightly. "Yours is the harder part. But I think we make a pretty good team."

It was not so much the words as the look in his eyes that caused Sheila to blush furiously. To hide her embarrassment she said, "It looks like plain sailing now. We'll have you out of here in no time, Eric. Won't we, Mr Matthews?"

But the solicitor had had his moment of glory. He said guardedly, "We mustn't rush our fences. The police won't just accept our word for this; they will want to satisfy themselves that the evidence justifies the assumptions. That will take time. I think the most we can hope for is that Mr Cawthorne will come up before the magistrate on the twelfth, as arranged, and that the police will then either offer no evidence or withdraw the charge. There might even be a further remand if they can't complete their investigations in time—although I don't envisage that. But it's another reason why we should put these new facts before them as soon as possible."

"You mean that it's unlikely I shall have to stand trial?" Eric asked.

"Very unlikely, I should say. Even without this new evidence it was not a strong case. Plenty of motive, of course. But you can't be convicted on that."

"It's Caroline I'm worried about," Eric said, frowning. "If the Hump made her keep her mouth shut before, why has she opened it now?"

"I wondered about that too," Sheila said. "I think it's because she's sorry for you—and also because it was easier to talk to me than to the police. I don't believe your possible guilt or innocence counts very strongly with Caroline. To her Grace was an erring wife who deserved what she got; and if you killed her you were justified."

"*Le crime passionel,*" Matthews murmured. "Miss Winter is not alone in her opinion."

"I hope she sticks to it, then," Eric said. "Incidentally, I had a letter from my headmaster this morning, Sheila. He says he has every confidence in my ability to prove my innocence. He also enclosed a cheque."

"How nice of him! Was that to help pay for your defence?"

"I'm afraid not." Eric gave a wry smile. "It was in lieu of a term's notice. Despite his belief in me, he considers that it would be wrong to involve the school in any scandal or notoriety that might arise from the trial. He hopes I will appreciate his point of view."

"Well, I don't," Sheila said indignantly. "I call it absolutely disgraceful. Poor Eric!"

"Oh, I don't mind. I'd think twice before going back there anyway. And he did say that he'd be pleased to give me a reference should I ever require one—which sounds to me like hedging on his confidence, eh? 'Mr Eric Cawthorne has been an assistant master at this school for the past four years, during which time he has not murdered a single boy.'"

The solicitor laughed and stood up. "Well, I must be off," he said, stuffing map and notes into his brief-case. "I have to be in court in half an hour. Can I give you a lift, Miss Loveday?"

Before Sheila could reply Eric said, "I'd like a few words alone with Miss Loveday—if that's possible. Can you wait for her? I won't keep her long."

Matthews nodded. He thought he knew what his client wished to say to the girl, and was annoyed that the knowledge should displease him.

"It's okay with me; I'll wait in the passage outside. But I'm afraid the authorities will insist on an officer being present."

Eric looked at the man through the window. "I suppose their tongues don't wag about what they overhear?" he said doubtfully. And, at the solicitor's shocked expostulation, "All right. Show the gentleman in."

But his gaiety departed when Matthews had left the room. With a quick glance at the officer standing stolidly just inside the door he said, "Do you think he's right, Sheila? Can Caroline's evidence get me off?"

"Of course," she said confidently. "And I did think you were rather unkind to the poor man, darling, in not showing *some* enthusiasm. It really was a clever piece of deduction."

"I know. But the fact is, it's all false."

"False?" Sheila stared at him. "What on earth are you talking about? It *can't* be false."

"I'm afraid it is. I didn't know whether to tell Matthews, or to leave him in ignorance and hope for the best. But I feel I must tell you. You see—well, I don't know what Caroline is up to—perhaps she's just overdoing the pity—but in actual fact I was never anywhere *near* Gavin Head that afternoon!"

10

INSPECTOR PITT received them in his office at police head-quarters. He still bore traces of his recent illness; the cough was there, although more subdued, and his voice was husky. "I lost it completely for a day," he told them, when Sheila asked how he was.

Matthews did the talking. Sheila admired the clarity with which he presented his case. Occasionally she glanced at the inspector's gaunt face in an attempt to gauge the effect on him of some particularly telling point, but for most of the time her eyes were fixed steadily on the handsome face of the young solicitor.

When Matthews had finished Pitt said quietly, "Thank you, sir," and then was silent again. Swivelling gently from side to side in his chair, he sat staring at his desk, a pencil tapping out a monotonous rhythm between his teeth.

Looking up, he caught Sheila watching him. He smiled.

"Ever thought of joining the police, Miss Loveday? You'd be welcome—for more reasons than one."

I wish I didn't blush so easily, she thought, as the warmth rose in her cheeks. But she was pleased at the compliment. She decided he was neither so severe nor so unpleasant (no, not unpleasant—inhuman) as she had originally thought him.

"I belong to a rival organization," she said, returning the smile. "Private enterprise."

But already he had turned to the solicitor, and was again the dour policeman.

"Just why have you come to me, Mr Matthews?" he asked.

"For several reasons, Inspector. Primarily, of course, because of the conversation Miss Loveday overheard between Kane and Drummond. Murder's your business, not mine. There is also this possibility that Mrs Cawthorne was murdered by the man Miss Winter saw with her. Miss Loveday could learn no details about time and place, but in your official capacity you might fare better; and if a stranger is involved the police have more chance of locating him than I have. And finally, as the bottom seems to be dropping out of the case against my client, I want to know if you are prepared to withdraw the charge."

Pitt took his time in replying. He said, speaking slowly, as though weighing the significance of each word before uttering it, "I'm going to be frank with you, sir. As you know, I was ill when the arrest was made. I was not even consulted; had I been, I think I would have advised against it. Mind you, I'm not saying the arrest was unjustified; merely that it was premature." He shook his head. "Experience has taught me caution in these matters, Mr Matthews. There's nothing more damaging to the police than an action for wrongful arrest."

The solicitor frowned. "Are you inferring that the police are going to try to make this charge stick, or at least to justify the arrest, simply to avoid my client bringing an action against them? Because if so, I must insist that——"

"There's no need to insist on anything, sir. I was not inferring, I was stating a fact." There was an edge to the inspector's voice. "Coming from a member of your profession, Mr Matthews, I am surprised that you should make such an unwarranted accusation."

The solicitor reddened. "I apologize—although, to paraphrase your own words, it wasn't an accusation, it was a query. But unnecessary, I agree."

Pitt smiled thinly. "Shall we stop sparring and get down to business, then? In the first place, I am certainly making no promises about what the police will or will not do until this new evidence has been thoroughly sifted." He paused. "Miss Winter, it seems, has become a key witness."

Sheila shifted uneasily on her chair. She had not repeated Eric's confidence to the solicitor. At the time it had given a shattering blow to her optimism, but on reflection she had decided that provided Caroline stuck to her story it did not matter whether it was true or false. No one but Eric could disprove it. And if the truth could not establish his innocence then a lie must do it. Surely in this case the end must justify the means?

She was suddenly aware that the inspector's keen grey eyes were fixed on her intently.

"There's no doubt in your mind, Miss Loveday, about the truth of Miss Winter's statement?" he asked.

"Of course not." That, unfortunately, was true. Eric had dispelled any doubt she might have had. "Why should she invent it? You've met Lady Humpleston, Inspector—but have you any idea what a dreadful old tyrant she is? For Miss Winter to volunteer that statement against her aunt's expressed wish (and Lady Humpleston's wish is as good as an order to her family) was quite something."

"Exactly. It shows Miss Winter fully realized its importance. So I can't help wondering why she forbore to mention it when I spoke to her."

"Perhaps she hadn't yet steeled herself to defy her aunt," Sheila said. "And she's very shy; it shows in her abrupt, rather unfriendly manner. You have to break down that barrier before you can win her confidence."

"Meaning that I didn't, eh? I'll see if I can do better next time." He turned to the solicitor. "Would you mind if I had a talk with your client this afternoon, sir? I think it might be profitable for both of us."

"Okay by me, Inspector, so long as I'm present."

Sheila allowed her thoughts to wander as they talked. How would Caroline stand up to a fresh interrogation by the police? How would she survive a severe grilling in court if it ever came to that? How did one defend a lie under pressure? (Or didn't she know it was a lie? Did she really believe she had seen Eric that afternoon?) Surely everything depended on the purpose behind the lie, and on how dear that purpose was to the girl?

Well, there could be only one purpose—to save Eric. But why

did she want to save him? Because she was sorry for him? Because she was in love with him? Because she was convinced of his innocence, and could see no other way to help him prove it? To spite her aunt? It could be any of those. Eric had suggested pity as the reason, but he had no basis for it. He was, she knew, as puzzled as herself.

Only Caroline could determine the mystery; but to ask her would be to bring the lie into the open. Caroline might then retract it; at best it would shake the girl's confidence in her ability to maintain it successfully. And Caroline was Eric's chief hope of establishing his innocence. As Matthews had said, let the police worry over who had killed Grace. Their task was to clear Eric.

But it was only human nature to ponder on the identity of the murderer. It had to be Kane or Drummond—or Grace's unknown lover; and because he was unknown, and speculation impossible, Sheila tended to disregard the latter. But Kane and Drummond—they had actually discussed murder. What was the inspector going to do about them?

When she asked him he was noncommittal. "I doubt if it was murder they were planning," he said. "More likely they were referring to Mrs Cawthorne's death."

"But they were planning *something*," she protested. "I heard them."

"Something, yes," he agreed. "And from your description of that basement room I might be able to put a name to it."

"What?" asked Sheila and Matthews together. But Pitt shook his head. "You can't ask a policeman a question like that," he said, smiling. "It's almost indecent."

"Indecent or not, we've asked it," Sheila said. "And it's mean of you not to answer. I don't believe you know, really," she added darkly. "You're just making a wild guess to tantalize us."

But Pitt was not to be drawn.

"Let's leave it at that, then, shall we? I'm guessing."

"All that junk," the girl went on. "Bits of wood, scraps of

muslin, an old flat-iron. What possible significance could they have for you?"

"Quite a lot, Miss Loveday." There was a distinct twinkle in the inspector's eye; he was obviously enjoying her perplexity. "And especially the flat-iron."

After Sheila and Matthews had left him that morning Eric's mood alternated between high hope and dark despair. His defence now rested on a lie. It was a good and useful lie, and he had no moral objection to accepting it. But what if the lie should be exposed? Might not the police assert that he had inspired it, thus making his position even more precarious?

At first he refused to see the inspector when the latter called at the prison in the early afternoon. He wasn't talking to any more policemen, he said sourly; if there had to be a discussion his solicitor could do the talking. That was his job. It was only with considerable difficulty that Matthews eventually persuaded him to change his mind.

Eliciting information was to Pitt, as to other skilled police officers, a matter of technique allied to experience. There was no set formula; the technique varied with the person to be interrogated and the information required. Eric Cawthorne could be neither bullied nor threatened; he was too resentful and suspicious to be coerced. To obtain his co-operation it was necessary to break down that resentment and suspicion by arousing his interest; to give information rather than appear to seek it.

"Your wife seems to have kept you very much in the dark about her financial affairs, Mr Cawthorne," he said. "Misled you, too. That mythical inheritance, for instance. So it may also surprise you to learn that the bulk of her income was paid into her bank in cash. What's more, she paid it in personally."

"In cash?" Eric exclaimed.

"Yes. Large sums, too; anything up to a thousand pounds at a time. They were paid in at irregular intervals, but in all they amounted to three or four thousand a year. Quite a tidy sum, eh, when you appreciate that it was probably tax-free? Any idea where it came from?"

The question came so naturally that Eric was surprised into answering it.

"Not me." The tone was less surly. "Have you?"

Pitt shook his head. "It wasn't only cash, of course. There were cheques from the sale of her paintings. Two years ago I imagine she was happy to get fifteen or twenty pounds apiece for them, but I see that lately she was asking four or five times that sum."

"She and Jim Upway held a joint exhibition of their work at the Strange Gallery in Baker Street last year," Eric said. "I believe it boosted her reputation considerably."

"I imagine it did. I was there the first morning, you know. One of her pictures—Gavin Head, it was called—appealed to me particularly. I might have been tempted to buy it if it had not been sold already."

"I remember it. She only finished it the day before the exhibition opened." Eric frowned. "I meant to ask her about that. But I never did."

"Ask her about what?"

"Why anyone should buy a picture without seeing it first. And he couldn't have seen it, you know. There was a 'sold' label on it even before the doors opened."

"Unusual," Pitt agreed. "The buyer was obviously an admirer of your wife's work. Or it might have been James Porter himself. I saw him the other day, and he told me he had bought one of her seascapes. Out of sentiment mainly, I suspect—although he didn't say so."

"And who might James Porter be?" asked Eric.

"You've never heard of him?" Pitt sounded surprised. "He's a partner in Sutcliffe and Cashell. They specialize in the cleaning and restoration of old paintings; a most reputable firm. It's odd that your wife should never have spoken of them to you. She worked for them for nearly five years."

Eric stared at him. His former animosity had vanished, ousted by curiosity.

"It seems to me, Inspector, that you know a great deal more about my wife than I ever did. Why? What is behind all this delving into the past?"

"Just routine police work, Mr Cawthorne." Pitt evaded the direct question. "Nothing unusual—we spend most of our time on it. Some of it pays off, but much of it doesn't."

"And is it paying off now?"

"It might. It's too early to say yet." He got up slowly from the hard chair, arching his long back. Matthews thought he looked tired, and suspected that he had left his sick-bed too soon. "Well, I must be off. Thank you, Mr Cawthorne. I won't detain you any longer."

The stock phrase was thoughtlessly uttered, and immediately regretted. But Eric seized on it. It revived all his former annoyance.

"But that's just what you are doing, Inspector. And apparently you intend to go on detaining me—even though Miss Loveday and Mr Matthews have produced cast-iron evidence that I did *not* murder my wife. You pop round for a social call and a nice, cosy chat about my wife's finances; but what good is that? You put me into this damned prison. Why the hell don't you get me out?"

The inspector was not in the least perturbed by this outburst.

"The magistrate committed you to prison, sir, not the police. Only he can order your release. And he won't do that until the charge is withdrawn or until he is satisfied that there is no case to answer."

"Then withdraw the charge, damn it!"

Pitt shook his head. "Your cast-iron evidence isn't cast-iron to me, Mr Cawthorne. Far from it."

That silenced him. None knew better than he how unfounded was that evidence. He said petulantly, "Oh, have it your own way, damn you! But at least tell me this. Those cash payments made to my wife. Are you suggesting that they were for services rendered—that she was no better than a rather superior call-girl?"

That shook the inspector. Shook and shocked him. Indignantly he denied that such a thought had occurred to him. But Matthews laughed. "I imagine that even the élite of that profession couldn't demand a fee of a thousand pounds. Or could they? I wouldn't know."

"Then where the hell *did* the money come from?" Eric demanded.

"That, Mr Cawthorne, is something I hope to find out very shortly," Pitt said.

Sheila was cooking lunch when Miss Lomas arrived. She came in a taxi, and from the battered and bulky suitcase Sheila knew that she had come to stay.

Miss Lomas had no apologies to offer. "I can't afford the hotel," she announced without preamble. "And if I'm to see this thing through I must stay somewhere. This was my sister's house, not Eric's, so I suppose I've as much right to be here as you have. Not that I'm trying to turn you out, mind you. There should be room for both of us."

"Thank you," Sheila said. While admitting to herself the truth of the woman's claim, she was appalled at the prospect of sharing the house with her. "I'll try not to get in your way."

"No need to be sarcastic, young woman," Miss Lomas said briskly. "Since I'm here you may as well learn to put up with me. I've got to put up with *you*." She dumped her suitcase in the hall and followed Sheila into the kitchen, eyeing the bright paint and modern equipment with approval. But the approval vanished when she saw the burnt chop and watery potatoes that were Sheila's lunch. "Not much of a cook, are you? From now on you'd better leave that to me. Cooking's something I *can* do."

"Have you had lunch?" Sheila asked, relieved that Miss Lomas's presence would not be entirely without compensation. She appreciated good food, but privately agreed with the other's opinion of her cooking. "There's another chop."

I

"I have, thank you. And if the chop's anything like that burnt offering I'm glad I have. But I could do with a cup of tea."

While she busied herself with the kettle and the tea-things she never stopped talking; most of her comments were acid, but Sheila got the impression that she was trying to be friendly. But do I want her friendliness? the girl wondered. Wouldn't it be easier if we maintained our former footing, so that I could ignore her when I felt like it? Having her tag along could be quite a handicap.

Miss Lomas said, "How's lover-boy bearing up? Oh, you didn't fool me with all that detective tomfoolery. You're far too pretty for that game."

·It was a double-edged compliment. "But I *am* a detective," Sheila said coldly.

"Are you? Well, you're a woman too. *And* you're in love with Eric." Sheila said nothing, but the tell-tale flush on her cheeks spoke for her. "A pity. You'd do better with that good-looking lawyer you've managed to pick up. Eric's all right; he can be quite entertaining when he's in the mood. But I've no illusions about him. Eric never loved anyone but himself; never did and never will. He'll get tired of you, same as he got tired of Grace." Miss Lomas sighed. "But what's the use? You're not likely to take *my* advice."

"I'm not," Sheila agreed. "And aren't you being rather personal?"

"And why not? I like personalities. Don't you?" She sat down opposite the girl, poured two cups of tea, and pushed one across the kitchen table. "You're quite convinced of the man's innocence, aren't you? Why?"

It was a question Sheila would have preferred to avoid; she didn't know the answer. Intuition, she supposed, was the basis of her conviction. But would Miss Lomas accept that?

Miss Lomas would not. "Don't believe in it," she declared firmly. "It's just a cloak for an inability to reason. Can't you do better than that?"

"Well, he doesn't *behave* like a guilty man," Sheila said

desperately. "Besides, I know Eric. He *couldn't* have done it."

"H'm! Not exactly a convincing argument, is it? You don't think it has anything to do with love being blind, eh?" And, when the girl vehemently denied the suggestion, "No, I didn't think you would. But if you weren't in love with him would you still believe in his innocence?"

Would she? She didn't know. "One can't answer a hypothetical question like that," she said. "I *am* in love with him."

"And would you still feel that way if you knew he were guilty? Would you still fight to get him off?"

"One can't just switch love on and off," Sheila said. "And why all these questions? What's behind them?"

"Inquisitiveness. Pure inquisitiveness, my dear. I like to know what makes people tick." She smiled; it was a broad smile that seemed to split her square, weatherbeaten face, and rather to her surprise Sheila found herself returning it. "You'll get used to me in time. People do—if they live long enough. How about showing me round the house if you've finished your tea? And call me Daffy if you feel like it. The name's Daphne, but the general opinion seems to be that Daffy's more suitable."

Miss Lomas was a practical woman, not given to enthusing. She accepted the living-room as a work of art, but not as a room. "Typical of Grace," she said, staring about her. "I prefer comfort myself. Imagine dusting those awful chandeliers!" She stumped over to one of the pictures and gaped at it for a moment. "Good heavens! Is that supposed to be Grace?"

"I think so. It was painted by one of the tenants here. A Mr Upway."

"He wants his head examined. So does Grace—for hanging a thing like that on her wall." Suddenly she remembered that Grace was dead. "Dear me! I shouldn't have said that, should I? But Grace and I never saw eye to eye about anything." She seated herself in an Adam chair, which creaked ominously. "Well, how's crime? Got that letter sorted out yet?"

"You mean the complication your sister referred to? No."

"And you a detective? Tut, tut! You're not trying."

The tone softened the criticism. But Sheila was not in a mood for humour; she considered the remark crude and ill-timed. "Oddly enough, I don't find that funny," she said.

"Failure's never amusing to the unsuccessful," Miss Lomas said cheerfully. "But don't let it rattle you, my dear; one can't win all the time. I dare say you've been more successful in other directions. Let's hear how lover-boy's defence is shaping."

"Why should I? You'll only criticize. And stop calling him lover-boy."

"You should never be afraid of criticism," the other reproved her. "Not if it's constructive—as I hope mine is. I don't pick holes just for the hell of it."

"Don't you? That *does* surprise me."

The tone was as provocative as the words. But Miss Lomas did not take offence.

"I've as many rights in this murder as you, young woman," she said mildly. "More, I'd say. Love—your boy-friend may be in danger of carrying the can for it, but it was my sister who was the victim; and if that didn't break my heart it certainly didn't please me. I hate to think of Lomases being pushed over cliffs."

"I'm sorry," Sheila said humbly.

Miss Lomas waved a large hand in recognition of the apology.

"Let's make a fresh start, shall we? Try a little co-operation. Not necessarily to save Eric—though that too, if he's innocent—but because neither of us likes the idea of some one getting away with murder. (That's the first time I've used that phrase in its literal sense.) I'm not sure how well-developed my deductive faculties are, but otherwise I'm reasonably sane—I think. And two heads are said to be better than one." Miss Lomas grinned. "And don't tell me you've got a spare head already. I know—that lawyer fellow. Well, his may be younger and more handsome and in better shape, but it isn't here—more's the pity."

Sheila gave her a grudging smile. "He's Eric's solicitor, not mine. And what difference do his looks make?"

"They'd make a hell of a lot of difference to me if I were your age." Miss Lomas sighed gustily. "Even now they make the blood circulate a little faster. You'd be surprised how——" She sighed again. "But I'm away off course. Let's hear the news, my dear."

Sheila had not meant to tell her anything; she was not even sure that it was right or wise to do so without first consulting the solicitor. But there was something compelling about Miss Lomas; without quite knowing why, Sheila did as she was bid. Only the fact that Caroline's statement was a lie did she keep to herself. That was something for Eric and herself alone.

Heavy brows knitted in concentration, Miss Lomas listened.

"It's a tangle, isn't it?" she said eventually. "Loose ends all over the place. But I agree with Eric about the boy-friends. That wasn't like Grace at all. If it had been me, now——" She slapped her large thighs, chuckling, and heaved herself out of the chair. "But that's life for you. How about a stroll round the garden? I think better out of doors."

Somewhat reluctantly (if they should chance to meet the Hump how would the old tyrant receive the news that there was yet another squatter in the East Wing?) Sheila led the way into the yard, pointing out the Drummond flat above the garage. As they passed through the archway they met Jim Upway. He was standing at the top of the steps that led down to the basement, so lost in thought that he did not notice them until Sheila spoke to him.

"Not thinking of calling on the Hermit, are you?" she said, when she had introduced Miss Lomas.

"Good heavens, no! Merely contemplating. Have you ever considered what a grim life a menial must have led in the old days? No light, no air, no mod. con., and those awful stone steps into the bargain. Can't think how they stuck it. Particularly with a Humpleston for lord and master."

"The windows aren't so small," Miss Lomas said, peering down into the area. "I suppose they're a modern improvement. But I most certainly wouldn't care to live down there. Fancy tackling those steps at night! Why aren't there any railings?"

"Melted down for guns during the war," Jim said. "And the Hump's too mean to replace them."

He strolled along the terrace with them. Miss Lomas was obviously impressed by his good looks, and urged him to talk about his painting. "I've just been admiring the portrait you did of my sister," she said, avoiding Sheila's eye. "I'd like to see some more of your work if I may."

"Get Sheila to bring you up one evening," Jim said. "My fans are always welcome."

They had nearly reached the end of the terrace when Lady Humpleston, with Caroline and Pompey in attendance, came round the corner of the house. The scowl that seldom left her face deepened when she saw them, and Sheila's heart sank. But she could not avoid the encounter, and with some trepidation she introduced Miss Lomas.

Much to her surprise, something like a smile appeared on the old lady's face.

"I'm glad to see you, Miss Lomas," she said. "It's about time some one was here to keep an eye on poor Mrs Cawthorne's treasures." She shot a malevolent glance at Sheila. "If, indeed, there are any left."

Sheila gasped. Recovering, she was about to make a suitably cutting retort, with some reference to the laws of libel, when the absurdity of the situation suddenly struck her. Unable to stop herself, she burst into uncontrolled laughter.

Nothing could have shaken the Hump more. Just occasionally she had received from some doughty opponent as good as she had given, but never had anyone presumed to treat her as a figure of fun. She was so flabbergasted that even words failed her; she could only stand there, glaring at the laughing Sheila, her mouth working silently, the gnarled fingers gripping her stick so tightly that veins and bones almost burst their way through the parchment-like skin. At last, when it seemed that she must explode with the anger bubbling up inside her, she banged her stick furiously on the terrace and hobbled away.

"Well, well!" Jim said. "If you never had an enemy before

you've got one now, my girl. Don't let the Hump catch you unawares on a dark night."

"I'm sorry," Sheila said, wiping her eyes, and still giggling intermittently. "It just struck me as so absurd, the way that old women accuses every one right, left, and centre—and without a shred of evidence. She's so impossible that she's farcical. It was rude of me, of course—but she can't complain about that after the way she spoke to me."

"You don't know the Hump, obviously. She can complain of anything."

Caroline had gone with her aunt. Now she reappeared and hurried up to them. She took no notice of Jim or Miss Lomas, but caught Sheila by the arm and drew her aside.

"That detective is here, Miss Loveday," she whispered, with a quick glance behind her as though she feared her aunt might be listening round the corner. "The one who came before."

"Oh! Does he want to see me?"

"I think so. He and another man are waiting outside the East Wing." Her voice sank even lower. "Does he know?"

"Know what? Oh, about your seeing Eric. Yes, he does. You'd better hang around in case he wants a word with you. I expect he will."

Caroline stared at her. Her lips parted; there was a desperate appeal in the dark eyes. Sheila wanted to reassure her, but she could think of nothing reassuring to say. It was a relief when Caroline turned away.

In silence the three of them watched her go. Jim said, "Police, eh? Well, you'll be safer with them than with the Hump. I'll fade out, I think."

"Me too," Miss Lomas said hastily. She made to follow Jim, but Sheila stopped her.

"Just a minute," Sheila said. "We're co-operating, remember. You had your turn—now it's mine. What did you mean when you told Mr Matthews yesterday morning that Eric might not inherit your sister's money?"

"Eh?" Miss Lomas was obviously embarrassed. "Did I say that?"

"You implied it, certainly."

"H'm! Well, it was just an idle thought. Wishful thinking, perhaps. I'm next in line after Eric."

"It was more than that," Sheila persisted. "What?"

Miss Lomas shifted uneasily from one broad foot to the other, watching Jim Upway cross the lawn. "It—I'm afraid it isn't my secret," she said.

"Then whose is it?"

"Well, it used to be Grace's. But now——" Miss Lomas paused to consider. "I suppose it's Eric's. And I wish him joy of it."

SHEILA watched as the inspector closed the door to the basement and locked it. He hesitated over the key, looked speculatively at Sergeant Rivers, and then handed it to her. "Put that away and don't lose it," he said. "And don't use it either."

"Aren't you going down there now?" she asked, disappointed.

"Not this way. But I might try the old-fashioned method of ringing the front-door bell."

For a detective, thought Sheila, he was very unenterprising. "Will you see the Drummonds as well?" she asked.

Pitt smiled. "You ask too many questions, Miss Loveday. It's the curse of our profession, I sometimes think. Now—may I have another look at the studio before I leave?"

She went upstairs with them. She could not understand Pitt's interest in the dead woman's paintings (presumably he was there as a detective, not as a connoisseur of art?), but after that last rebuff she thought it wiser not to ask. Apparently his search was unsuccessful, for when he left he took nothing with him, and there was no hint of triumph on his gaunt face.

"Anything else?" she asked hopefully.

"Not for you, Miss Loveday," he said. "Sergeant Rivers and I are now about to pay a few social calls on your neighbours."

From the sitting-room window she watched them go through the arch and disappear in the direction of the basement. He's an old meanie, she thought; I've done all the spade-work, and now he's crowding me out. Why can't he be co-operative?

But Miss Lomas was still out in the garden, and there were more ways than one into the basement flat. If Pitt was making a frontal assault she would infiltrate from the rear. He should have hesitated longer before handing over that key, she told herself gleefully as she unlocked the door. I'll show him!

Walter Kane's swarthy face was expressive, and it registered considerable distaste when he opened the door of his flat to be confronted by the police. His previous encounter with them had been brief and uneventful, part of the routine inquiry into Grace Cawthorne's movements on the day of her death. He had declared himself unable to help, and they had left without further questioning. Why were they back now? he wondered uneasily.

"Still on the Cawthorne job?" he asked, as he led the way into the sitting-room. "I thought you'd got that taped ages ago."

"Just tying up a few loose ends," Pitt told him. "How well did you know the deceased, sir?"

"I didn't. Not to speak to, that is; just a nod when we happened to meet. It's the same with the others here—'cept that some of 'em don't even bother about the nod. I'm not their sort."

It was stated as a fact, without bitterness. And it was a fact Pitt could easily believe. He looked round the room they were in. It was comfortably, even expensively furnished; pictures and ornaments were lacking, but there was a television set and an expensive-looking radiogram, and the carpet had a thick pile. Walter Kane might not be "their sort," but he wasn't poverty-stricken. So why the old clothes, the threadbare appearance?

"It was not until more than twenty-four hours after she died that Mrs Cawthorne was found," Pitt said. "That's a long time, Mr Kane, when one considers that her body was plainly visible from the cliff-top. And the cliff walk is quite a favourite with the people here, isn't it? I believe you were out that way yourself the next morning?"

"Me?" The man hesitated. "I may have been. But it's too long ago to be sure."

"Nine days. Last Tuesday week," Pitt reminded him. "It

was probably a coincidence, but you were seen just above the spot where the body was lying. You didn't see it?"

"If I'd seen it I'd have reported it, wouldn't I?" The truculence sounded forced. "No, I didn't. The tide was in."

So at least you looked down, thought Pitt. Why? "You weren't looking for her, I suppose?" he asked.

"Of course I wasn't. I didn't know she was dead."

Pitt nodded. One of his handicaps as a detective was an inability to unbend with some one he disliked. And he had no liking for Walter Kane.

"It was just a thought," he said. "It's not important. But you're a lucky man to be able to take a stroll on a Tuesday morning when you feel like it. Most of us have to work for a living."

"I work," Kane said. "I'm a dealer."

I'm sure you are, Pitt thought. But a dealer in what? He said, "On your own, sir? You're not in partnership with Mr Drummond, by any chance? I know he's a friend of yours."

So far Kane's attitude had been cautious without being outwardly antagonistic. Now it changed. It was as though he were forcing himself into anger as a cloak for a growing uneasiness.

"Who told you that?" he demanded. "Absolute rubbish. We're not friends and we're not partners."

"No?" Pitt feigned astonishment. "I'm sorry. But he's one of the two people from Mulgerry known to visit you, so I thought——"

"What business is it of yours who visits me?" A slight stutter had crept into Kane's speech. "Can't I have a visitor without the police sticking their noses in? And what've my job and my visitors got to do with Mrs Cawthorne getting herself killed?" There was obviously more to come, but he stopped abruptly. Anxiety had replaced anger as he asked, "Two visitors? Who's the other?"

"Mrs Cawthorne," Pitt said.

Kane stared at him. Still staring, he backed to a chair and sat down. "Why would she come here?" he asked slowly.

The inspector shrugged. "I can't imagine. A mutual love of painting?" His eyes travelled slowly round the bare walls. "Or aren't you interested in art sir?"

Kane shook his head. "I don't know what you're talking about. Some one's been pulling your leg good and proper, I reckon."

Pitt decided that the time for plain speaking had arrived. He abandoned his show of friendliness with relief.

"Some one certainly has, Mr Kane. For if Mrs Cawthorne didn't visit you, then why the carpeted stairs to the East Wing, the well-oiled locks and hinges? For you to visit her, perhaps?"

The man fumbled in his pockets for a cigarette. He took his time over lighting it. When he spoke the stammer was more pronounced.

"W—what do you w—want from me?" he asked.

"Information, Mr Kane. Information about your relationship with Mrs Cawthorne. You used to visit her, didn't you? Why? And why the secrecy? And don't come the love and passion act. I'm not buying that one."

The other shook his head. "That's my business."

"It was. Now I'm making it mine." Taking a chance, he said, "You were up there on the afternoon she died, weren't you?"

"Y—yes." Kane was really frightened now. "But I didn't see her, Inspector. There was a man upstairs with her. I could hear them talking. And I didn't know w—when Cawthorne might be back, so I hopped it."

Pitt said eagerly, "Who was the man?"

His eagerness was a mistake. Kane was suddenly aware that he had been talking unnecessarily, that the detective was largely guessing. He said sullenly, "I don't know."

Under his breath Pitt swore softly; impetuosity, so foreign to his nature, had lost him what might have been vital information. It did not increase his good humour to know that Rivers had been listening, had no doubt appreciated his error. "How were you able to get into the East Wing without Mrs Cawthorne's co-operation?" he asked. "Wasn't the door kept locked?"

"Yes." Pitt saw the relief on the man's face, and scowled. "I don't know w—why it was open that afternoon. Maybe this chap called just as she was coming down to see me, and she forgot——"

He stopped abruptly, realizing his mistake. Pitt saw it too.

"So she did visit you here, eh?"

The other took a quick puff at his cigarette, and stubbed it out. "Sometimes," he admitted.

"And you're not saying why?"

"No, I'm not."

"Well, no doubt you know what you're doing." Pitt tried to sound casual. "All the same, if I were in your shoes I'd do a lot of heavy thinking during the next few days. You could find yourself in a very nasty spot, my friend."

He licked his lip nervously. "W—what do you mean?"

Pitt countered with another question. "What time was it when you heard Mrs Cawthorne talking to this man?"

"Around five o'clock."

"H'm! And an hour later she was dead. That brings you right into the picture, doesn't it? You say you didn't see her, but you were probably the last person to hear her. Apart, of course, from this man who was with her upstairs. But it might be argued that there wasn't any man upstairs, Mr Kane; that there was only you. Add to that your reluctance to explain what you were doing in the East Wing, and . . ."

"Good God, man! You're not suggesting *I* killed her, are you?" He was half out of his chair, leaning forward. "Why, she was the last person I'd want to get rid of. She was . . ."

He paused. "She was what?" Pitt asked.

Kane shook his head. "Nothing. Leave me alone, will you? I've got to think."

"Go ahead and think, then. We're in no hurry."

Kane stayed on the edge of his chair, his head bowed in his hands. Rivers moved restlessly about the room. It seemed to him that they were getting nowhere very fast, and presently he said,

"Would it be all right to take a quick look round the flat, sir?"

"If Mr Kane doesn't object."

"But I do object." He looked up quickly. "I'll have no busies searching my premises. Not without a warrant."

"That could be arranged," Pitt told him. "But what have you got to hide, Mr Kane? A stolen picture?"

His mouth fell open. It was obvious that the question was unexpected and unwelcome.

"W—what picture?" he asked.

"Two days after Mrs Cawthorne died a picture was missing from her studio. And you are the only person with access to the East Wing. You see the connexion?"

"It wasn't me," he said earnestly. "I swear it wasn't. I haven't been up there since she died. I couldn't. The door was locked."

"But you tried, eh? Why?"

Kane shook his head mutely. He sat staring at the carpet while Pitt watched him. Sergeant Rivers wondered how much more prodding would be needed to break the man down. He's a wretched-looking specimen, he thought. Lady Humpleston must just love having him around.

Slowly the man sat up and squared his shoulders. To the watching detectives it was indicative of a decision, yet somehow it accorded ill with his appearance.

"Listen, Inspector," he said, and there was a hoarseness to his voice that had not been there before. "I know what your game is. You're in a jam, aren't you? You've arrested the wrong man, and now you're running round in circles looking for the right one. That's it, isn't it? Only the right one doesn't happen to be me, see?"

"And how do you know we've arrested the wrong man, Mr Kane?"

"Because I——" He hesitated. He lit another cigarette, and offered the packet to the two policemen. Both refused. "I just know, that's why."

Pitt said slowly, "You're in a bit of a jam yourself, aren't you?"

"You can say that again." The quick puffs at his cigarette betrayed his nervousness, but his voice was steadier. "This ruddy murder has mucked things up good and proper."

"And what do you propose to do about it?"

"I—well, I was reckoning we might do a deal." He glanced quickly at the inspector, but the latter's face was inscrutable. "We've both got our troubles, eh? I can put you on to the chap that killed Mrs Cawthorne, but if I do I sink myself. I had nothing to do with the murder; it's just my ruddy luck that him and me's mixed up in something else—something you chaps wouldn't like the smell of. And once you get your hooks into him you'll smell it good and proper. He's going to talk." He ran a finger round the inside of his collar. His neck was long and knotted, with a prominent Adam's apple. "See what I'm getting at, Inspector? You make things easy for me and I'll make things easy for you."

Pitt shook his head. "I see all right. But it's no go, Kane. The police don't bargain; the most I can promise is to put in a good word for you at the proper time." His thin lips twitched into the ghost of a smile. Sergeant Rivers smiled also. It was always a significant moment when his superior dropped the courtesy title in addressing a prospective 'client.' "If it's any consolation to you a whiff of that smell you refer to is already in my nostrils. Now—how about a statement?"

Kane shrugged resignedly. "Okay. But to-morrow. There's things I have to see to first."

I bet there are, thought Pitt. And a good bonfire would take care of quite a lot of them. "No time like the present," he said hopefully. "If you were to come down to the station with us——"

"No," Kane said flatly. "To-morrow."

"I can have a search warrant in a couple of hours," Pitt told him. "Added to what I know already it could be enough to put you away for a nice long stretch."

"Okay. Go ahead and arrest me. But in that case it's no deal —you'll get no statement out of me, not to-morrow or any other day. I know how to keep my mouth shut when I want to."

Pitt hesitated. He thought he knew now what Kane's racket was, but he had been largely bluffing in saying he could prove it. That would take time—time which a search of the flat, made before the man could destroy incriminating evidence, might shorten considerably. Yet he had no doubt that Kane meant what he said; no deal, no statement. How much was that statement worth? The murder of Grace Cawthorne was Pitt's immediate assignment, and he was fast coming to the conclusion that the police had been wrong in arresting her husband. If Kane could put a name to the man who was with her that afternoon— as he was sure he could—that error could be rectified. But what guarantee was there that the man would keep his word?

He decided to take a chance.

"Right," he said briskly. "I'll give you until to-morrow. But I'm sticking my neck out—you know that as well as I do. Double-cross me to-morrow, my friend, and I'll make it my business to see that you have a long, long stretch in which to regret it."

Kane nodded. "I'll see you're all right, Inspector."

He sounded almost patronizing. Pitt hesitated again, knowing how wrong his decision could be, how disastrous its consequences might prove to himself. Then he said curtly, "You'd better. Come on, Rivers, let's go," and strode into the hall.

Kane went with them. As he opened the front door he asked, "Do I have to come to the station to-morrow to make that statement?"

"I'll collect you personally," Pitt told him.

At the top of the steps Rivers said, "Taking a chance, aren't you, sir? What if Kane decides to run?"

"Of course I'm taking a chance. I had to. But he won't run far, I'll see to that."

"And this other chap—Drummond? Didn't you say he was mixed up in it?"

"Up to the neck, unless I'm very much mistaken. But I can't touch him. Not until I've got that statement."

Rivers shook his head. "I don't like it, and that's a fact," he said anxiously.

"I don't like it either, damn you!" Pitt snapped at him. "But it's my responsibility, not yours, so stop moaning." A spasm of coughing shook him. "Now let's see what we can get out of the Winter girl."

It was Mrs Winter, who opened the door of Lady Humpleston's apartment to them. They were obviously expected, for she did not inquire into their business, but showed them straight into the large drawing-room. It was similar in size and design to the sitting-room in the East Wing, but in need of decoration and repair. Damp patches showed through the faded wallpaper, the tapestries and carpet were worn, the windows cracked, and the paintwork peeling. Even the air, thought Pitt, could do with freshening.

On a Victorian chaise-longue at the far end of the room, with cushions plumped behind her, sat Lady Humpleston. Her right foot rested on a leather pouffe; the inevitable stick was beside her. She made no gesture of welcome to the two policemen, but stared at them frostily, her beady eyes alert.

There was no sign of Caroline. Pitt looked from one to the other of the sisters inquiringly. "It was Miss Winter I called to see," he told them.

"My niece is indisposed," Lady Humpleston said coldly. "It will be quite impossible for you to see her this afternoon."

"I'm sorry." Since Sheila had already told him that it was Caroline who had warned her of his arrival, Pitt knew that the woman was lying. "Miss Winter's indisposition must have been very sudden. I understand she was out in the garden with you a short while ago."

Since she could not refute this Lady Humpleston did not deign to reply. Mrs Winter said, "My daughter is far from strong, Inspector. She has these sudden attacks."

"I'm sorry," Pitt said again. "But it seems that your daughter

K

may be able to give us vital information concerning Mrs Cawthorne's death. It is essential that I should see her as soon as possible. Perhaps you would be good enough to tell her that?" And, as Mrs Winter neither acknowledged his request nor moved to go, he added, "I'll wait for her reply, if you've no objection."

Mrs Winter looked indecisively at her sister. Lady Humpleston said sharply, "Sit down, please. I wish to talk to you."

They sat down. Pitt felt his temper rising, and said brusquely, "Please make it brief then, Lady Humpleston. This is not a social call. I am a busy man."

She glared at him. "I have every intention of making it brief. I merely wished to inform you that Miss Winter's health is immaterial; well or ill, I will not allow her to be interviewed by the police or anyone else. If there are questions that must be put either her mother or I will answer them for her. I can assure you we are perfectly capable of doing so."

At another time Pitt might have been amused by this dictatorial assumption of authority. But the risk he had taken with Kane still worried him, and he said angrily, "That is absurd, Lady Humpleston, and you know it. No one can answer for Miss Winter but herself."

The Hump was also in an ill-humour; Sheila's laughter still rang in her ears. But she knew that she could not ride roughshod over the police as she did over her own family. In a slightly more placatory tone she said, "I don't think you quite understand the situation, Inspector. My niece now realizes that the man she saw near Gavin Head that afternoon was *not* Mr Cawthorne. She is a kind-hearted girl, and a mistaken desire to save him from the consequences of his terrible crime no doubt coloured her imagination. A case of wishful thinking, I am afraid." She settled herself more firmly against the cushions. "I must apologize for any inconvenience her mistake may have caused you, but you will appreciate that there is no longer any need for an interview that would undoubtedly distress her and would profit you nothing."

"I appreciate nothing of the sort, Lady Humpleston," Pitt said firmly, controlling his rising temper. "Your niece may or may not have been mistaken, but I must insist on speaking to her personally." He stood up and turned to Mrs Winter. "Will you please tell your daughter I am here, madam?"

"No, Ellen." Lady Humpleston snapped out the command before her sister could move. "I am the only person who gives orders in this house, Inspector. And I say that my niece is not to be disturbed. If you refuse to be reasonable there is no more to be said."

Pitt clenched his fists. "There is a lot more to be said, Lady Humpleston; but not now. I imagine the reason for your present attitude is to avoid publicity for your niece. I'm afraid you have achieved exactly the opposite result. Since you refuse to let me see her, she will be subpœnaed to appear as a witness at the trial. Good day to you."

He left Sergeant Rivers in the drive, and returned, still fuming, to the East Wing. The engaging smile that accompanied Sheila's greeting helped to calm him, but the smile with which he attempted to return it was still a very wintry effort.

"What's wrong?" she asked, peering up at his gaunt face. "Didn't you have any luck?"

" 'Chanced my luck' would be a more accurate description," he said. He held out his hand. "I think I'd better have that key back now. How much did you manage to overhear?"

Sheila blushed. "I—how did you know I was there? Did I make a noise?"

Pitt shook his head. This time his smile was more natural.

"Knowing you, Miss Loveday, it was the logical conclusion."

She breathed a sigh of relief. "Thank goodness! But it was a waste of time anyway; I didn't hear a thing until just as you were leaving. Something about a statement, and that you were calling for him to-morrow." Her eyes widened. "Did you *expect* me to listen? You did, didn't you? That was why you gave me the key?"

"I believe in assisting a professional colleague where possible," he said gravely.

Sheila curtseyed, dimpling. "Thank you, sir. Will you please assist me some more, and tell me what happened?"

"That, Miss Loveday, would be carrying chivalry too far."

She nodded. She had not expected him to comply. "And Caroline?" she asked anxiously. To Eric, and therefore to her, Caroline was more important than Kane. But when Pitt told her of the Hump's autocratic behaviour she was shocked and worried.

"The old tyrant!" she exclaimed. "There's nothing wrong with Caroline. Did you——" She hesitated. "Did you believe her when she said that Caroline had changed her mind about seeing Eric?"

He attributed her hesitation to a natural concern as to how Caroline's change of mind might affect her lover.

"No. When one thinks it over the likelihood is that Miss Winter is sticking to her statement. If she had given way to the old despot there would have been no objection to my seeing her, I fancy."

Sheila was filled with a tremendous feeling of relief. The Hump, unbeknown to herself, had been right about Eric if not about Caroline; and through her the inspector, who would probably have exposed the falsity of Caroline's statement had he been allowed to question her, was now convinced it was genuine.

It was odd how providence worked, the girl reflected. But also very comforting. In this instance it had certainly been on Eric's side.

"It's dreadful to think that anyone could refuse help to an innocent man merely to save her family from unwelcome publicity," she said sadly.

"To do the old lady justice, I don't think she sees it like that," Pitt said. "She believes in Mr Cawthorne's guilt as you believe in his innocence—intuitively. And I suppose intuition can work as surely in one direction as in another."

Miss Lomas did not return to the house until after the inspector had gone; she had been for a walk, she said. She seemed to have lost interest in her sister's murder; and although she inquired about the inspector's visit and listened attentively while Sheila told her, she made no searching probe into detail. Sheila pressed her again to explain why Eric might not inherit his wife's money—what the 'secret' was that had once been Grace's and was now Eric's. And again Miss Lomas refused the information.

"It's dirty linen," she said. "That's something I prefer not to handle."

"Whose? Grace's or Eric's?"

But Miss Lomas would say no more, except that since it had no bearing on Grace's murder it was the concern only of Eric.

They were having a late tea when Matthews arrived. Sheila was not expecting him, and he gave no reason for his visit apart from expressing a desire to "talk things over." But he made no attempt to discuss them at once. Sheila attributed this to the presence of Miss Lomas, and when the latter had gone up to her room after the meal she turned to him expectantly.

"Well?" she asked eagerly. "What's new?"

He told her of his visit to the prison with Pitt earlier in the afternoon. He told it in great detail; but it did not seem to Sheila to amount to much, nor to warrant a special visit to discuss it when she would in any case be seeing him in the morning.

When she said so he looked embarrassed. "Or am I being dense?" she asked. "Is there something particularly significant about Mrs Cawthorne having been paid large sums of money in cash, and having worked for this firm of art dealers?"

"No more dense than I am," he admitted. "There must be a significance, or Pitt wouldn't have been so interested. But I'm damned if I know what it is. It occurred to me at the time that this James Porter might be the nigger in the woodpile—the stranger Miss Winter referred to. Pitt said he bought the picture out of sentiment. But I don't know. It's a very long shot in the dark."

Sheila agreed that it was. He looked so crestfallen at his inability to cheer her with anything concrete that she did not question him further, but related for the second time what she knew of the inspector's visit to Mulgerry. She told him also of Miss Lomas's refusal to reveal the mysterious 'secret.'

This last piece of news brought more response than the first. "She is probably right in saying it has nothing to do with the murder," Matthews said. "That is, unless——" He paused. "I've sent my clerk up to Somerset House to make a few inquiries."

"Why Somerset House?"

"If Mr Cawthorne is not to inherit it must have something to do with birth, death, or marriage."

Somehow he managed to bring the conversation round from Eric to herself, asking her questions about her job. He did not find it humorous, as did most people; rather he seemed unhappy that she should be doing it.

"I had to earn a living somehow," she told him. "The job offered, and I took it. I'd be no good in an office. For one thing, I can't type."

"But isn't it embarrassing—even unpleasant—at times?"

"Not often. Occasionally it's quite amusing."

"All the same, I wish you didn't have to do it," he said.

There was no mistaking the concern in his voice. It was almost as though he had a proprietary interest in her, Sheila thought—and allowed the imagery to progress a little further. What would he be like as a lover? Involuntarily she found herself comparing him with Eric. He lacked the compelling male magnetism that had drawn her to Eric; but he would probably be more tender, more considerate, more—more dependable. And he was certainly better-looking. His eyes . . .

Stop it! she told herself sternly. Don't start getting ideas about Charles Matthews when you're as good as engaged to Eric. It's—it's indecent.

Matthews himself was confused by his feelings towards the girl. His interest in her went further than the interest occasioned in him by most pretty girls. He had an instinctive desire to protect her, to make her happy; her smile or her laughter gave him a sense of contentment, even exhilarated him. Was he in the elementary stage of falling in love? That would be absurd; he had known her for less than forty-eight hours. It would also be embarrassing, since she was not the sort of girl he *ought* to fall in love with. Another man's girl-friend—and that man his client.

The latter thought disturbed and annoyed him, and he fell into a moody silence. Instinctively Sheila guessed that his thoughts had been running on similar lines to her own, and that he had spurned them as she had done. The knowledge embarrassed her; and though she had previously found herself happy in his company it was a relief when he rather abruptly decided to leave.

Matthews was not the last visitor to the East Wing that day. Connie looked in after supper; Jim had told her of Miss Lomas's arrival. "It'll be nice for Sheila, having some one with her," she told Daffy. "It's not good to live alone when one—or—or a friend is in trouble. One lets things go; I know I do. I'd certainly never bother to cook myself a meal. I'd make do on tea and biscuits and the occasional egg."

"I don't mind being on my own," Sheila said. "I'm used to it." But that sounded uncivil towards Daffy (she thought of her as Daffy, although so far she had not managed to address her as such), and she added, "But you're right about the meals. We've just eaten a positive banquet that Miss Lomas conjured up out of practically nothing. She's a wonderful cook."

Miss Lomas shook her head. "I can cook, but I'm not *that* good. It's a matter of contrasts, Mrs Upway. Sheila's so bad that any decent cook becomes a *cordon bleu*." She said frankly, "I like your husband. I think he's charming."

"So do I. And so does he," Connie said. "No, that's unfair. He's not really conceited." She turned to Sheila. "He tells me the inspector was here this afternoon. What did he want?"

"Caroline," Sheila said. "But the Hump wouldn't let him see her. She said she was ill."

"Ill my foot! Why, I saw her out just now with the dog. Or I think it was her."

"They will probably keep her shut up during the day, and let her out at night," Miss Lomas said dryly. "Just in case there's a detective waiting to pounce."

"Caroline's not the only night prowler," Connie said. "Mike Drummond and the Hermit were in the yard just now, and having quite an argument. They didn't notice me—I'd got my sneakers on." She lifted one foot as evidence. "But Mike sounded really cross about something. That's odd, isn't it? I mean, I didn't think they knew each other well enough to argue."

Sheila thought she knew what the substance of the argument had been. The inspector's visit was getting results, if only in causing dissension between the two conspirators.

Connie did not stay long, and after she had gone Sheila and Miss Lomas sat talking. Or rather, Sheila listened while Daffy did the talking. Daffy's conversation was entertaining without being demanding, and Sheila found it a relief to relax in listening. It prevented her from thinking—and she realized that she had done a lot of thinking in the past few days. It was good to give her brain a rest.

But it was not long before her eyelids began to droop, and the yawns became more frequent. Daffy saw them and said briskly, "Time you were going to bed, young woman, by the look of you. My best cracks are getting nowhere, and I hate to waste them."

Sheila murmured a perfunctory apology; she was too sleepy to worry about being polite. But some of her sleepiness vanished when Miss Lomas said casually, "I'll just take a stroll round the block, and then I'm for bed too."

"A stroll? What on earth for?"

"Fresh air," Daffy said. "Can't sleep without it. But don't

worry, I'm not expecting you to accompany me. You go to bed; I shan't be long."

Sheila never knew whether she was long or not. Almost as soon as she closed her eyes she was asleep.

She came downstairs the next morning to the delicious aroma of coffee and frying bacon. Normally her breakfast consisted of toast and tea, but that morning she felt hungry enough to tackle all that Miss Lomas had prepared. When she told Daffy this the woman nodded understandingly. "That's because you haven't had to cook it yourself. Makes all the difference. I used to fiddle with breakfast myself when I was young. I've learnt better since. Nothing like a good breakfast to start the day."

But she did not eat a good breakfast herself. "Off me oats," she explained, when Sheila remarked on this. "It doesn't happen often, believe me. I'm positively gluttonous as a rule."

They were still at the table when there came a shrill scream from outside. The two women looked at each other, startled. Then Sheila put down her cup with a bang, slopping the coffee into the saucer as she jumped up, and made for the door. Miss Lomas was slower to react, but she too got to her feet and followed the hurrying Sheila into the sitting-room.

In the courtyard outside stood Nadia Drummond. Hands over her eyes, she was still screaming. "What is it, Nadia?" Sheila shouted, leaning out of the window. "What's happened?"

If Nadia heard her she took no notice; the screaming continued. "She's hysterical," Miss Lomas said needlessly. "We'd better go out to her. But not that way," she added, as Sheila began to clamber over the window-sill. "Not for me. I prefer the more prosaic front door, thank you."

Nadia had stopped screaming by the time Sheila reached her, but her hands still covered her eyes, and her body was shaking. Sheila put an arm round her, and the other started in terror.

"It's all right," Sheila said soothingly. "There's nothing to be frightened of." She looked quickly round her; there was no one else in the yard. "What was it, Nadia? What happened?"

Nadia shuddered and went limp. Sheila thought she was

going to faint, and tightened her arm. But Nadia did not faint. She said, taking her hands away from her eyes and pointing behind her, "D—down there. In the area."

Sheila turned. Miss Lomas had come into the yard, and was standing at the head of the steps, peering down into the area. She looked up and caught Sheila's eyes.

"There's a man down there," she said quietly. "And from the way he's lying I'm afraid he's dead."

12

Pᴵᵀᵀ did not reach Mulgerry until late in the morning; Sergeant Rivers, together with the "print and picture boys," as he called them, had already been there some hours when he arrived. "We haven't moved anything except Kane," Rivers told him, leading the way down the steps. "We had to move him, of course; he was stiff. But the boys say they got some nice pictures."

"Any idea what happened?" Pitt asked, stepping carefully.

"Well, it looks like an accident—as though he slipped coming down the steps. No sign of foul play. Just fell and broke his neck, poor chap."

Pitt frowned. "You think so?"

"No. That's what I was *meant* to think. That's what I would have thought—if it hadn't been for those," Rivers said cautiously.

Pitt looked where he pointed. He had noticed the croquet set on the previous day; it had stood alongside the steps. It still stood there; but now the thin plywood top and sides of the box were smashed. So were some of the mallets; they were still in the box with the iron hoops. The balls were scattered over the area.

Rivers was watching his reaction to the scene. "He fell on the box," he said in explanation. "Went over the side, not down the steps."

With his foot Pitt trundled a ball along the stone surface.

"I suppose it's these you don't like, eh?" And when Rivers nodded, "The sides of the box caved in. They could have been forced out when he hit it."

"They could have been," Rivers agreed. "But were they?" He shrugged his broad shoulders. "Your guess is as good as mine, sir.

But fatal falls are becoming just a little too frequent around these parts for them to be accidental, I'd say. Mrs Cawthorne's wasn't. It's my bet that this one wasn't either."

"How do you suggest it was done?"

"Simple. Two or three of those balls on one of the top steps. You wouldn't see them in the dark. But step on them . . ." The sergeant made an expressive gesture. "Bingo! You've had it."

Pitt picked up one of the balls and placed it on a step. Slowly it rolled towards the edge and toppled over, to bump its way down to the bottom.

"How do you make them stay put?" he asked.

"A couple of strips of wood; one at the front, one at the side. Just enough to stop 'em rolling of their own accord." He picked up a thin lath. "That's what put me on to it. It doesn't belong."

Pitt walked down the area to a door and pushed it open, to reveal a coal-cellar containing, in addition to coal and coke and a pile of kindling wood, several broken pieces of furniture and an old mattress.

"It belongs there," he said, closing the door. "Or somewhere similar. Yes, you could be right. A nasty trick—but not necessarily a fatal one. I've known men survive a bigger drop than that. Whoever played it was taking a chance; he couldn't be sure his victim would die."

"Well, this time he was lucky. It worked. Kane couldn't be deader."

The inspector stooped to examine a damp patch on the outer wall of the area; there was damp on the stone beneath also. "Did it rain at all last night?" he asked.

"No."

"Some one must have spilt water here, then." He straightened his back, and a fit of coughing seized him. When it was over he said, wheezing, "Any prints?"

"A few. Poor, though—and most of 'em Kane's, I expect." Rivers tapped the steps with the piece of wood still in his hand. He said, not looking at the inspector, "You—er—your luck didn't hold, did it? You're not going to get that statement now. Some one's made sure of that."

"Kane's luck wasn't working too well either," Pitt said glumly. "If he'd talked yesterday he'd probably be alive to-day, poor chap."

"You hadn't figured on this possibility?"

"Of course I hadn't," he snapped, angry because he knew now that he ought to have considered it. "I didn't realize he was a fool as well as a crook. I thought he wanted time to clean up his own nest—not warn whoever it was that he was going to double-cross him."

"And who do you think that was? Drummond? Or the chap Kane said was closeted with Mrs Cawthorne the day she died?"

"They could be one and the same. But I'm not dealing in riddles at this stage. Let's have a look round the flat. You've got his keys, I suppose."

Apart from the old kitchen Pitt found little to interest him, but here he was surprised that Sheila's description should still tally so closely. He had expected change, but there was no evidence of it. None of the items she had mentioned was missing; even the shavings and scraps of muslin still littered the floor around the work-bench. Using the dead man's keys, he unlocked both chest and cupboard; the former was empty, the latter held an assortment of junk that he decided to examine at his leisure. Right now there were more important things demanding his attention.

"What was the approximate time of death?" he asked Rivers.

"Midnight—give or take a little."

"Any help from the other occupants of the house?"

"Not a whisper. I've questioned them all."

"All?" Pitt asked sharply.

Rivers grinned. "No, not the girl. The old lady nearly threw a fit when I asked to see her. But I'm told her room is on the far side of the house, so she is unlikely to have heard anything if no one else did. Oh—I haven't questioned Mrs Upway or Drummond yet. They'd gone off to work before we arrived."

"And Mrs Drummond?"

"Can't get a thing out of her, sir. Hysterical type, if you ask me. Or maybe she's just not used to finding corpses."

"Maybe not." Pitt grunted. "Your 'all' is a bit thin, isn't it? Where's Mrs Drummond now?"

"In the East Wing. Miss Loveday is looking after her."

"I'd better see her, then. She should have calmed down by now."

At the top of the steps he paused, mechanically acknowledging the salute of the uniformed constable posted there. His eyes travelled slowly up the mellowed stone of the house to a window immediately above. "Whose room is that?" he asked, pointing.

"A Miss Lomas's. She's staying with Miss Loveday. She didn't hear a thing, she says."

Pitt looked down into the area at the smashed croquet set.

"When Kane hit that box he must have made quite a racket. And wouldn't he have cried out as he fell? Screamed—shouted—made *some* vocal noise? She must be a damned heavy sleeper to sleep through that."

The sergeant shrugged. "Well, she did. Says she was in bed by ten-thirty, and slept solidly until just after seven this morning." He clicked his tongue. "That croquet set puzzles me most. Odd place to keep it, and odd thing for Kane to have had. Can you see him playing croquet with the old lady on a summer afternoon?"

It was Miss Lomas who opened the door of the East Wing to them. Her face was grave, but she looked neither depressed nor upset by her experience. She said calmly, "You'll want to see Miss Loveday, eh? She's upstairs with Mrs Drummond. I'll get her for you."

She left them in the sitting-room. They could hear her measured tread on the stairs, and after a pause the fleeter movement of Sheila hurrying lightly down them. Pitt sighed, remembering his own youth. Was he becoming ponderous in his old age? The years had given him experience, but they had taken away some of the drive and enthusiasm of his early days in the

Force. Crime had become just a job of work; it was no longer an adventure.

"How is Mrs Drummond?" he asked, when the girl joined them.

"Better. Do you want to see her? I've left Miss Lomas with her; she seems scared of being alone." Sheila looked anxiously from one to the other of the two policemen, and settled on the inspector. "Was Kane murdered, Mr Pitt, or was it an accident?"

"It *looks* like an accident," Pitt said truthfully. "But naturally we're not taking that for granted."

"Grace Cawthorne's death looked like an accident too, didn't it?" she said. "It—it's rather terrifying for the people here, not knowing who is going to be next."

Pitt nodded. "Is that what's frightened Mrs Drummond?" he asked.

"Partly. Seeing Kane's body upset her, of course. But she isn't only scared, Inspector; she's worried and angry as well. She's got husband trouble, you see." Sheila smiled wryly. "You'll probably hear about that when you see her. I did. At the moment I think it's uppermost in her mind."

"I'll go up now, if I may," Pitt said.

He moved towards the door, but Sheila stopped him. She said, "You won't have seen Mrs Upway yet, so perhaps I ought to tell you that she overheard Kane and Drummond arguing last night." She gave Rivers an apologetic glance. "I'm sorry, Sergeant. I clean forgot it when you spoke to me."

"What time was this?" Pitt asked.

"About nine o'clock." She told them all she could remember of what Connie had said. "I know one shouldn't jump to conclusions, but—well, it does look suspicious, doesn't it? Particularly as Drummond has disappeared. Or so his wife says."

"What?" Pitt almost bellowed the word. He gave Rivers a baleful glance. "You told me he'd gone to work."

The sergeant reddened. "I thought he had, sir."

"You thought!" He turned to the girl. "Anything else?"

"Not to do with that." The dimples reappeared in her cheeks, and some of the tension left her. "But Lady Humpleston pulled a fast one on you, Inspector. Caroline Winter is now taking her exercise later in the day, instead of after tea. Mrs Upway saw her last night."

"So much for her indisposition, eh?" Pitt did not smile; he was too annoyed for that. "Now she is only to be allowed out after dark—like the dog."

"With the dog," she corrected him. "He's never allowed out on his own for fear he might dig up the flowers." She frowned. "I call it scandalous to keep the poor thing shut up all day. Particularly in a lovely place like this."

Rivers thought it scandalous too; he was an ardent dog-lover. But when he started to express his indignation the inspector silenced him. "You can keep that for another time," he said. "Right now it's Drummonds, not dogs, that interest me."

Nadia was sitting in an armchair in what had been Grace's bedroom and was temporarily Sheila's. As the police came into the room she sat up quickly, her hands gripping the arms of the chair. Her eyes looked bigger than ever, the smudged lipstick and mascara accentuating her pallor. Sheila had done her best with the blonde hair, but it still had a slightly dishevelled appearance. It was plain that for once events had ousted her looks from Nadia's mind.

Sheila hurried to her and put a reassuring hand on her shoulder; she did not particularly like Nadia, but anyone in trouble could count on her sympathy. Pitt said, hoping he sounded more optimistic than he felt, "We won't bother you for long, Mrs Drummond; I know you've been through a very unpleasant experience. But there are one or two queries that just won't keep, I'm afraid."

Nadia stared at him. Miss Lomas, after a brief nod to the two men, left the room. Sheila wondered whether she was expected to leave also, and looked questioningly at Pitt. He shook his head.

"Mrs Drummond would probably prefer that you stay."

To the detectives' surprise (but not to Sheila's) Nadia at first answered Pitt's questions readily enough; Sheila understood the different emotions struggling for supremacy in that shallow little mind. Her voice was pitched higher than usual, so that the words had a brittle sound, but otherwise there was no show of hysterics. Only the occasional clenching and unclenching of her plump fingers, and the strained look on her white face, betrayed the conflict within.

She had got up and cooked the breakfast that morning at the usual time, she said; but her husband did not appear. Nor did he answer when she knocked on his bedroom door, and she had gone in to find the room empty. Her first thought was that he had left early to visit a distant client, and that there would be a note explaining his absence. But there was no note, and his bed had not been slept in. Anxious and annoyed, she had gone first to the garage; finding it empty, she was about to return to the flat when she remembered that he had had a visitor the previous evening. Maybe he could tell her where her husband was.

And there Nadia stopped. After an interval Pitt said quietly, "So you went to see him, eh? And found him dead? That's it, isn't it?"

"Yes," she said, without hesitation, but with a shudder at the remembrance. Sheila guessed that the pause had been deliberate, a cue for the inspector to prompt her. Furious as she was at her husband's behaviour, and fearful of its possible consequences to herself, she still could not bring herself voluntarily to name Kane as the visitor. As a sop to her conscience as a wife she needed to have it dragged out of her.

Does she believe her husband to be a murderer? Sheila wondered.

Pitt was wondering the same thing. He said, "Did you see Kane at your flat last night, Mrs Drummond?"

Nadia shook her head. She was in bed when he arrived, she said. At first she could hear only the low murmur of their voices in the sitting-room, and did not know who the visitor was. Then suddenly the voices were raised, as though in argument, and she

L

had recognized Kane's. That had surprised her; it was the first time, to her knowledge, that he had ever visited the flat.

"Have you any idea why he should have called last night?" asked Pitt.

No, she had not. Nor could she say when Kane had left. She had fallen asleep while they were still talking.

Pitt tried further back. "I gather that you and your husband occupy separate rooms. Was that a permanent arrangement, Mrs Drummond?"

"It wasn't. Not before Wednesday." The blue eyes glittered. "But things'll have to be very different when he comes back if it isn't to stay permanent."

Very different indeed, thought Pitt. The way they're shaping at present, he'll be lucky if he comes back at all. "You quarrelled on Wednesday, didn't you? Why?"

Again the hesitancy. It's like a steeplechase, thought Sheila. She gallops quite readily down the straight, but has to be given a lead over the hurdles. Or over the more difficult ones.

"I—it was a private matter," Nadia answered.

"Most domestic quarrels are," Pitt said dryly. "Was it by any chance connected with the key you found in your husband's pocket?"

Nadia looked up quickly at Sheila. But there was no accusation in her eyes. I believe she's *glad* I told him, Sheila thought. I've saved her the embarrassment of having to tell him herself.

"Why ask me if you know already?" Nadia said.

"I only know the framework," Pitt told her. "Suppose you fill in the details?"

She repeated what she had told Sheila, the anger mounting in her as she recalled her husband's deception. But that was not enough for Pitt. She had known for some time of her husband's association with Grace Cawthorne; that alone could not be the cause of her present anger against him. Even the finding of the key had not, apparently, precipitated the quarrel; it was on the Tuesday she had confided in Sheila, yet it was not until the following evening that the final bust-up had occurred. There must be something more—something that had been brought into the open on the Wednesday.

But to prise this something from her proved more difficult than he had expected. Here he could not give her a lead; and without it Nadia could not bring herself to make this final and most damning betrayal. She remained obstinately mute to all his pleading.

In desperation he said sternly, "You obviously do not realize the gravity of your husband's position, Mrs Drummond, so let me enlighten you. At nine o'clock last night he and Walter Kane were overheard in a violent argument." (The 'violent' was an invention that Pitt considered justified.) "Later Kane visited your flat, where the argument was continued; and by midnight he was dead. Highly suggestive, don't you think, when we add to that your husband's sudden and unexpected disappearance? Wait, please——" as Nadia started to protest. "There is reason to believe he was also involved in Mrs Cawthorne's death. The key alone is evidence of that. Your explanation is that she gave it to him, that they were lovers. Well, you may believe that—but I don't. Mrs Cawthorne must have taken a key with her when she left this house on the afternoon of her death, but it wasn't in her bag when we recovered that the next day." He paused impressively. "I suggest your husband took it, Mrs Drummond. And I want to know why."

Nadia's reaction was immediate, and pitiful in its intensity. For a brief moment she stared open-mouthed and wide-eyed at the inspector; then her lower lip began to quiver and her eyes to fill with tears, and she burst into violent sobbing, rocking her body back and forth in the chair. Sheila put an arm round her in an attempt to comfort her, but the gesture was quickly repulsed.

It was partly remorse and partly self-pity that moved her. She was fond of Mike, so far as she was fond of anyone but herself. Despite his unlikely appearance, he was a satisfactory lover. He had money, he was generous, he was indulgent; she required no more in a husband. But his interest in Grace Cawthorne had wounded her vanity badly; despite his repeated protests that she had interpreted it wrongly, to Nadia there was only one reason for a man's interest in a beautiful woman. Grace's obvious contempt for herself had enlarged the wound. Nor was it only her vanity that was hurt; she feared for her comforts also. Mike's infatuation for another woman might prove costly. His pockets were deep, but they were not bottomless. A time might come when she would feel the pinch.

She had welcomed the news of Grace's death, but her relief had been short-lived. Mike had changed; he was moody and depressed, he paid her less attention. The suspicion grew in her that it had been more than an infatuation, that he had been in love with Grace. She had not believed his account of how he had come by the key any more than she had believed him before. His sudden flight during the night convinced her that he had gone for good.

It was in this mood of fear and anger that she had started the interview with the police. It had never occurred to her that Mike might have killed Kane, but in her spite she was only too willing to bolster the suspicions shown by the police. Let him suffer as she was suffering. His suffering would be short compared with hers.

And now, suddenly, it seemed that she had been wrong. According to the police, Mike had *not* been Grace's lover; what he had told her about the key might well be true. And if she had been wrong about Grace, might she not also be wrong about Kane? Perhaps Mike *had* killed him; not intentionally, of course —Mike was too kind—but accidentally. He might even have killed Grace. She did not know. She was no longer sure of anything except that she, in her foolish anger, had done her best to ruin him. And in ruining Mike she had ruined herself.

It was that latter thought that was uppermost in her mind now.

Gradually the sobbing ceased, her body stilled. She took her hands away from her tear-streaked face and said in a broken whisper, "I—you're wrong, Inspector. Terribly wrong. Mike wouldn't kill anyone. He—he was kind and—and gentle." At the thought of Mike's kindness the tears began to flow again, and she stared through them beseechingly. "Please, you've got to believe me. You've just *got* to."

Pitt said quietly, "I did not say that your husband killed Kane or Mrs Cawthorne; I said the evidence pointed that way. And the police believe in evidence, Mrs Drummond—and only in evidence." His voice assumed an almost pleading note. "No doubt it seems to you that by telling us how your husband came into possession of that key you may incriminate him further. But are you really in a position to judge? Why not leave it to the police to decide, Mrs Drummond? If your husband is innocent the truth can't harm him."

His earnestness, the knowledge that she had already said so much, her basic belief in Mike's innocence, decided her. Haltingly (she had been so angry at the time that it was difficult to recall exactly what Mike had said) she told them what she could. But not quite all. Mike had said he needed the key to recover something from the East Wing. She did not mention that he wanted to recover it before the police arrived.

For a few seconds after she had finished talking there was only the sound of her tearful sniffing to break the silence. Then Pitt said, "Did he give you no hint at all as to why he failed to report Mrs Cawthorne's death, or what it was he needed so urgently from here?"

She shook her head. But Pitt thought he could make a guess at the answers to both questions, and did not pursue them. He said, "Can you remember if your husband was at home that afternoon, Mrs Drummond?"

He was not, she said. Mike had left soon after breakfast, saying he would be late home; but in fact he was back by six-thirty. His unexpected appearance in the kitchen had startled her; she had not heard the car return. And then, just before seven, the telephone had rung. She did not hear the conversation, but when she questioned him he said it was from an important client who was kicking up a fuss about an order that had gone astray. It had obviously upset him; he was silent during the meal, and afterwards had gone for a walk—a most unusual thing for Mike to do. He was away for nearly an hour.

"What was your husband's business, Mrs Drummond?" Pitt asked.

Nadia frowned. "I don't know exactly. Something to do with paint, I think." Mike had never volunteered information about his work, and she had not been sufficiently interested to ask him. So long as it was lucrative she was content. "Inspector, what—what are you going to do? About Mike, I mean?"

"The first thing is to find him. You've no idea at all where he might be?" She shook her head. "Does he own a passport?"

"Yes. Sometimes he has to go abroad on business. To France, mostly. But only for a few days at a time."

"What is the make and registration number of his car?" Rivers asked. It was the first time he had spoken during the interview, and Nadia started at the unexpected sound of his voice.

Pitt watched him write down the answer. Then he said, "It might help us considerably, Mrs Drummond, if you would allow us to look over the flat." And, as she hesitated, "You have a perfect right to refuse, of course—in which case I shall apply for a search warrant. I'm trying to save time, that's all; but it's entirely up to you."

She made no objection. They would find nothing in the flat, she thought, that could damage Mike.

Pitt wasted no time over the search. He went quickly from room to room, with Nadia trailing listlessly behind him. At Drummond's desk he paused; but it was locked, and she did not have the key. "He always carries it with him," she said.

"Are there any outhouses that go with the flat?" he asked.

"No. Only the garage."

Drummond and Kane shared the large garage between them; they were the only occupants of Mulgerry to own a car. Kane's elderly blue van was there now, leaving enough space for at least two more cars. At the back, stacked almost to the beamed roof, was an untidy pile of garden implements and old furniture.

It was this seeming junk that attracted Pitt's interest. He

walked slowly along it, his eyes probing where his fingers could not reach. Nadia stood by the entrance watching him, her mind far away.

They were still there when Rivers arrived. He had stayed in the East Wing to telephone Drummond's description to headquarters. He said cheerfully, "Thinking of making an offer for that lot, sir? They tell me there's good money to be made in junk nowadays."

Pitt did not answer. Dust was thick on most of the furniture; but in one corner, where a pile of broken chairs rested precariously on a high-backed settee, it was clear that the dust had recently been disturbed. He said to Nadia, "Do you mind if we pull some of this stuff down? We'll put it back for you."

"Please yourself," she said. "It's not ours. It belongs to Lady Humpleston."

Carefully they removed the interlocked chairs, expecting an avalanche of furniture to descend upon them at any moment. But it seemed that this pile had been stacked separately from the rest, and Pitt's hopes rose.

"That'll do," he said eventually. Kneeling on the settee, whose springs twanged dismally beneath his weight, he leaned over and stretched an arm down behind the high back. His groping fingers caught the feel of wood and canvas, and with an exclamation of triumph he grasped the picture and drew it up.

Nadia came over and watched as they examined it. As Eric had said, it was a view from the studio window. Not one of the artist's best, Pitt thought, but the brushwork and treatment were typical.

Nadia recognized it too. She said sharply, "Grace Cawthorne painted that, didn't she? What's it doing here?"

"Your husband put it there, I fancy," Pitt told her. "This, Mrs Drummond, is why he needed that key so desperately, why he told no one that Mrs Cawthorne was dead. Once that fact was known the police would appear on the scene, and his chance of getting hold of this picture would be gone. He had to get there first."

Nadia stared at him. "You mean—that was all he wanted? One of her pictures?"

"That's all." Pitt put the canvas down and reached for his notebook. "I'd like to take this away with me if you've no objection. I'll give you a receipt, of course."

"I don't want a receipt," she said. At the brittle sound of her voice he looked up quickly, recognizing the advent of tears. "I don't want the picture back either. When you've finished with it you can burn the damned thing."

So much had happened since she had visited Eric the previous morning that it astonished Sheila to realize that it *had* been only the previous morning. It worried her too that she had thought about him so little, and then only as one of the many characters who had recently became part of her daily life, and not as some one special. Yet he *was* some one special. He was her lover.

It was this feeling of guilt that spurred her to visit him that afternoon. She did not really want to go; she was tired after all the excitement, and prison was a depressing place. Even Eric was depressing—although that wasn't his fault, poor dear. One could hardly expect him to be cheerful with a charge of murder hanging over him.

But seeing Matthews again cheered her. Perhaps that was because he was so unfeignedly glad to see her. The embarrassment that had clung to their last meeting was no longer present, and he greeted her with that warm smile of his that showed all his beautiful white teeth. He fussed over her, sent for a cup of tea; and his eyes seldom left her face as he listened to what she had to tell him. It was all very unprofessional—and very welcome.

When she told him of Kane's death his first reaction was one of dismay. "You ought not to stay there," he declared. "It isn't safe. Let me get you a room in Tanmouth?"

"You'll do no such thing," she said firmly. "I'm on a job. Remember?"

He pleaded with her, but she was adamant; she was staying at Mulgerry until Eric was free. He said ruefully, "Well, I don't

like it. I don't like it at all. But thank goodness you've got Miss
Lomas with you. She's a tough old bird if ever I saw one."

Sheila laughed. "She's not so tough as you think. But don't
let's talk about me. What happens now? How does this affect
Eric?"

"Directly, it doesn't affect him at all. The two deaths could
be unconnected, however wild an assumption that may seem. But
indirectly—well, the police have quite a problem on their hands.
If Kane was murdered——"

"Mr Pitt didn't say he was," she pointed out.

"No. But also he didn't say he wasn't. And would he show
such acute interest in the missing Drummond if he thought
Kane's death was an accident?" He shook his head decisively.
"'No, Miss Loveday. The police are looking for a murderer, and
this time they certainly cannot accuse Mr Cawthorne. He has an
extremely watertight alibi."

He had stopped referring to Eric as 'our client,' Sheila noticed.
Was that out of consideration for her, or because he was beginning to think of Eric as a person? "What's the problem, then?"
she asked.

"Are they to look for one murderer or two? Two is improbable,
but not impossible. If they plump for one they must rule out
Cawthorne, since he couldn't have committed the second crime.
Yet they cannot charge Drummond on both counts when they
still hold Cawthorne on the first. Not unless they charge them
jointly."

"Then why don't they release Eric?"

"As I see it, for two reasons. This second murder may add to
their existing doubt about Cawthorne's guilt, but it doesn't
actually refute the evidence on which he was arrested and
charged. Only Miss Winter can do that, it seems. And since Lady
Humpleston denies them access to her, they must wait until she
appears as a witness in court." He smiled. "Added to which is
the fact that Inspector Pitt happens to be a very cautious man."

"What do you think he'll do?"

"I think he'll play it safe. He'll hang on to Eric, and hold

Drummond (when he catches him) for questioning on the second charge. Do you happen to know if Drummond had a passport?"

"His wife said he had."

"With a fair start, then, he could have left the country. However, that's Pitt's worry, not ours. There are still three clear days before Mr Cawthorne is due to appear in court again, and by that time the police may have decided to withdraw the charge. I think it's highly probable that they will. But if they don't— well, Miss Winter's evidence should do the trick." He grinned at her boyishly. "And just in case Lady Humpleston again proves awkward, we've arranged for a summons to be served on the girl. She can't ignore that."

"Suppose she does? Lady Humpleston, I mean. You know what she is."

"In that case the justice would almost certainly issue a warrant for Miss Winter's arrest. I doubt if Lady Humpleston would chance that calamity." He looked up expectantly as his chief clerk came into the room. "Ah, there you are, Simmonds. I expected you before this. Any luck?"

The clerk nodded. "I've got the copies here, sir." He tapped his brief-case and looked doubtfully at the girl. "Shall I come back later?"

"Miss Loveday is an interested party," Matthews told him. "We'll tackle it here and now."

Eric was in a black mood. His had never been a stable character, and the boredom and restrictions of prison life were taking their toll. They had been irksome from the start; now, with his innocence so clearly established by Sheila and Matthews, they were doubly so. At the beginning, he conceded, the police might have had some slight justification for holding him. They had none now.

Sheila's heart sank when she saw him; she knew him well enough to recognize the look on his face. Nor was it only his expression that worried her. Eric had never been particular over his appearance; now he looked positively scruffy. He had not shaved, his hair was tousled from lying on the bed, there was grime under his finger-nails. His suit was badly creased, and there were food stains down the front of his jacket.

If he's angry and fed-up now, she thought unhappily, what is he going to be like when he's heard what Matthews has to tell him?

Eric started off with a grouse. He said, "Late, aren't you? I expected you this morning, as usual. When you hadn't come by lunch-time I thought you'd forgotten me. What kept you?"

"Quite a lot of things." She was irritated by the surliness of his greeting, but tried hard to make allowances for it. "Do you want to hear about them, or would you prefer to go on grousing?"

He had the grace to look abashed.

"I'm sorry. It's just that I'm thoroughly cheesed off. This place seems to get more bloody every day." He rubbed a hand over the stubble on his chin. "My apologies for the bristles. I just couldn't be bothered to hack them off."

She was instantly repentant of her own display of irritation.

"It's all right," she said, smiling at him. The fact that he considered an apology necessary was more important than the apology itself. "Even visiting here gives me the shudders. I can imagine what it does to the residents."

"I'm not a resident yet; merely a lodger." His voice was more alert. "Come on, let's hear your excuses for being late. And they had better be good, or I'll take my custom elsewhere."

He was looking at Matthews as he spoke, but Sheila cut in quickly. The solicitor had only bad news to tell. That could wait.

Eric was not a good listener. Sheila tried to give him the facts succinctly and in order, but he interrupted so frequently that eventually she became confused. After a particularly lengthy comment from him she said irritably, "I wish you'd listen, Eric. All these interruptions put me off. Now I've forgotten where I'd got to."

He was genuinely surprised. "I'm sorry. I thought my views might matter. I know these people better than you do."

"Of course they matter. But couldn't you wait until I've finished?"

After that he kept his remarks to a minimum.

Matthews watched them both as she talked, prompting her occasionally when she faltered but otherwise saying nothing. Although his ears were attuned to her voice, his mind kept wandering. He believed Eric to be innocent and was sorry for him; but he could not like him. It worried him that Sheila should, as he believed, waste her sweetness and beauty on a man who would appreciate them so little.

Or am I just plain jealous? he wondered.

"So Drummond's the man, is he?" Eric said, when Sheila had finished. "Well, it's nice to know it wasn't me. After five days in this hole I was beginning to think the police might have been right."

"You're jumping to conclusions," Matthews told him. "About Drummond, I mean. Granted things look black for him. But then they looked black for you, didn't they, at one time?"

Eric grunted. "They still do. Three more days of that damned wall, those damned locks and keys, and I'll probably go crazy. All right—so I'm still not in the clear. What next?"

Once more Matthews tried to forecast the probable course of events. But his dislike for his client had increased. Eric had expressed no horror at Kane's death, no interest in the recovery of his wife's picture apart from an impersonal curiosity. Most unpleasant of all, although he had immediately identified Drummond as his wife's murderer, he had evinced no animosity towards him. Either prison had dulled his emotions, the solicitor decided, or he was an extremely insensitive person.

His dislike made it easier to broach the matter that had been the main purpose of his visit. He said, "I suppose you knew that your wife had been married before, Mr Cawthorne?"

Eric stared at him. "What on earth made you ferret that out? It has nothing to do with Grace's death." And then, as the solicitor made no answer, "Of course I knew. I forget the chap's name, but I know he was much older than Grace; she married him while she was still in her teens. It wasn't a success, and she left him after a year. A few months later he was killed in a motoring accident."

Matthews shook his head. "He wasn't killed in a motoring accident, Mr Cawthorne. He died of lung cancer last year."

Sheila was watching Eric's face, afraid of what she might see there. But at first he did not appreciate the significance of the information. With a puzzled frown he said slowly, "That's odd. I wonder why Grace told me——" Then the full impact hit him, and he sat up with a jerk. "Last year? Good God, man! You don't know what you're saying!"

"I'm afraid I do. There's no doubting the accuracy of the information. My clerk checked the records most carefully."

"But that means he was still alive when we got married! It—we committed bigamy, damn it!"

"It wasn't your fault," Sheila said soothingly. "You didn't know."

"Of course I didn't know! But did Grace? That's the point."

Matthews shrugged. "How can we tell? But the inference is that she did. Why else should she have lied to you about the date and manner of his death?"

"Well!" Eric took a deep breath. "We're finding out quite a lot about my late wife, aren't we? She invented a legacy that didn't exist, she was paid large sums in cash for nobody knows what services, she was a liar and a bigamist and an adulteress. Quite a formidable indictment, isn't it? Is there anything else to come, I wonder?"

Sheila did not blame him for his bitterness; as he said, it was a formidable indictment. But she knew that he still had not realized the full significance of what the solicitor had told him. He had not yet considered its effect upon himself.

"Do the police know about this?" he asked sourly. "Are they going to charge me with bigamy as well as murder? If so I think I'll ask the Governor here to reserve me a better room. Something a little more cosy, and with a finer view. I'm likely to become his best customer before I'm through."

Matthews gave a somewhat sickly smile, uncertain whether his client was being humorous or merely bitter. "I don't think you need worry on *that* score," he said.

Eric noted the emphasis. "On what score, then?"

"Well, Mrs Cawthorne died intestate, so her next of kin will automatically inherit. That isn't you, Mr Cawthorne. Legally you have no claim to any share in her estate."

"You mean I get nothing? What happens to it, then?"

"Unless your wife had issue by her first marriage—and there is no confirmation of that—presumably it goes to her sister, Miss Lomas."

"Daffy!" The word was almost explosive. "Why, they couldn't stand the sight of each other! Grace would never have left it to *her*. Yet because of some damned legal quibble Daffy walks off with the lot. What a bloody farce!"

Matthews refrained from pointing out that his wife had also had no intention of leaving it to him. Sheila said softly, "I'm terribly sorry, Eric dear. Really I am."

Eric did not heed her. "Daffy!" he muttered. He ran his fingers through his hair and clutched the back of his head. "Of all the bloody luck!" He looked up quickly. "Does she know?"

"I think so," Sheila said. She looked at Matthews. "Isn't that what she's been hinting at?"

It was a thought that she found rather disturbing. The solicitor had laughed at her when, on their first meeting with Miss Lomas, she had suggested that Daffy might have murdered her sister. There had been no motive, he had said. But that was where he had been wrong. Daffy had had a very strong motive, if only they had known.

The same thought had occurred to Matthews, but he did not voice it until he was driving her back to Mulgerry. He wanted to warn without alarming her, and he did not want to do it in front of Cawthorne. He was too concerned for her safety to trust himself to speak casually.

"I still wish you'd let me find you a room in Tanmouth," he said.

"No." There was a long pause. Then Sheila said quietly, "You're thinking of Miss Lomas, aren't you?"

With a sigh of relief he admitted that he was. "It seems ludicrous to suspect her. And I don't, of course. But—well, while there is even the faintest possibility of her being a murderess it gives me the shivers to think of you sharing that house with her."

Sheila was glad that the traffic made him keep his eyes on the road ahead. She knew that she was blushing furiously; there had been no mistaking the real concern in his voice.

"You mustn't worry," she said, her voice not quite steady. "I'll be in no danger."

She hoped fervently that that last assertion would not be proved false.

13

IT would be difficult under any circumstances to behave
naturally towards a person whom one suspects may have
been guilty of murder. When that person happens to be
one's sole companion in a lonely country house, in the near
vicinity of which two people have recently met a violent death,
it must become almost impossible. Certainly Sheila found it so.
Charles Matthews had said it was ludicrous to suspect Miss
Lomas, and at the time she had agreed with him. But that had
been in the car, with his comforting presence beside her. It did
not seem so ludicrous later.

Miss Lomas met her at the door, and together they watched
the solicitor's car turn and move slowly down the drive. As it
disappeared through the gates on to the road Sheila decided that
she had never felt so alone, so vulnerable, as she did at that
moment. And it was not only the large, red-faced woman beside
her that made her feel so. There was something else on her mind;
something that she had hitherto stubbornly refused to recognize,
but which was now looming so large that she knew she could
not avoid it for long.

"You look tired," Miss Lomas said. "Eric in a bad mood?"
She did not wait for an answer, but went on, "Why not lie down
on your bed for an hour? I'm just going to start preparing the
supper, and I certainly don't want you in the kitchen." She gave
Sheila a playful pat on the back, but to the girl it felt like a
knife in the ribs. "Up you go, my dear. I'll call you when the
meal's ready."

Sheila accepted the suggestion without demur; she *was* tired,
mentally as well as physically. But although she lay down on the

bed she did not sleep; the thought of Daffy moving about below, the fear of what she might be plotting, kept her awake. She would have felt more relaxed had she been able to lock the bedroom door; but to do that would have announced to Daffy, as clearly as any words could do, the fear and suspicion that now beset her. And that, thought Sheila, might force Daffy's hand.

It was a relief when Daffy called her, a relief to go downstairs and face her fears openly; she no longer had to strain her ears to listen, or to wonder uneasily at the silences. And gradually, under the cheerful heartiness of Daffy's chatter, suspicion lessened and fear began to fade. It was ridiculous to think of this outspoken but friendly woman as a murderess.

With the pleasant contemplation of hunger about to be satisfied Sheila started on the large plate of crab salad that Daffy had placed in front of her.

After a few moments Miss Lomas said, smacking her full lips, "Delicious, eh? Shellfish are a real weakness with me. I ought to be scared of them—nearly died of food poisoning once after eating crab—but I just can't resist them. And this tastes all right, doesn't it? It's so damned difficult to know if they're fresh."

As if to show her confidence, she skewered a large piece of crabmeat and popped it into her capacious mouth, to devour it with obvious relish.

Slowly Sheila put down her fork, her appetite gone as suddenly as it had come. She remembered that it had been at Daffy's suggestion that she had gone upstairs to rest; had there been a sinister motive behind the apparently kindly thought? The salad had not been served from a dish; it was already attractively laid out on plates when she came downstairs. Was there poison in her portion? Was that why Daffy had not wanted her in the kitchen while preparing the meal? And was this casual reference to food poisoning intended as an alibi, to be trotted out again later when the pain started?

"Goodness me! You haven't finished, have you?" Miss Lomas said, eyeing her companion's plate with dismay.

"I—I'm not hungry," Sheila stammered. "I thought I was—

M

it looked so tempting, the way you'd done it—but I'm afraid my eyes were bigger than my stomach."

"That doesn't make them very big, does it? Try to eat a little more, just to please me," Miss Lomas urged. "Such a pity to waste it. I didn't put you off with my talk about food poisoning, did I? There's nothing wrong with *this*."

"I'm sure there isn't," Sheila said hastily. "It's just that I'm not hungry." She pushed her chair back and stood up. "I'll make the coffee while you're finishing."

At least she could then be sure of the coffee.

Am I being foolish? she wondered, as she stood over the stove watching the milk move sluggishly in the saucepan. Even if Daffy *did* kill Grace, she had a motive for that. She wanted Grace's money. But why should she kill *me*? I've got nothing she wants, I'm no danger to her. In fact, I'd be more of a danger to her dead than I am alive. With only the two of us in the house it would be too obvious.

She shuddered. She was being both foolish and morbid, she decided. It did not make her feel any the less foolish when Daffy said, "Mind if I finish up your salad, Sheila? If you're quite sure you don't want it, that is. Terribly non-U behaviour, of course, but I hate to see good food wasted. Particularly crab."

"Go right ahead," Sheila answered. But as she watched the other gobble up the food she had shunned her hunger returned, and her annoyance at her foolish fears increased. Yet she was not completely reassured. It was not poison she had to fear; poison had not been the unknown murderer's weapon. Sergeant Rivers had said that Kane was killed by a simple form of booby trap, and Daffy could have done that. She had gone for a short stroll before bed that evening, Sheila remembered with some misgiving.

"And how's our Eric?" asked Miss Lomas, sipping her coffee. "Bearing up?"

Sheila's answering nod lacked conviction. She was reminded that Daffy's secret was a secret no longer; to tell her so might be to discourage her from any further attempt at murder that she might be contemplating. She would know then that she was no longer outside suspicion.

Miss Lomas evinced no surprise when told. She said, "It was bound to come out sooner or later, I suppose. How did Eric take it?"

"He was rather stunned," Sheila admitted.

"I bet he was. Losing money he fondly believed to be his would hurt him like hell. Eric was expensively reared. His father was a wealthy man until the crash."

"You can't blame Eric for that."

"I'm not blaming him. I'm even rather sorry for him." She put down her cup and eyed Sheila keenly. "Is this going to make any difference to you, young woman?"

Sheila knew what she meant. But it was not offensively said, however badly expressed, and she did not take offence.

"Yes," she said. "But not the way you think."

"You don't know what I think." Miss Lomas smiled at her. "You've fallen out of love, haven't you? Eric isn't quite the lover-boy you thought him. And now you don't like to tell him so for fear he may attribute it to the fact that he is now jobless and penniless. That's it, isn't it?"

"Yes," Sheila agreed. "That's it, more or less." She was surprised at the older woman's perspicacity, for she herself would admit to no reason for her change of heart. In a desire to unburden herself, and momentarily forgetful of fear and suspicion, she said wearily, "But how can I tell him? After all he's been through, to have that for a finale! It would be downright cruel."

"Are you sure you're looking at it straight?" Daffy asked. "Is it really because you don't want to be cruel? Isn't it rather your pride that's at fault? You can't stomach the thought that Eric (or anyone else, for that matter) should think ill of you?"

"Oh, no, it isn't that," Sheila protested. "At least—well, I don't think it is. But which would be most hurtful to Eric? To throw him over now—hit him when he's down, so to speak—or to marry him knowing that I don't love him? And I don't, I'm afraid. I thought I did, but—well, I don't."

"And why not?" asked Miss Lomas.

"I don't know. But he's different, somehow. I know he's had a rough time, and that could be partly responsible. But it shouldn't be able to change his character—his whole personality. Those are something in a person that *nothing* should change."

"They haven't changed in Eric either," Daffy said. "It's just that you're seeing him properly for the first time. Up to now it's been romantic, aery-faery stuff between the two of you. Now you've seen him when he's up against it, and he hasn't shown up so well." She drained the last of her coffee. "I think you're right, my dear. Charles Matthews is far more suitable."

Once more Sheila felt the fiery red in her cheeks.

"Mr Matthews doesn't enter into it," she said stiffly. "This is just between Eric and me."

But she knew it wasn't. And she knew that Miss Lomas knew she knew it wasn't.

She wondered if Charles Matthews knew it too.

Mike Drummond was arrested in Fulham the following afternoon. He had made no attempt to leave the country; perhaps he knew that the ports and airfields would be watched, and chose the more probable safety of a district with which he was familiar. Nor did he try to evade arrest, or to deny his identity, when stopped by the police. He accompanied them meekly to Fulham police-station, where the warrant for his arrest was read to him and he was detained pending the arrival of the Tanmouth police.

Pitt sent Rivers up to London to collect him. He was becoming increasingly concerned at the lack of progress his investigation into the two murders was making; there were too many suspects and too few clues. Kane and Drummond had drawn what might prove to be a red herring across the trail. If that could be eliminated the road ahead might be easier to follow.

He awaited Rivers's return with impatience.

Drummond was wearing one of his favourite loud checks (apparently it had not occurred to him that his taste in dress might attract attention), and his manner was almost as obtrusive. The meekness he had shown on his arrest had vanished during the journey. "Horrible flow of language your friend's got," Rivers told Pitt. "If I were you I'd book him for obscenity. It couldn't miss."

"Who was he swearing at?" Pitt asked, surprised. "You?"

"Not me. No one in particular. He just swore. I think it helped to relieve his feelings."

The inspector watched Drummond's face with interest as the charge was read out to him by the station sergeant.

" . . . did receive a painting by Renoir entitled *Man With A Stick*, the property of the Earl of Hobden, knowing it to have been stolen when receiving it," the sergeant concluded.

Drummond waved the subsequent caution aside.

"So the ruddy fool *did* talk. I thought he would." He swore blasphemously, his rich, plummy voice making the oaths sound curiously unreal. "What makes me puke is that it was so damned unnecessary. If he'd kept his mouth shut you couldn't have pinned a thing on either of us. And now . . . " He sighed mournfully. "It was that bloody murder that did it. It got him so scared he wouldn't listen to reason."

"We have the picture," Pitt reminded him. "How would you have explained that?"

"I wouldn't. I'm not a fool, Inspector; you didn't find it on *my* premises. The garage, and all that junk in it, belong to Lady Humpleston. If it hadn't been for that fool Kane you'd have had to charge *her* with receiving."

It was a thought that fascinated the inspector. But he had too much on his mind to indulge in idle fancies, however appealing. "Do you wish to make a statement?" he asked.

"Later, maybe," Drummond said. "Could I have a word with you first? Sort of off the record?"

Pitt took him into his office; an informal chat might tell him more than a written statement. He was surprised at the spirit the man was showing. From the look of him he would have expected him to fold easily.

"Supposing you manage to pin this label on me?" Drummond asked, accepting a cigarette. "What'll I get?"

"Well, the maximum for receiving is fourteen years; you knew the original stealing to be a felony. And I have an idea the police in other counties will be preferring charges against you. That Renoir was only one of many, wasn't it?"

Drummond nodded. "It's the missus I'm worried about, Mr Pitt," he said earnestly. "I've got enough salted away to take care of her for the next four or five years, but it won't stretch to fourteen. Not the way she likes to spend money, bless her! And Kane——" The thought of his late partner sent him off into another string of oaths—only to pull himself up sharply. "Here—how about Kane? Does he get off lightly for grassing, damn him?"

Pitt looked at the man's plump, undistinguished face and wondered about many things; but mostly he wondered just how natural his behaviour was. Everything pointed to the fact that Drummond had killed Kane. But if he *had* killed him he had done so to prevent Kane from making the promised statement; he must know that Kane was dead and that the statement had never materialized. Why, then, was he assuming the opposite? Did that mean that he was not the killer? This couldn't be bluff. It would be carrying bluff too far to incriminate himself as Drummond was doing now.

The inspector shook his head, as much in answer to his own thoughts as to Drummond's question.

"Kane won't be getting off lightly," he said. "You've no cause to envy him."

But during the long pause Drummond's mind had moved on.

"Fourteen years!" he said bleakly, shifting his neck uneasily in its tight-fitting collar. "That's a hell of a stretch." He thought of Nadia and her flirtations, and wondered how long it would be before the flirtations developed into something more permanent. Certainly not fourteen years. "But they wouldn't give me the maximum, would they, Inspector? I didn't cause any trouble when they arrested me, and I'm not giving any now.

I'm doing all I can to help you; if you want that statement you can have it. That'll make it easier for me, eh? I mean, the judge'll take that into consideration, won't he? Lop a year or two off the sentence, perhaps?"

"He might," Pitt said. "But don't bank on it."

Drummond shrugged his plump shoulders. "How about a cuppa before we get started? I'm thirsty."

"I'll send for one," Pitt said.

The idea had first occurred to him, Drummond said, about five years previously, when he read of the high prices being paid for pictures by famous artists. He and Kane had done a few jobs together (in Drummond's opinion Kane was the cleverest burglar then unknown to the police), and they broke into a country house near Reading and collected a Vermeer and a Raphael. Complications arose, however, when they tried to dispose of them; there was a ready market paying good prices in America and on the Continent, but the difficulty was to smuggle them out of the country.

It was while he was considering this problem that he met Grace Lomas. The information that she worked for a firm specializing in the restoration of old paintings, and that she was also a promising artist, intrigued him. Here was the accomplice he needed. He set himself to cultivate her acquaintance.

The task was not easy. Grace was unresponsive to his friendly overtures; it was only by lavish spending, and by assuming an interest in art that he did not possess, that he eventually got to know her better. He discovered that, apart from a passion for clothes, she had little in common with other women of his acquaintance. Men, and having a good time, were unimportant to her; it was the antique shops and art galleries, not the theatres and restaurants, that drew her, and she dreamed of the day when she would have the money to buy the things she saw there.

He tested her first on the Vermeer, giving her a fictitious tale of how he had bought it in good faith for a customer abroad, only to learn later that it was stolen. He could not afford to lose the large sum of money involved, he told her; would she be willing, in return for a handsome slice of the profits, to disguise it sufficiently for him to smuggle it out of the country?

Grace did not hesitate; she was not only willing, she was eager. But it would not be enough to paint a new picture over the original, she said. The frame and canvas would betray its age; it would also have to be lined. This she could do (it was the main part of her job with Sutcliffe and Cashell), but she would need the tools of her trade and a place in which to work. It could not be done in the bed-sitter which was her present home.

Drummond rented a flat for her near his own, just off the Fulham Road. But Grace's taste in furniture was expensive, and he took the opportunity of reminding her that the sale of one picture would not justify such extravagance. Was she prepared to go into partnership with him on a grand scale? There would be no lack of material for her to work on. And Grace had laughed her rather unfriendly laugh and had said that of course she was. Did he take her for a fool? She had guessed from the start that there would be more than the one picture.

She made such a good job of the Vermeer and the Raphael that he was able to dispose of them easily. They became a 'four-man' team. Kane and an accomplice 'acquired' the pictures, Grace disguised them, and Drummond disposed of them. And they made money. Lots of money.

"Who was the fourth man?" Pitt asked, interrupting for the first time.

Drummond shook his head. "Me and Grace and Kane, we're finished," he said. "What I'm telling you now can't hurt any of us. You've had it all from Kane; this is just another angle on the same story. But the fourth chap—he's still in business. I'm not grassing on him." He had been doodling on a piece of paper as he talked. Now he looked up quickly. "Or did Kane spill that too?"

"No," Pitt said, happy that he could stick to the truth. Even to a crook like Drummond he did not enjoy having to lie. "He didn't mention anyone else."

"Grace gave up her job with Sutcliffe and Cashell," Drummond went on; "the money the firm had been paying her was chicken-feed to what she was making now. But it wasn't long before she became dissatisfied with her surroundings; she was beginning to spend money the way she had always wanted to spend it, and the Fulham Road wasn't the right setting for the things she was buying. There wasn't room for them, either. She wanted a house in the country, she said, somewhere near the sea; an old house, with large rooms and high ceilings, and a studio where she could paint undisturbed by the noise of traffic. One of these days, she declared, she would be a fine painter in her own right. It was only a question of time."

The country-house setting appealed to Drummond also. He had not long been married, he was making big money; it was time to cut adrift from the Fulham Road and spread his wings. There was also the consideration that in a remote rural area the police would be thin on the ground. And who would expect to find a big-time crook (it pleased his vanity to think of himself thus) in such surroundings?

It was Grace who found Mulgerry; as soon as she saw it she knew that nowhere else would do as well. She suggested that the basement flat, with its communicating door to the East Wing, would be ideal for Drummond; either he or Kane had to be near her, although they must appear (at any rate at the beginning) to be strangers to one another. But a basement flat did not fit into Drummond's plans, and he knew it would not suit Nadia. Kane should take it instead.

Kane raised no objection; it did not matter to him where he lived. He had been a small-time thief until he had teamed up with Drummond, but his new affluence appeared to make no difference to his mode of living. He wore the same old clothes, and led the same lonely, unenterprising existence. In an unusual burst of confidence he had once told Drummond that he had taken to crime simply because he was too lazy to work; but he did not want riches, only enough money to keep him in idleness. His one fondness (it was not strong enough to be called a passion) was for music. The little money he spent went on gramophone records.

"You were an oddly assorted trio, weren't you?" Pitt remarked. "How did Mrs Cawthorne take to Kane as an associate and near neighbour?"

"I think she liked him better than she liked me." Drummond's tone implied that such a preference was strange. "Grace and me, we never did hit it off. And she scared Kane stiff with her grand manner. He didn't like it at all when we fitted up the old kitchen as a workroom for her; that was where she did the lining. He was always clearing out for a walk when she was down there, in case she might ask him to help her." Drummond shook his head. "But it wasn't only Grace. He just didn't like people. All he wanted was to be left alone. Prison should suit him fine."

Pitt wondered idly whether Kane's spirit, wherever it might be, was finding its present surroundings more congenial than his earthly ones had apparently been.

He sent for more tea.

Kane and Grace moved into Mulgerry at about the same time; the Drummonds arrived six months later, when the flat over the garage had been modernized according to their tastes. ("It all came out of my pocket," Drummond said. "The Hump, blast her, wouldn't do a thing. Take it or leave it, that was her attitude.") But life was not as peaceful as he had hoped it would be. It was essential that he should visit Grace occasionally, and alone; and this led to trouble with his wife. She accused him of infidelity—an accusation he could do little to disprove, since she did not know (and he did not want her to know) the real nature of his activities. Even Grace's marriage did not allay her suspicions. It actually augmented them, since Drummond now had to confine his visits to the East Wing to periods when Cawthorne was away in Sheffield. That to Nadia was proof that the association was clandestine and libidinous, and a threat to her marriage.

But the enterprise profited, even though they were not greedy. Grace had become so expert at her part in it that, when she and Jim Upway held a joint exhibition in London, she had actually included two of the disguised pictures among her own work—taking care to mark them as sold before the first day. They had hung there undetected throughout the exhibition, to be dispatched abroad later by the unsuspecting gallery-owner!

"You'd never had it so good, eh?" Pitt commented. "I'm surprised Mrs Cawthorne should have jeopardized so lucrative a set-up by taking to herself a husband for whom she appears to have had no great affection. Didn't you point out the dangers to her?"

Drummond nodded vigorously.

"You bet I did! But Grace—well, it was difficult to know what made her tick. She wanted roots, she said. She had the house and the furniture, and she wanted a solid, respectable husband to go with them."

"And who more respectable than a schoolmaster?" Pitt murmured. "Particularly as he also happened to be the son of a peer. But why Cawthorne if she didn't love him?"

Mike Drummond shrugged, spreading his hands wide. He had no confidence in his ability to explain the vagaries of women.

"Maybe she thought she did. He looks a pretty ordinary type to me, but my wife says he's got something." Pitt nodded, recalling that Sheila Loveday had also fallen for that 'something.' "And his being away at boarding-school most of the year made things a lot easier. She could do her work without having him around." He grinned feebly. "Cawthorne didn't think much of the arrangement, I reckon—her down here and him up there. But he couldn't shift Grace."

"Business first, eh? Did she ever consider confiding in him? With your approval, of course."

"No." The negative was decisive. "He belonged to the other side of her life—the respectable side. She wouldn't mix 'em."

Pitt thought it made some sort of sense. He shifted in his chair and leaned across the table, smothering a cough.

"All right. Now let's get down to the murder. And don't try to skip your own part in it. We're not entirely without information on that, you know."

"I didn't have any part in it," Drummond said quickly. A note of fear had crept into the rich voice. "Don't you start getting ideas like that, Inspector. It isn't funny."

"It wasn't meant to be," Pitt said. "And whether you had any part in it or not, you were one of the first to find the body. Your wife told us that."

"She did?" Drummond was startled. He said sadly, "I didn't think she'd do that to me."

Pitt felt a twinge of pity for the man. "You shouldn't have run out on her," he told him. "She thought you'd left her."

"She ought to know I wouldn't do that." He looked pleadingly at the inspector. "Can I see her, Mr Pitt? Just to put things right between us?"

Pitt nodded. "When we're through with this."

The first he knew of Grace Cawthorne's death, Drummond said, was when Kane telephoned him that evening to say he'd seen her body lying on the rocks below the cliffs. That had shaken him badly. He had no liking for Grace as a person, but without her technical skill he and Kane were finished. His agitation increased when he remembered that the Renoir was still in the studio. She had completed the lining about a week before her husband had come home for the holidays, but how far had she got with the painting itself? An unnatural death would involve the presence of the police; was the Renoir sufficiently disguised? And even if it was, how were they now to get possession of it?

He met Kane out on the cliff after dinner. Kane had already made an attempt to recover the picture; but the communicating door to the East Wing was locked, although it had been unlocked earlier in the day. That means of access was barred to them, then, until another key could be cut. And that would take more time than they had at their disposal. They had to act before Grace's death became public.

With the aid of his torch they could see the body, already being lapped by the incoming tide. That gave them some comfort. When the tide went out during the night it would take the body with it. Grace would be missed, but no one but themselves would know that she was dead.

And then they found her bag, with the key in it. That was a real stroke of luck. They would no longer have to break into the East Wing (for Kane that would have been easy, but it would have resulted in unpleasant police activity), they could walk in whenever they wished. It was unlikely that the picture would be missed. Grace had told them that her husband seldom went into the studio, and that he had no interest in art. It was probable that he did not even know of its existence.

Their luck did not hold sufficiently to enable them to recover the picture that same night; they found the front door bolted. But time was less urgent now. Drummond remembered that he and Nadia and the Cawthornes were having dinner with the Upways the following evening; that could be their opportunity. Grace would not be present—and neither would he. And in the unlikely event of Cawthorne declining to attend without his wife they would have to think again.

To allay any possible suspicion that might arise later he left Mulgerry as usual the next morning, keeping in touch with Kane by telephone. Kane went out along the cliff about ten o'clock to satisfy himself that the sea had done its job; but the tide was in, and there was nothing to see. He had met Cawthorne on his way back, and that had startled him; even at that early stage he was getting jumpy about the possibility of Grace having been murdered, Drummond said. It seemed he had already formed his own suspicions.

Drummond returned home for lunch. That was unusual, but he had no option; Kane in his isolation might be unaware of the latest developments. He was relieved to learn from Nadia's chatter that Cawthorne appeared to be unperturbed by his wife's absence. And if Grace had left a note saying she had gone to London so much the better. He did not understand it, but it made his task much easier. There would be no policemen yet.

He left the flat soon after tea. Nadia was suspicious when he told her he would be unable to attend the dinner-party (she assumed that his appointment was with Grace), but for once he paid her no attention. He returned at eight, to find the East Wing and his own flat in darkness, and Kane waiting for him. The coast was clear, Kane said. Both Nadia and Cawthorne had gone to the Upways.

They stored the Renoir in the chest in the basement until they could dispose of it. Drummond didn't want it in the flat; Nadia would form her own conclusions were she to find it. "And we moved it down to the garage the day before yesterday," Drummond said. "It was due to go to the States on Monday."

"It won't be going now," Pitt said. "But you seem to have skipped very lightly over Mrs Cawthorne's death, and the events immediately preceding it. Isn't there something more you have to tell me?"

Drummond hesitated. Then he said, "No, not me. And that's gospel, Mr Pitt."

"I doubt it. What about Kane's visit to the East Wing that afternoon? I don't think you mentioned that."

The man stared at him. "Of course I didn't. You asked about me, not about Kane. Didn't he tell you?"

"Partly. Now I'd like the rest."

Drummond shrugged. "You'd better ask him, not me. I wasn't there."

Pitt decided that this was the moment of truth. Bluff had taken him a long way. Now he must dispense with it. "I can't do that," he said quietly. "Kane is dead."

It took Drummond a few seconds to assimilate this. When he did the look of incredulity on his face was absolute.

"Dead? But he can't be! Why, I was——" He paused, realizing that death, particularly in Mulgerry, could be sudden. "Good God, how awful! When, Inspector? What happened?"

"Thursday night. He broke his neck. Fell down the steps leading to the basement."

"The poor devil!" The incredulity was still there as he stared wide-eyed at the inspector. Then his expression changed. He said, with mounting indignation as the truth clarified in his mind, "If

he was killed Thursday night you couldn't have got that statement from him, damn it!"

"I didn't," Pitt agreed equably.

Drummond banged his fist on the table. "So you pulled a fast
one on me, did you? That's a dirty bit of trickery if ever there
was one." His face was suffused with anger. "All right, so you've
got your statement. But it'll be no damned use to you. I won't
sign it."

"You tricked yourself, Drummond," Pitt told him. "I never
said Kane made a statement; you just assumed it." His voice
hardened. "And don't think you're out of the wood yet. Kane's
death was no accident; some one killed him to prevent him from
talking. And who profited most from Kane's silence? You might
ask yourself that before you start shouting your head off."

The blood drained from the man's cheeks as quickly as it had
mounted.

"You think I killed him? You must be crazy." But Pitt did
not look crazy, and the hard, accusing look was still on his face.
"God damn it, Inspector, I'm not a murderer! I've never willingly
harmed anyone in my life. I couldn't—I'm just not built that
way. And Kane—why, we've been partners for years."

"Maybe. But murderers aren't types, and Kane was no longer
your partner. He was about to ditch you—and you knew it."

"Of course I knew it. That's why I cleared out, wasn't it? If
I'd killed him I could have stayed put; I didn't have to do both,
it was one or the other. I tell you, I never even touched him."

You didn't have to touch him, thought Pitt; not if Rivers was
right about the croquet balls. You didn't have to be anywhere
near him. But there was sense in what Drummond said; that,
and his readiness to talk, and his obvious astonishment at the
news of Kane's death, were all in his favour. It was not part of
the inspector's policy, however, to assuage the man's apprehen-
sion too soon. A frightened man was a talkative man, and there
was still more that Drummond could tell him.

"All right, so you didn't kill him. But the evidence points
your way, Drummond. You were heard arguing with him, he

went to your flat with you and stayed late; and it seems probable that he was killed on the way home. That needs some explaining, doesn't it?"

"No, it doesn't. It explains itself." He wrung his hands in a gesture of despair at the detective's stupidity. "Of course I argued with him! What else would you expect me to do? Clap him on the back and tell him how pleased I was that he was going to ditch me? But the damned fool wouldn't budge. He said you'd as good as put the finger on him for Grace's murder, and the only way to clear himself was to tell the truth. The fact that it would land us both in stir didn't count with him at all. It was the murder that scared him. He just couldn't get his mind off it." Drummond screwed up his eyes in bewilderment. "That's crazy, isn't it? He was as innocent as you or me, Inspector; you knew that, didn't you? It wouldn't have made sense for him to have killed her. Neither of us liked Grace; but even if we'd been the murdering kind we wouldn't have done away with our bread and butter."

"You have a point there," Pitt admitted. "Just what *were* you planning to do about that same bread and butter if we hadn't caught up with you?"

Drummond frowned. "We hadn't got it properly figured out. It was the lining that stumped us. Artists are two a penny, but there can't be many with the technical skill that Grace had. *And* with no scruples about how they use it."

That's just as well, Pitt thought. "So Mrs Cawthorne's death had practically put you out of business, eh? My heart bleeds for you. It must have been a tragic moment."

"It was," Drummond said, ignoring the sarcasm. "But we'd have made shift somehow. We'd already got a chap lined up to do the painting; he took a bit of persuading, but he hadn't much choice. And Kane reckoned he——"

"Just a minute," Pitt said. "Who was the unwilling artist? Or is that a trade secret?"

Drummond hesitated. He glanced across at the stenographer, and then back at Pitt.

"That was something I hoped you wouldn't ask me," he said slowly. "I was hoping Kane might have told you. I never did like grassing, you see, and——" He shook his head. "Well, he has it coming to him, I reckon. It was Jim Upway."

The inspector was not surprised. Upway was on the spot; he was also hard up. But Drummond had said that he needed persuading; had he then had moral scruples? And why was a choice denied him?

"Jim doesn't suffer from scruples," Drummond said, when the question was put to him. "Not that sort or any other, I fancy. And he didn't have a choice because we didn't give him one."

"Blackmail, eh? What had you got on him?"

"Murder," Drummond said briefly. "He was the chap who was with Grace that afternoon, up in the bedroom."

14

JIM UPWAY was alone in the flat when the police called that evening. Connie had gone across to the garage flat to see that Nadia was all right; the school had broken up on the Friday, and during the holidays she was less averse to spending part of an evening away from her husband. She was worried about Nadia, who, when she had spoken to her that morning, had been convinced that her husband had left her—and, what was far worse, had left her without provision. Nadia did not take easily to adversity; since the previous afternoon she had alternated between moods of black despair and vicious anger. Connie, to whom to love was to trust, could not understand the anger. But she tried, without much success, to console and cheer her.

"What, again?" Jim said, as he opened the door. "Working late, aren't you? It's nearly seven. You'll have your union down on you if you're not careful, Inspector. But come in, do."

Pitt ignored the pleasantry. He and Rivers muttered a formal greeting, and followed Jim into the barrack-like sitting-room. "Sit down, won't you?" their host said, flinging cushions into the corners of the settee. "My wife's over with Mrs Drummond at the moment, but she'll be back shortly. Now—what can I do for you? I suppose you're still working on poor old Kane's demise? Have you found Mike Drummond yet?"

"We have," Pitt said. "But it's Mrs Cawthorne's death that brings us here now, Mr Upway. It seems you were not entirely frank with us about that. You forgot to mention, for instance, that you were with her in her bedroom that afternoon. Why was that?"

"Oh!" Both surprise and anxiety were depicted on his handsome face, but he hesitated only momentarily. "How on earth did you dig that up? I thought it was a well-kept secret. As for why I didn't mention it——" He shrugged. "Well, I should have thought that was obvious. One never does, does one? Not when both parties are married, Inspector. It could lead to considerable unpleasantness."

"That is no excuse, Mr Upway, and you know it. Mrs Cawthorne was killed very shortly after your visit, and it was your duty to give the police every assistance in your power."

"I didn't think it was relevant," Jim said weakly.

"It was, and it still is. But to save further prevarication, sir, I may as well tell you that we have a statement from Drummond that confirms everything Kane told us the day before he died. We know that you quarrelled with Mrs Cawthorne that afternoon, and we know why. Kane overheard you, and——" The inspector paused. "But I don't have to tell you that, do I? It was on the strength of what Kane overheard that they persuaded you to work for them."

Jim had been standing with his back arched against the mantelshelf. This sudden (although not altogether unexpected) attack made him feel the need for greater support, and he sat down heavily in the nearest armchair.

"I see. You know quite a lot, don't you? Although you're wrong on one point, Inspector. It wasn't a quarrel—just a mild argument."

"And what preceded it?" asked Pitt.

Jim frowned. "Can't you guess? I'm no saint where women are concerned, and Mrs Cawthorne was extremely attractive. She was also a grass widow for most of the year; with my wife away all day it was bound to happen sooner or later. I had expected it to be sooner."

"All right, so it happened. But you are being too vague, Mr Upway. I want more detail."

"Sordid, aren't you?" The smile he gave them was forced. "Well, I went round to the East Wing just before four, as near as I can remember. The Cawthornes had had a row that after-noon—quite a man-sized row—and I hoped she might be in the mood to revenge herself on her husband; I'd seen him go out earlier, so I knew she was alone. I'd been trying to make her for months, but I'd never got very far. I hoped this might be my opportunity."

He and Cawthorne are supposed to be friends, Rivers thought, with acute disgust. It makes you think. Pitt said drily, "I presume it was."

"Yes. She began by fending me off as usual—and then, quite suddenly, she capitulated. We went upstairs to the bedroom. We had started to undress when she noticed that she hadn't drawn the curtains; she insisted on doing that, even though no one could see in. I think it was really to darken the room; there was an oddly virginal shyness about her when it came to love-making." He paused. There were slight beads of sweat on his forehead. "Do I have to go on with this, Inspector? Are such intimate details really important to you?"

"They're not," Pitt told him. "It's what happened afterwards that interests me."

"Oh, afterwards." He frowned at the memory. "That was quite shattering. Without being unduly modest, I had thought it was simply through a desire to be revenged on her husband, and not because of my personal charm, that she had surrendered. But apparently I'd got it wrong; she'd fallen for me good and proper. She insisted that we should get our respective spouses to divorce us, and marry and live happily ever after."

The irony in his voice told his listeners, without further ex-planation, that the proposal had not been to his liking.

"That really put me on the spot. I hadn't the slightest wish to divorce my wife; I happen to love her. I regarded what had happened as a pleasant, extra-marital interlude—not as the heart-searing, cataclysmic event that she seemed to think it. But when I pointed this out to her she flatly refused to believe me. She thought that what had happened to her must have happened to me also, and that my avowed intention of sticking to Connie was merely an heroic, self-sacrificing gesture. And it was a gesture she wasn't going to let me make." He sighed. "It was all very emotional. Quite the opposite to what I had expected from such a normally level-headed woman."

"So what?" asked Pitt, as the other paused.

"So we went on arguing. I pointed out that she had been mistaken before; she had married Eric thinking she loved him. Couldn't she be mistaken again? But no, she said, she couldn't. There was a world of difference; this was the first time that the physical act of love had meant anything to her." He scratched the back of his head, frowning. "The devil of it was, she wouldn't agree to wait. What had happened that afternoon had changed her whole life, she said, and she couldn't live a lie. She was determined to tell her husband as soon as he returned, and she expected me to tell Connie. Nothing I said—and I said plenty, I assure you—could budge her from that." He laughed bitterly. "You're getting your money's worth, I hope, Inspector. Is it detailed enough for you?"

Pitt nodded. He was fascinated by the statement that Grace Cawthorne had declared herself unable to live a lie. She had done that very successfully in her business affairs; why should it have been different in love?

"And how did it result?" he asked.

"It didn't. My wife was due home, I couldn't go on arguing indefinitely. Besides, I could see it would be useless. I just walked out on her."

"What time was that?"

"A quarter-past five. I remember, because when I got home I noticed on the table a letter I had meant to post, and I took it down at once. The postman is erratic, but it's not safe to rely on his calling later than five-thirty."

If ever a man had spoken against his own interests, thought Pitt, Jim Upway had done so. He had shown that he had had the strongest of motives for murder. Was it a coincidence that Grace Cawthorne had died so opportunely? Certainly Kane had not thought so; both he and Drummond had been convinced that Upway had killed her. And there had been opportunity as well as motive. He had no alibi for that vital half-hour before six-fifteen. He had said he was alone in the flat, but there was nothing to show that he had not been out on the cliffs with the woman, making a final plea which, when rejected, had culminated in her death.

When Pitt explained this to Jim the latter was really shaken.

"Good God, man! I don't need an alibi, do I? There's no suggestion that I killed her, surely."

"Kane thought so, didn't he?" From the look on the other's face Pitt knew that he had scored a hit. "As for suspicion, that's fairly widespread. Unfortunately, nearly every one at Mulgerry seems to have had a motive for murder. Until to-day we didn't know of yours, or we might have investigated you more closely."

"But you don't call an argument a motive, do you?" Jim protested.

"Not the argument itself. It's the point at issue that matters. In this instance your whole marriage was at stake. That's quite a sizeable issue, isn't it?"

"Well, I didn't kill her. And that's that."

"Not quite that, Mr Upway," Pitt said quietly. "Not so far as the police are concerned. If you were not out on the cliffs with Mrs Cawthorne I should very much like to know exactly what you *did* do during the half-hour before your wife returned."

"I told you—I was here." But it was evident that that was not enough for the inspector, and he went on grimly, "And I wasn't far off panicking, either. It looked like the end of the road for me. I remember I was in the bathroom when I heard the noise of a front door being shut violently. I was sure it came from the East Wing, and I had the dreadful suspicion that Grace had gone out to meet my wife and tell her what had happened. I couldn't see into the courtyard because of the gable, so I came in here to watch the drive. But there was no sign of Grace. It seemed I'd guessed wrong."

"You must have been glad you had," Rivers said.

"You're telling me! But I was still uneasy. I went back to the bathroom; from there I could see the cliffs, and I thought it possible that Grace had gone for a walk in that direction. That might mean she had had second thoughts, that she wasn't going to act in a hurry. If she was prepared to sleep on it I might even be able to talk her out of it altogether."

"Did you see her?" Pitt asked.

"Not at first. I'd almost given up when I spotted her in the distance; she must have gone round by the garage, instead of taking the short cut across the lawn. I only got a brief glimpse of her, and then she was lost in the trees. But it was enough to ease my mind considerably. I looked like living to fight another day."

"You're quite sure it was Mrs Cawthorne? It wasn't Miss Winter, for instance? She was out that way during the afternoon, and they were about the same height. At that distance it would be difficult to tell them apart."

"It certainly wasn't Miss Winter," Jim said decisively. "I'd seen her earlier, and she was wearing a grey tweed suit. This woman had on a bright yellow coat." He shook his head. "But I couldn't swear it was Grace, of course. I just assumed it was. Wishful thinking, perhaps—though it seems I was right."

"Did Mrs Cawthorne own a yellow coat?"

"Goodness knows! But from the size of her wardrobe I imagine she had one of nearly every colour under the sun."

Pitt remembered another accusation that Drummond had made—that it was Upway who had killed Kane. Kane might have told him, as he had told Drummond, that he intended making a statement to the police; a statement that would incriminate all three of them, but that would be more dangerous to Upway than to the other two. "He'd have murdered me too, I dare say, if I hadn't had the sense to clear out," Drummond had said. "I knew as much as Kane about him and the woman. Jim knew that."

"When did Kane—or was it Drummond?—approach you about taking Mrs Cawthorne's place in their set-up?" he asked.

"Wednesday," Jim said promptly. That was a day he was

unlikely to forget. "And it was Mike Drummond who spoke to me."

"What exactly did he want you to do?"

"Paint over their ruddy pictures for them. I turned it down flat. It was then he told me they knew about my being in the East Wing that afternoon, and what Kane had overheard. If I didn't play ball, he said, they would make their knowledge public. He even threatened to make it look as though I'd killed Grace. It wouldn't be difficult, he said. No distortion of the facts; a little embellishment here and there was all that would be necessary." He snorted. "Nice friend *he* turned out to be."

And a nice one you are to talk about friendship, thought Rivers.

Pitt said, "And the blackmail worked, eh? You agreed. It must have been a great relief to learn on Friday that Kane was dead and that Drummond had gone."

Jim's eyes narrowed.

"It was. But don't let that give you ideas, Inspector. I didn't kill Kane—I wasn't that disgruntled. Between ourselves, I'll go so far as to admit that, once I was committed, the task was not entirely repugnant to me. I'm no more averse to easy money than the next man. But that, of course, is not for publication."

You're even more of a scoundrel, thought Pitt, than I had imagined. "Were you at home all Thursday evening?" he asked.

"I was. But again I can't prove it. My wife was here with me most of the time, but I was alone for about three-quarters of an hour while she went down to the East Wing to see Miss Loveday."

Pitt sighed inwardly. Again that vital gap. "To return to Mrs Cawthorne," he said. "What was your reaction when you heard the next day that she was missing?"

"I didn't know what to think. Suicide didn't seem to fit Grace. When her husband told me that she had gone up to London I decided she had left him for good, and that I would be hearing from her later. I was thankful she had apparently said nothing about me in the note she had left him."

"And when her body was found? What then?"

Jim shuddered. "That was hell. I felt it *had* to be suicide." He paused, listening. There was the sound of a key turning in the front-door lock, the sharp clatter of high heels on a wood-block floor. He said hurriedly, keeping his voice low, "That'll be my wife, Inspector. For the Lord's sake don't mention any of this to her. She believes in me—as a husband, I mean. If she has to be told I'd rather tell her myself."

Pitt nodded. From the hall came Connie's voice. "Where are you, darling?"

Jim cleared his throat. "Here. In the sitting-room. There's——"

"I found Caroline strolling around with the dog, so I brought her up for a drink," Connie said cheerfully. "What with both her aunt and the police hounding her, life's pretty grim for the poor girl at present. I thought——" She pushed open the door and halted abruptly, eyeing the two policemen with surprise and some dismay. Behind her stood Caroline.

The men had risen at her entrance. But none of them spoke. They stood there staring at her in silence, a look of incredulity on the faces of all three which, in the case of Jim, was tinged with horror.

Connie was wearing a vivid yellow coat!

She was the first to recover her composure. With a smile for the two policemen she said brightly, "Good evening. I'm sorry— I didn't know we were interrupting anything."

Pitt stepped forward quickly, holding the door for her.

"You're not, Mrs Upway. We're very glad to see you. You too, Miss Winter. I've waited some time for this opportunity."

Caroline said nothing; her pale face was expressionless, but the dark eyes were fixed steadily on the detective. Connie turned sharply, all contrition.

"Oh, Caroline, I'm so sorry. I didn't know they were here— honestly I didn't."

"It doesn't matter," Caroline said. There was no reproof in the soft voice. "I don't mind talking to them. It was Aunt Alice who objected."

Connie shook her head. "She'll never forgive me for this. She'll think I deliberately tricked you into meeting them." She sighed, and moved farther into the room. "Oh, well—the damage is done now. We'll all have a drink and forget it." She turned to her husband. "Jim, you get—hey, what's the matter? You look as though you'd seen a ghost. Are you feeling all right, darling?"

He forced a sickly smile. He would not be the first to tell her about the coat, although he knew the question must be put. "It's stuffy in here," he said hoarsely. "I think I'll open a window."

Connie watched him anxiously as he walked across the room. "I hope you haven't been bullying him, Inspector," she said lightly, her eyes on her husband's back. "You don't get that drink if you have."

"If you don't mind, Mrs Upway, we'll cut out the drinks." She looked at him then, aware of the gravity of his voice. "I have a few questions I must ask you."

"Must?" She shrugged. "Sit down, Caroline, won't you? It seems I'm the one to be put on the spot, not you." She pushed a chair forward for the girl, and sat down herself. She was still wearing the yellow coat, unaware that it was the cynosure of all their eyes. "How can I help you, Inspector?"

"On the day Grace Cawthorne died, Mrs Upway, you did not arrive home until six-fifteen." Pitt spoke slowly, choosing his words with care. "That was late for you, wasn't it? Yet on that day you left the school earlier than usual—at half-past four. It would take you about half an hour to come home on your cycle, I imagine. How did you occupy the other hour and a quarter?"

Connie stared at him, puzzled. "Isn't it rather late to start asking questions like that, Inspector? It's nearly a fortnight since Mrs Cawthorne died. You can't expect my memory to be *that* good."

"You might put it to the test," Pitt said quietly.

"Well, I'll try. I know I was late home—six-fifteen is probably about right—but I certainly don't remember leaving the school early. It's usually nearer five before I get away. However, if you say it was four-thirty I'm prepared to take your word for it. I've no doubt you made it your business to find out." Pitt nodded. "As for how I filled in the time—well, first I did some shopping (it always takes longer on a Monday, plugging the gaps that the week-end makes in the larder); and then, on the way home, the bike packed up on me."

"What was the trouble with it?"

"Not being a mechanic, I wouldn't know. It was probably the carburettor, or the plug, or something. Anyway, it just petered out. I stood there looking helpless until a passing motorist took pity on me and stopped. After he'd put it right I came home."

"With no more trouble?"

"None whatever. It's gone like a bird ever since."

Pitt took a deep breath. This was something he found distasteful, but it had to be done. He could see no other way.

"You said your memory might be at fault, Mrs Upway. Well, perhaps you were right. Isn't it just possible that you got back to Mulgerry at your usual time that evening, and that you took a walk along the cliff before coming home?"

There was more colour now in Connie's cheeks. She said, with unaccustomed sharpness, "It isn't possible at all, Inspector. And if you are suggesting——"

"I am asking questions, not making suggestions," Pitt interrupted her. "Can you remember what you wore that day?"

"A fortnight ago? Really, Inspector!" There was little humour in her laugh. "Why should I remember? At the time it was just like any other day. It wasn't until the following morning that we learned that Grace was dead."

"Not *quite* like any other day. You had a breakdown," Pitt reminded her. "Did you know that there was an old croquet set in the area outside the basement flat?"

Connie stared at him.

"You ask the strangest questions, Inspector. But as a matter of fact, I did. I pointed it out to Miss Winter early last week— Tuesday, I think it was," She turned to Caroline for confirmation, and Caroline gave a barely perceptible nod of her dark head. "She told me it used to be kept in the coal-cellar there, along with some other odds and ends. Mr Kane must have moved it out and forgotten to put it back. Why? Is it significant in any way?"

"Very significant, Mrs Upway. While Kane was absent from his flat on Thursday evening some one placed the croquet balls on the steps. When he came home he slipped on them and fell."

There was a great stillness in the room, broken only by gasps from the two girls. Before anyone could speak Pitt went on, his long, gaunt face and quiet voice adding solemnity to the words, "It might be wiser, Mrs Upway, if you were to say no more at this stage. But I must warn you that whatever you do say will be taken down, and may be given in evidence. Do you understand?"

"I understand perfectly," Connie said, her voice well under control. But her husband, who throughout the interview had stood gazing unseeing out of the window at the gathering night, now wheeled sharply.

"Wait a minute——" he began wrathfully. But Pitt cut him short.

"You wait a minute, sir." The inspector's voice was curt. His task was not an easy one, and he wanted no interruptions. He turned to the girl. "Mrs Upway, we have been unable to trace any motorist who stopped to repair your machine for you on the afternoon of Mrs Cawthorne's death. I suggest to you that there was no breakdown, and that you returned here at five-fifteen—at least half an hour earlier than usual. And I suggest it was because of something you saw then"—there were exclamations of protest from Caroline and Jim, but Pitt took no notice—"that you followed Mrs Cawthorne out to the cliff and—after an argument, perhaps—deliberately pushed her over the edge. Isn't that what happened?"

"It isn't," Connie said. "But please go on, Inspector. You intrigue me."

"I will. We now come to last Thursday. On that evening you went out to visit Miss Loveday, and by your own admission you overheard an argument between Kane and Drummond. You say you didn't stop to listen—but I think you did. And I think it was because of what you heard Kane say then—that he knew who had killed Mrs Cawthorne, and that he intended making a statement to the police the next day—that you laid that trap for him. You knew the croquet set was there. It was a simple matter to place the balls on the step, hoping that in the dark they would not be seen and that Kane would fall and kill himself. And that, Mrs Upway, he very conveniently did."

He paused. Connie asked quietly, "Is that all, Inspector?"

"Not quite all," he told her. "There are two other significant factors. One is the coat you are wearing, Mrs Upway. A woman in a yellow coat was seen going towards the cliff at about the time Mrs Cawthorne is believed to have been killed. The other is your motive in killing her. You knew——"

"No!" Caroline said sharply. She was on her feet, eyes blazing in her pale face. "No, you mustn't."

Pitt turned to her.

"I'm sorry, Miss Winter. I understand your scruples, but as a policeman I can't afford such luxuries. Certainly not where murder is concerned. And Mrs Upway knows already that——"

"No!" Caroline said again. She was behind the armchair, her long fingers gripping the high back. "She doesn't know. And she didn't kill Grace Cawthorne. I did."

15

Eric returned to Mulgerry the next morning, with Pitt and Matthews in attendance. Pitt had done his best to hasten his release, but Eric did not think it necessary to thank him for that service. He was still smarting under a sense of grievance —of several grievances. The loss of his inheritance rankled no less strongly than his arrest and imprisonment; but whereas there seemed to be nothing he could do about the former, he was determined to do something about the latter. Apart from the indignities and privation he had been made to suffer, his arrest had cost him his job. Pitt had told him that Rivers's hand had been forced by the knowledge that he was planning to go abroad, but Eric refused to accept that as an excuse; he was innocent, therefore he had had every right to go where he wished. The police should be made to pay, and pay handsomely. He would have a talk with Matthews and instruct him to institute proceedings.

Miss Lomas was in the kitchen when he arrived. "We may as well provide a decent lunch for his homecoming, poor man," she had said to Sheila that morning. "I'll spread myself a bit." And Sheila had pointed out that it was no longer Eric's home; it was Daffy's, together with everything in it. Eric hadn't got a home. "Well, he can stay as long as it suits him," Daffy had retorted, in the gruff tone she adopted whenever she happened to be in a generous mood. "And so can you, my dear. Although under the circumstances it might be wiser if you didn't."

Sheila knew what she meant; and as she welcomed Eric home with a kiss and a warm embrace she avoided the searching gaze of the solicitor behind him. Eric would expect that welcome, since she had said nothing to him of her change of heart. It would be kinder, she had decided, to postpone that until after his release. Now she wondered if she had been right. In prison her desertion would have been just one more trial added to the many that beset him. Now it must stand alone—a prominent, and perhaps a sole, focus for grievance.

As she turned to lead the way into the house she realized with a sinking heart that she might never be able to bring herself to tell him the truth. He might have to discover it for himself.

Daffy joined them in the sitting-room. She had opened a bottle of wine to celebrate the occasion, but the little gathering remained an awkward one. Each had his or her particular cause for tension. Eric had left Pitt in no doubt about his intention to sue the police for wrongful arrest. Nor was that the only cloud on the inspector's horizon. He had a nagging doubt of the correctness of his behaviour towards Connie Upway the previous evening; she had accepted his explanation, but it distressed him that he should have had to resort to such methods to extract the truth. Charles Matthews was aware of a sense of impending loss. Witnessing the embrace with which Sheila had greeted Eric had made him realize that very shortly she would be going out of his life for good; and although he had ceased trying to analyse his feelings towards her, he knew that he would miss her. Sheila was preoccupied with what she had to say to Eric. She kept rephrasing the words, trying to find the least hurtful combination. But they always amounted to the same thing—that she was jilting him. Miss Lomas too was worried about Eric, suspecting that he regarded her as a thief and an interloper. She had the uncomfortable feeling that she ought to do something about him; Grace had never meant her to have that money. And Eric himself, glad as he was to be free, was too intent on revenge to be carefree. Pitt was an enemy, Matthews a potential one; the man was far more interested in Sheila than such a brief acquaintance warranted. Freedom itself was trammelled with care. He had no home, no money, no job. Even Sheila's embrace had lacked the fervent warmth he had anticipated.

"Poor Caroline," Sheila said. "What she did was monstrous, but I can't help feeling sorry for her. From all accounts her life has been a pretty miserable one; it's dreadful to think of her spending the rest of it in prison. Did she tell you why she did it, Inspector?"

"She told me a lot of things, Miss Loveday. None of them made pleasant hearing."

"Pleasant hearing or not, suppose you tell us?" Eric said belligerently. "Me, anyway. I spent a whole week in prison because of that damned girl, and I'm entitled to know what happened."

"Not entitled," Pitt said. While appreciating that the man had cause for bitterness, he was human enough to resent it being focused on himself. "But I'll tell you, none the less. She did it to shield Mrs Upway from the discovery of her husband's infidelity."

"Rather drastic—but effective, I suppose," was Daffy's comment. "But is that all we get? Have another glass of wine to loosen your tongue, Inspector. You're not on duty now."

Eric frowned as he watched her pour it out. She had opened a bottle of vintage hock—1949, an excellent year—and it pained him to see good wine wasted on a policeman.

"That miserable life you referred to, Miss Loveday, is probably responsible for the deaths of two people," Pitt said, gazing abstractedly into his glass. "Had Miss Winter received any affection at home she might not have responded so whole-heartedly to Mrs Upway's kindness. As it was she came near to idolizing her. So you can imagine how she felt when she discovered that Mr Upway was having an affair with Mrs Cawthorne.

"She went out with the dog as usual after tea that afternoon. But going through the trees near the garage she chanced to look up—and there, framed in the bedroom window as she reached up to draw the curtains, was Mrs Cawthorne. She was half undressed—and behind her, his arms around her, was Mr Upway."

So that explains the curtains, thought Eric. And it was probably the sound of Grace shutting the windows that had attracted Caroline's attention. He supposed that he should feel angry, or indignant, or hurt at this affront to his dignity as a husband; cuckolded husbands usually did. But he felt only indifferent. Even the fact that Jim had been the nearest approach to a friend that he had had at Mulgerry, and that it had been Jim who had cuckolded him, seemed unimportant. Mulgerry and its people had never loomed large in his life; there had always been something unreal about it. And now he was finished with Mulgerry for good.

He did not think of Grace. Grace had become unreal too. Since her death he had learned so many things about her that in retrospect she now seemed an entirely different person from the Grace he had married. Or thought he had married.

"Miss Winter stayed in the trees with the dog for nearly an hour," Pitt said. "I don't think she knew why; she says she was so horrified that she just couldn't think what to do. When Upway eventually came out she still had not made up her mind, and she decided to go for a walk to think it over. But first she went back to the house for a coat—the yellow coat; she was cold after standing for so long. Mr Upway saw her walking back as he put his letter in the hall, but he had returned to the flat by the time she came out again. And Miss Winter did not see him."

"Perhaps it's a pity she didn't," Daffy said. "She might have vented her spleen on him instead of on Grace."

"It wasn't spleen, Miss Lomas. She didn't say so, but I'm quite sure that her only thought was to preserve Mrs Upway's happiness. Even when, as she walked along the cliff, she saw Mrs Cawthorne, her first impulse was not to kill but to plead with her."

"That must have been difficult for Caroline," Sheila said. "I don't know her well, of course, but even to me she seems to have much of her aunt's arrogance and pride. She wouldn't enjoy pleading. And she didn't like Grace Cawthorne, either. She told me so."

Eric said bitterly, "Dammit, what is this? She goes in for wholesale slaughter—and here you all are, talking about her as though she were a noble, unselfish creature with not an evil thought in her head. Daffy's right—it *was* spleen. She wasn't considering Connie, she was considering herself. Connie was her friend, and she didn't want to lose her; and she knew damned well she *would* lose her if Jim and Grace cleared off together. Connie wouldn't stay here on her own." He refilled his glass with hock. He had been drinking steadily, and it was not only indignation that made him look flushed. "She's like that damned aunt of hers, selfish to the core."

Pitt shrugged his thin shoulders.

"You may be right, sir. But I still don't think she had any thought of murder when she first spoke to your wife. It was only when her pleading was contemptuously rejected, when Mrs Cawthorne told her that she and Upway were in love and would be going away together, that she lost her head, or her temper, or whatever you like to call it, and attacked her."

"With intent to kill, you mean?" Miss Lomas asked.

"Perhaps. She seems rather hazy about that. Apparently Mrs Cawthorne turned her back on her with some taunt or other, and this so infuriated Miss Winter that, without conscious thought of what she was doing, she made a wild rush at her. Perhaps neither of them realized how near they were to the edge. One violent push was all that was necessary, it seems; Mrs Cawthorne had no chance to resist or avoid it." Pitt shook his head. "Whether she meant to kill or not, she shows no remorse for what happened. None whatever. She regards it as the lesser of two evils. It was better that a wicked woman should die, she says"—Pitt looked apprehensively at Eric, but the latter showed no concern at this description of his dead wife—"than that a good woman like Mrs Upway should be robbed of her happiness."

"She's mad, of course," Eric declared loudly. "I told you, she's just like her aunt. You've met the Hump, Inspector. Ever come across anyone crazier? Hard, too. Hard as granite."

"She's not mad in the legal sense," Pitt said. "Or I don't think so. And she's not entirely hard; there are weak spots in the granite. Her fondness for Mrs Upway is one. She could even feel pity for you, Mr Cawthorne." ("Which is more than can be said of some people," Eric muttered.) "That is why she invented the lie that she had seen you near Gavin Head that afternoon."

"It could have been pride, not pity," Sheila suggested. "Pride would not permit her to allow another to be punished for what she had done."

"And who was the stranger she saw with Grace?" Eric asked. "Did she tell you that?"

"There was no stranger, Mr Cawthorne. There was only Mr Upway. She invented the stranger with the same purpose as she did everything else—to protect Mrs Upway. To have told Miss Loveday the truth would have defeated that purpose."

He thought it unnecessary to point out—as he wondered why no one else had pointed out—that Caroline Winter need never have mentioned that Grace Cawthorne was an adulteress. That she had done so was evidence of her deep-rooted hatred of the woman. She could not resist the opportunity to expose her.

"And Kane?" Miss Lomas asked. "She was in no danger from him, was she? Why did he have to die?"

"The same reason again. She too heard Kane and Drummond arguing that evening; but, unlike Mrs Upway, she stopped to listen. She heard enough to realize that Kane was going to make public the secret she was determined to keep. So Kane also had to be silenced." Pitt shook his head. "She was horribly thorough in her single-mindedness."

"It's sad, isn't it, to think of the death and pain and sorrow she has caused—and all to no purpose?" Sheila said. "Because Connie can't be kept in ignorance much longer. About her husband, I mean. It's bound to be mentioned at the trial, isn't it?"

"I'm afraid so," Pitt said. "I don't see how it can be avoided."

"Good heavens! The man is human after all," Eric exclaimed, with exaggerated astonishment.

Pitt ignored the taunt. Matthews, who up to now had been content to listen, his eyes dwelling appreciatively on Sheila whenever he felt himself unobserved, said slowly, "If Miss Winter is as single-minded in her purpose as you suggest, Inspector, she may plead guilty and refuse to put up and defence in mitigation."

"It would be in keeping," Pitt agreed. "I can't see her agreeing to a plea of insanity, which would be the only possible defence."

"I saw Connie earlier this morning," Sheila said. "All this has upset her terribly; you know how she worries about people. And I don't think the grilling you gave her last night helped, Inspector. Even to be suspected of murder, no matter for how short a time, must be pretty shattering."

"You're telling me!" Eric exclaimed. "I had it for over a week. But what's this about Connie? Don't tell me you actually suspected her of murder, Inspector. That would be too rich."

"Not quite. But I had to pretend to suspect her." Pitt remembered that Eric knew nothing of what had transpired the previous evening, and told him briefly. "I hated myself for doing it, but I could see no other way. I banked on Miss Winter's devotion to her friend being stronger than her instinct for self-preservation."

Sheila said thoughtfully, "It must have shaken your confidence, Inspector, when Connie walked in wearing that yellow coat."

Pitt shook his head. "It didn't, you know. Or only momentarily. I haven't a very high opinion of Mr Upway, I'm afraid, but I don't think he would willingly betray his wife. He was as shocked and surprised as I was. Therefore he didn't know she had a yellow coat. Therefore she hadn't had it very long. And she hadn't. Miss Winter gave it to her only two or three days ago. One of many presents, I gather. She told Mrs Upway that it had shrunk after being worn in the rain, and was too small for her."

"So much for her devotion, then," Eric said brusquely. "She deliberately tried to incriminate Connie."

"Oh, no. She was unaware that anyone had seen her that afternoon. She may not even have remembered wearing the coat."

"She ought to," Sheila said. "She told me she was soaked through by the time she got home."

Eric nodded. "And another thing, Inspector. Where did she get the money for all those presents to Connie? Did she tell you that? No? Well, I will. She got it from Grace."

"From Grace?" exclaimed Daffy. "Why on earth should Grace give her money?"

"I'll tell you. Grace found her wandering about upstairs one day; she'd brought a message from the Hump, and had simply walked in without bothering to ring. I suppose the front door was open. Anyway, there she was. Grace was furious with her."

"I don't blame her," Daffy said. "What cheek!"

"Damned cheek," Eric agreed. "But typical Humpleston. Neither Caroline nor her aunt could get used to the fact that Mulgerry was no longer all theirs. The point is, though, that it wasn't like Grace. Grace was a snob, and she wanted the Hump to think well of her; she wouldn't have lost her temper with Caroline except for a very good reason. Well, I think she had one. I think she was about to start work on a stolen picture, and was terrified that Caroline might have seen it in the studio and recognized it. From a newspaper photograph, perhaps." He paused for breath. "Well, I think Caroline did. And I think Grace gave her money to keep her mouth shut."

"Blackmail, eh?" Pitt shook his head. "It seems most unlikely."

"So did murder, once. But it happened. And if you ask Jim Upway I bet you'll find that those presents to Connie—or the better ones, certainly—started from then."

"Well, you may be right, sir. But we can't know for sure unless Miss Winter decides to confess—which is an unlikely contingency, I should say."

"So should I," Sheila agreed. "It would be even more out of character than the blackmail itself. But to return to last night, Inspector. I still don't see why you had to badger Connie. Why didn't you just arrest Caroline when she walked into the room?"

"Lack of evidence, Miss Loveday. There was only her statement to you to connect her with Mrs Cawthorne's death. And she could have retracted that."

"Her statement to me? But that only concerned Eric. How could it implicate her?"

"Because of the discrepancy in time. She said she went out after tea—and so she did. But Mr Upway saw her in the grounds at five-thirty—which meant that she was lying when she said she saw Mr Cawthorne near Gavin Head at a quarter to six. But even that didn't amount to much. It could have been merely a mistaken attempt to provide an alibi for a friend."

"We weren't friends," growled Eric.

Pitt ignored this. "There was not much more against her on the second count, either. She was out with the dog on Thursday evening, and she knew about the croquet set. I took that for granted even before Mrs Upway told me, since it was unlikely that anyone other than Lady Humpleston and her family would be croquet-players. Certainly not Kane—either here or anywhere else. But the only direct evidence was the damp patches on the wall and floor of the basement area. Although I did not realize it at once, that was where the dog had urinated. And since Pompey is the only dog here, and Miss Winter the only person to exercise it, that seemed to give a direct lead. But no more than that." A clock chimed in the hall, and he looked quickly at his watch. "Time I was off. There'll be a whole lot of paper work piling up in my office."

"Oh, no, you don't," Sheila said. "Not until you've explained how you knew in advance what Kane and Drummond were up to."

"From your description of their workroom, you mean?" Pitt gave one of his rare smiles. "I'm afraid the detective in me can't claim any credit for that. It so happens that I know something of the restoration and lining of old pictures."

"And what exactly is lining?" Daffy asked.

"Replacing an old or worn canvas," Pitt told her. "I won't attempt to describe the process in detail, but roughly it is this. Paper is pasted on to the face of the picture, which is then placed on a smooth, level table so that the back can be cleaned by means of pumice-stone or a knife; and a new piece of canvas is then glued on and pressed down by hand. When it is nearly dry it is further flattened by a hot iron, placed on a new stretching frame, and the paper removed from the face by a damp sponge. And it was all there, Miss Loveday. Rolls of paper, muslin (muslin is sometimes used instead of canvas, or pasted over the paper when the backing is particularly rotten), pumice-stone, glue and paste (often mixed with creosote to resist the effects of damp), the smooth-topped table, wood for the stretching frame, and the iron. Particularly the iron—as I think I said before."

"But why that heavy, old-fashioned thing? Why not an electric iron?"

"Because of the weight; something like fifteen to twenty pounds is necessary. It has to be broad, too. The ironing is perhaps the most tricky part of the operation. There must be no heavy pressure; the iron has to be glided over the surface, and only experience can enable one to judge the correct temperature which is so essential. If the iron is too cold you won't get an even surface; too hot, and you'll probably discolour the paint or destroy the new canvas." He shook his head. "It's no job for the amateur, I assure you. Kane and Drummond were lucky to find an expert in Mrs Cawthorne."

Eric drained his glass. "Wonderful woman, wasn't she?" he said bitterly. "Liar, cheat, bigamist, adulteress, and crook. You can be proud of your sister's memory—eh, Daffy? And to think that the Hump once described her to me as a really good woman! That shows you just how fine a judge of character the old basket is."

Miss Lomas looked at him with distaste, disdaining to reply.

But Sheila was filled with sadness at his bitterness—sadness for Eric, and sadness for herself.

"Poor Lady Humpleston," she said. "Unpleasant though she is, I can't help feeling sorry for her. The doctor was here last night, and again this morning; she must be in a bad way. Think what it must have done to her pride to learn that her niece is a murderess. I wonder the shock didn't kill her."

"Don't waste any pity on the Hump," Eric said. "She won't have any for Caroline, you can be sure of that. It's only herself she'll be thinking of, now as ever."

And that, thought Sheila, is probably true enough.

"I'm off," Pitt said. "Thank you for your hospitality, Miss Lomas. I don't often taste wine as good as that." I bet you don't, Eric muttered to himself. And it's me you should be thanking, not Daffy. "Ready, Mr Matthews?"

"I'll see you out," Sheila said.

They were at the car when Pitt said, "Excuse me a moment, will you? There's something I forgot to ask Mr Cawthorne."

Matthews gazed after him. He said, trying to sound briskly cheerful, "Is he being tactful? Perhaps he thinks—no, he can't do. He knows about you and Cawthorne, doesn't he?" Sheila blushed as he took her hand and held it. "Well, it only remains for me to say good-bye. With great reluctance, I may add."

"You make it sound dreadfully final," she said, trying to match her tone to his. "Sheffield isn't completely inaccessible, you know."

"It isn't the journey that deters me," he told her. "It's your prospective husband. I don't think he likes me."

"He doesn't like anyone at present," she said. "He's at war with the whole world, himself included. But he'll get over it."

She was tempted to tell him that Eric was no longer her prospective husband. But he might interpret that as an invitation to take Eric's place; and although he had made it plain that he admired her she could be sure of no more than that. Nor was she completely sure of herself. It was not Charles Matthews who had killed her love for Eric, but Eric himself. She had rushed impulsively into love once; she would not make the same mistake again.

She comforted herself with the thought that, despite the finality of his good-bye, this was unlikely to be their last meeting. Inspector Pitt had warned her that she would probably be called as a witness at Caroline's trial, and no doubt Charles Matthews would be there too. They could go on from there—if they both wished it.

"Good-bye," she said, withdrawing her hand from his as the inspector reappeared from the house. "And thank you for all you have done. You've been very patient."

He gave her a rather stiff little bow, but his smile relieved the formality.

"It is I who should thank you. Our partnership has given me nothing but pleasure. I only regret that success inevitably cut it short."

As the police car drove away Connie came across the courtyard from the direction of the garage. Sheila waited for her.

"How's Nadia?" she asked. "I presume you've been on your usual errand of mercy."

"She's surprisingly cheerful." Was there the faintest trace of bitterness in Connie's voice? "She's seen Mike, and apparently she is not the abandoned, destitute wife she thought she was. Mike has left her nicely provided for." She sighed. "I think I ought to see if there is anything I can do for poor Mrs Winter. It's her I'm most sorry for; she must love Caroline in her own peculiar way—although I doubt if the Hump does." She rubbed her eyes. Sheila could see that tears were very near the surface. "Why, oh why, did Caroline do such a dreadful thing?" wailed Connie. "Apart from everything else, couldn't she see how pointless it was? How could she possibly imagine that after five years of marriage I don't know my own husband?"

Sheila stared at her. "You—you *knew*?"

"Of course I knew. Oh, not about Grace—although I guessed it was likely to happen. But Grace was only one of many. She wouldn't have made any difference."

"And you didn't mind?"

"Oh, yes, I minded. What woman wouldn't? But I married Jim with my eyes open, and I didn't expect marriage to change him. The important thing is that he loves me; if I have to share him occasionally that's not so very dreadful, is it? And as long as he continues to love me I'll continue to forgive his little brief amours."

"Forgive? You don't mean that Jim tells you when——"

"Good heavens, no! That is important too—that he should have his secrets, and that I should never appear to suspect. Important to him—and therefore important to me. I don't think our love would have lasted long if it had been punctuated by servile confessions and petty jealousies. Jim would have lost his self-respect, and I should have come to despise him." Connie smiled. "I know people think I'm a blind fool. Well, I'm not blind; and if I'm a fool I'm a happy one. Or happier than I'd otherwise have been. So is Jim—I hope."

There was a lump in Sheila's throat as she watched Connie walk away. The Hump had referred to Grace Cawthorne as a good woman. How wrong she had been! But how aptly, Sheila thought, that description fitted Connie Upway.